Ladies and Gentlemen

By

Irvin S. Cobb

Ladies and Gentlemen
by Irvin S. Cobb

Copyright © 2024

All Rights reserved.

No part of this publication may be reproduced, stored in a retrieval system, or transmitted in any form or by any means, electronic, mechanical, photocopying or Otherwise, without the written permission of the publisher.
The author/editor asserts the moral right to be identified as the author/editor of this work.

ISBN: 978-93-62761-00-2

Published by
DOUBLE 9 BOOKS

2/13-B, Ansari Road
Daryaganj, New Delhi – 110002
info@double9books.com
www.double9books.com
Tel. 011-40042856

This book is under public domain

ABOUT THE AUTHOR

Shrewsbury, Irvin Cobb (June 23, 1876 – March 11, 1944) was a Paducah, Kentucky-born author, humorist, editor, and columnist who moved to New York in 1904 and lived there for the rest of his life. As the highest-paid staff reporter in the United States, he worked for Joseph Pulitzer's newspaper, the New York World. Cobb also published almost 60 books and 300 short tales. Some of his works were made into silent films. Several of his Judge Priest short stories were adapted for two feature films directed by John Ford in the 1930s. Cobb was the second of four children born in Paducah, Kentucky, to Kentucky natives. Reuben Saunders, M.D., is credited with finding in 1873 that injections of morphine-atropine were effective in treating cholera. Cobb grew up in Paducah, and many of his later works were inspired by events and people from his upbringing. Cobb was afterwards dubbed the "Duke of Paducah." Cobb attended public and private elementary schools before enrolling in William A. Cade's Academy to study law. Cobb's father became an alcoholic when he was 16, following the death of his grandfather. Cobb began his writing career after being forced to drop out of school and find jobs.

CONTENTS

A Lady and A Gentleman 7
The Order of the Bath 24
Two of Everything... 47
We of the Old South.. 65
Killed with Kindness... 86
Peace on Earth 101
Three Wise Men of the East Side 125
The Cowboy and the Lady—And Her PA 138
A Close Shave 157
Good Sam 164
How to Choke a Cat Without Using Butter 182

A Lady and A Gentleman

THERE were the hotel lobbies; they roared and spun like whirlpools with the crowds that were in them. But the streets outside were more like millraces, and the exits from the railroad stations became flumes down which all morning and all afternoon the living torrents unceasingly had poured. Every main crossing was in a twist of opposing currents. Overhead, on cornices and across window-ledges and against house-fronts and on ropes which passed above the roadway from one building to another, hung buntings and flags and streamers, the prevalent colors being red and white; and also many great goggle-eyed and bewhiskered portraits of dead warriors done on sail-cloth in the best styles of two domestic schools—sign-painting and election-bannering. Numbers of brass bands marched to and fro, playing this, that, and the next appropriate air, but when in doubt playing "Dixie"; and the musicians waded knee-deep through an accumulating wreckage of abandoned consonants—softly dropped *g's*, eliminated *r's*. In short, the United Confederate Veterans were holding their annual reunion, this being the evening of the opening day.

For absolute proof that this really was a reunion of his kind, there was visible here and there a veteran. His average age was eighty-three years and some odd months. He was feeble or he was halt or sometimes he was purblind. Only very rarely did he carry his years and his frame straight. He was near to being swept away and drowned in a vast and fragrant sea of gracious, chattering femininity. His daughters and his granddaughters and his nieces and his younger sisters and, very rarely, his wife—they collectively were as ten to one against him. They were the sponsors and the maids of honor and the matrons of honor and the chaperons; they represented such-and-such a camp or such-and-such a state, wearing flowing badges to attest their queenly distinctions; wearing, also, white summery gowns, the most of them, with touches of red. But the older women nearly always were in black.

Here and there moved the Amazonian figure of one among them who had decked herself for this great occasion in a gray uniform with bullet buttons of brass in twin rows down the front of the jacket and with a soldier cap on her bobbed hair—nearly always it was bobbed—and gold braid at the seams of her short walking skirt. A crafty stylist even had thought out the added touches of epaulets for her straight shoulders and a pair of black cavalry boots; and she went about much admired by herself and the rest.

You see, it was like this: In the days when there were many of them, the veterans had shared their reunions with their women. Now that they were so few and so weakly, their women would let the veterans share the reunions with them. It was very much like this—a gorgeous social event, the whole South participating; with sentiment for its half-erased background, with the memories of a war that ended nearly sixty years before for its fainting, fading excuse; with the splendid promise of balls and parties and receptions and flirting and love-making and match-making for its assembly call to the campaigning rampaging young of the species.

Only over by the river at the big yellow pine auditorium did the puny veteran element yet hold its own against the dominant attendant tides of the newer generations of its descendants. "General Van Brunk of Texas, honored leader of the Trans-Mississippi Department, will now present the important report of the Committee on History," the octogenarian commander-in-chief was announcing to those fifteen hundred white heads that nodded before him like so much ripened cotton in the bolls. So General Van Brunk, holding the typewritten fruitage of one year's hard work in his palsied hands, took the platform and cleared a shrunken throat and began.

But just then the members of the Orphan Brigade of Kentucky—thirty-two of them, no less—marched down the middle aisle with a fife-and-drum corps at their head and a color-bearer bearing a tattered rag on a scarred staff, and everybody rose up shakily to give the Rebel yell, and nobody, not even General Van Brunk, ever heard a word of General Van Brunk's report. It was ordered spread upon the minutes, though, while the commander-in-chief stood up there with his arms outstretched and wept a welcome to the straggly incoming column. He was an Orphan himself.

The proceedings were proceeding according to custom. The orator chosen to deliver the annual oration would have an easy time of it when his hour came next day. "Comrades of my father," he would say and they would applaud for five minutes. He would mention Jackson and they would whoop for seven minutes; mention Lee and that would mean ten minutes of the same. And so on.

At a quarter to ten a certain portly churchman—lately a chaplain with the A.E.F.—who by invitation had come down from Minneapolis to bear an affectionate message to these old men on behalf of the American Legion, wormed his way out of a side door of the auditorium, his job done. Inside his black garments he was perspiring heavily. The air of the packed hall had been steaming hot. He stood for a minute on the sidewalk, grateful for the cooling wind of the May night and trying to decide whether he ought to turn east or west to get back to his hotel. He was a bishop of the Episcopal Church and he had the bishop's look and manner. On his arm he felt a bony clutch, like the clutch of a parrot's foot.

A bent shell of a man was alongside him; it was this shell had fastened its skeleton fingers upon his sleeve. Out of a head that was just a skull with a brown hard skin stretched over it, a pair of filmed eyes looked up into his face, and from behind an ambush of dense white whiskers came a piping voice saying:

"Howdy, son."

The bishop was startled and secretly amused. He was used to being called "Father"—frequently his collar and vest deceived Romanists—but he couldn't remember when anyone had addressed him as "son."

"Good evening, sir," he answered.

"Son," quavered the other—he must be all of ninety, the bishop decided—"say, son, I heard you back thar—part of whut you said. You done fust-rate—yep, fust-rate, fur a Yankee. You air a Yankee, ain't you?"

"Well, I was born in Nebraska, but I live now in Minnesota," said the bishop.

"That so? Well, I'm an Alabama boy!"

All at once the bishop ceased to be amused. As the talon released its fumbling hold on him and the remnant tottered away, the bishop's right arm came up smartly but involuntarily in a military salute.

"He calls himself a boy!" quoth the bishop, addressing no one in particular. "I know now why they fought four years against such odds!"

Suddenly he was prouder than ever of being an American. And he, a stranger to these parts, felt the pathos of it all—the pathos of age and decrepitude, the pathos of the thronging shadows of an heroic Lost Cause, the gallant pathos of these defeated men who even now at their time of life would never admit they had been defeated—these things, thrown out in relief against this screen of blaring brass and pretty young girls and socially ambitious mothers and general hullabaloo.

But this story, such as it is, is not concerned with this particular reunion so much as it is concerned with the reactions to the reunion of one surviving Confederate who attended it. He was not an imported orator nor a thwarted deliverer of historical reports, nor yet the commander of some phantom division whose main camp ground now was a cemetery. He was still what he had been back yonder in '65—a high private of the rear rank. He was fond of saying so. With him it was one favorite little joke which never staled.

He was a very weary high private as he trudged along. An exceedingly young and sleepy Boy Scout was his guide, striving to keep in stride with him. First the old man would tote his small valise, then the Scout would take it over for a spell.

They had ridden together on a street-car. At a corner which the guide thought must be their corner, they got off. They were entering an outlying part of the city, that much was certain, at least. The last high-dangled example of the art preservative as practiced by local masters of outdoor advertising service—it was labeled with the name of President Jefferson Davis, so it must be a likeness of President Davis—was swinging aloft far behind them. Those thin broken sounds of distant band-music no longer came to their ears. The houses were getting scarcer, getting to be farther apart. They stumbled in the darkness across railroad tracks, thence passed on through a sort of tunnel that was as black inside as a pocket. When they came out from under the culvert they found themselves in a desert so far as stirring life went.

"Shore you're not lost, sonny?" asked the old man for the second or third time.

"No, suh, I think not." But the youngster's tone had lost its earlier manful conviction. "It oughter be right down this way somewhere. I guess we'll strike it soon."

So they went ahead. The veteran's trudge became a shamble. The Scout's step became a drowsy stagger. That Scout was growing very tired in his legs; they were such short legs. He had been on duty since breakfast time.

It was the high private's turn to carry the grip. He halted and put it down to ease his cramped hand and to breathe. His companion lurched with a bump against the telephone pole and gave a comatose grunt.

"Look here, little pardner," said the old man, "you act like to me you're mighty near played out. Whereabouts do you live?"

"Clean over—over—on the other side of town from here." The child spoke between jaw-stretching yawns. "That car-line back there goes right past our house though." His voice was very wistful as he said that.

"Tell you what, then. It'd be wrong to keep you up any longer. But me, I'm one of these here old-time campaigners. You hand me over that piece of paper with the name and the number and all on it, and then you put out for home and get yourself a good night's rest. By myself I'll be shore to locate the place we're hunting for. Anyway, you've done enough good deeds for one day."

That Scout might be sleepy, but sleepy or not he had a bounden service to perform and would have so stated. But the veteran cut short those plucky semiconscious protests of his, and being outargued, the boy surrendered a scrap of cardboard and bade his late charge good-by and good night and set out on his return to civilization.

Under a near-by electric this old-time campaigner adjusted his glasses and studied the scribbled face of the card. Immediately above his head a street-marker showed on the lamp-post where the light would fall on it, and next he looked up and spelled out the lettering there. He merely was reconfirming a fact already confirmed.

"This is certainly the right street," he said to himself. "But the question is—which-a-way is the right house? The thing for me to do, I reckin, is to roust up somebody and ask—if I can find anybody awake."

Diagonally opposite, he made out the square bulk of a sizable two-story structure. It must be a dwelling, for it had a bit of lawn in front of it; it must be tenanted because a patchy dullish crescent of illumination made outlines for a transom above the door. Maybe somebody over there might be smart enough to tell him.

He went across, moving very slowly, and toiled up a flight of porch steps. There were only four of the steps; he would have taken his oath there were a full dozen of them. He fumbled at the door-jamb until he found a knocker.

To his knocking the response was immediate. From the inner side there was the scraping sound as of a heavy bolt being withdrawn. Next a lock clicked, and then discreetly, almost cautiously, the door opened a few inches and the face of a negro girl was revealed to him in the dim glow of a heavily hooded light burning behind her in the entry hall. She squinted hard at him.

"Whut you want yere this time o' night, mista?" she demanded. Her manner was not hospitable; it bordered on the suspicious.

"I'm looking for an address," he began.

"Dis can't be it."

"I know that. But I thought maybe somebody here might help direct me." From his growing exhaustion the intruder fairly was panting. "I'm sort of lost."

"Oh, so tha's it? Wait a minute, then." Still holding the door slightly ajar, she called rearward over her shoulder: "Miss Sissie! Oh, Miss Sissie!"

"What is it?" The answer came from back of her.

"They's a ole, kinder feebled-up lookin' w'ite gen'elman out yere w'ich he think he's lost his way."

"Wait, I'll come talk to him."

A middle-aged tall woman, who was dressed, so the stranger decided, as though expecting stylish company, appeared now at the door and above the servant's shoulder eyed him appraisingly. He tried to tell her his mission, but his voice weakened on him and trailed off. He caught at the door-casing; he felt dizzy.

The white woman elbowed the black one aside.

"Come on in," she ordered. "Get out of the way, can't you, Pansy?" She threw this second command at her maid. "Don't you see he's about ready to drop? Pick up his valise. There, that's it, mister. Just put your weight on me."

She half-lifted him across the threshold and eased him down upon a sofa in the hall. The negress closed and barred the door.

"Run make some hot coffee," her employer bade her. "Or maybe you'd rather have a little liquor? I've got plenty of it in the house." She addressed the slumped intruder.

"Nome, I never touch anything strong. But I reckin a cup of coffee would taste good to me—if I'm not putting you out too much? You'll please have to excuse me, ma'am, for breaking in on you this way, but I—" Remembering his manners, he got his hat off in a little flurry of confusion.

"Where were you trying to get to?"

With difficulty he brought his card forth from his pocket and she took it from him and read what was written upon it.

"You're a good long two miles and a half from where you belong," she told him sharply.

"But ain't this Bonaventure Avenue?"

"Yes, North Bonaventure. You came out Lawes Drive, didn't you?—the wide street where the trolley-line is? Well, you should have gone south when you turned off. Instead of that you came north. These people"—she consulted the card again—"Philipson or whatever the name is—are they friends of yours?"

"Well, yes, ma'am, and nome. I've never met them. But they're taking in one old soldier during the reunion, the hotels and the boarding-houses and all being so full up. And a gentleman at Tennessee Headquarters—that's my headquarters, ma'am—he gave me that card and sent me there."

"Send you alone?" Her angular shoulders, bare above a low-cut evening gown, shrugged impatiently.

"Oh, nome, one of these here little Boy Scouts he came with me to show me the way. You see, ma'am, it's rightly my own fault, my not being all settled before dark. But I didn't get in on the steam-cars till about six o'clock this evening and I didn't want to miss the opening session at the big hall. So I went right there, packing my baggage along with me, just as soon as I'd got me a snack of supper, me not wanting to miss anything, as I was saying to you, ma'am. Then when the speechmaking and all was over, me and this little Boy Scout—he'd stayed right along with me at the hall—we put out to find where I was to stay. But he couldn't hardly drag one foot behind the other. Poor little wore-out fellow, I reckin he'd been running around all day. So a few minutes ago I made him go on home, me figuring I could find the house my own self. And—well, here I am, ma'am, imposing on your kindness and mighty sorry to do it, too."

"Never mind that part of it."

"But just as soon as I can get a dram of hot coffee in me I expect I'll feel stronger and then I'll be shoving along and not bother you any more. I reckin that long train ride and the excitement and everything must 'a' took it out of me, some way. There was a time when it wouldn't have bothered me at all—not a bit. Still, I'll have to confess I'm getting along, ma'am. I'll be eighty-four this coming ninth of August."

"Listen to me: You're not going to stir another inch tonight. You stay right here and tomorrow morning I'll decide myself whether you're fit to go trapesing off across to the other side of town."

"Oh, ma'am, I couldn't do that!"

"Why couldn't you?"

"But, ma'am, are you taking in any visitors during the reunion?"

"I wasn't aiming to." Her voice was grim. "But I'm fixing now to do that very little thing, whether or no."

"But honest, now—I—" He scuffled with his tired feet. "It's mighty good and mighty sweet of you, ma'am, but I'd hate to impose on you like that."

"No imposition. There're five spare bedrooms in this house—and nobody in any of them. And nobody going to be in any of them, either, while you're here—except you. I think you'll be comfortable."

"I know I'd be comfortable but—"

"Then it's all settled. By the way, I don't know your name yet?"

"My name is Braswell—Nathan Braswell, late high private of the rear rank in the Eighteenth Tennessee Infantry. But up at Forks of Hatchie—that's my home town, ma'am, a little town up in West Tennessee—they call me the Reverend Braswell, sometimes."

"Reverend?" Her eyelids narrowed. "Are you a minister?"

"Oh, nome. But sometimes when we're short on a preacher I make out to take the pulpit and read the Scriptures and make a little kind of a talk—not a regular sermon—just a little kind of a religious talk. And I'm purty active in church work generally. So I reckin that's why some people call me the Reverend Braswell. But I never use the entitlement myself—it wouldn't be becoming in a layman."

"I see. You preach but you're not a preacher. I guess you practice what you preach, too. You look like a good man, to me—and a good man can be set down anywhere and not suffer by it; at least that's my opinion. So, Mr. Braswell, right here is where you camp."

"Just as you say, ma'am." His surrender was complete now, his weariness was, too. "Probably you're right—if I tried to go any further tonight it's likely I wouldn't be much good tomorrow and I want to be spry and fresh so I can knock around and see if I can't run across some of my old pardners in the army. But excuse me again—you got my name but you ain't told me yours?"

"Call me Miss Sissie, if you want to. That's what nearly everybody does call me. Or else just plain Sis."

"All right, Miss Sissie, just as you say." He bowed to her with a grave simplicity. "And I'm sure I'm very much beholden to you, ma'am. It ain't every day that an old fellow like me is lucky enough to run into such a lovely nice lady as you."

He drank his coffee, and, being helped to his feet, he went upstairs with some aid from the lovely nice lady and presently was sound asleep in a clean bed in what he regarded as a very fine bedroom indeed. Its grandeur impressed him even through his tiredness.

Coming back down after seeing him properly bestowed, the mistress of the house hailed the colored girl. "Pansy," she said, "this place is out of business until further orders, understand?"

At that, Pansy seemed deeply puzzled. "But, Miss Sissie," she expostulated, "don't you remember 'at a suttin party—you know, Mista J. W. B.—is 'spectin' to be yere most any time wid—"

"Did you hear what I told you?" A quality of metallic harshness in Miss Sissie's voice was emphasized.

"Yessum, but you know yo'se'f how that there party, Mista J. W. B., is. He'll shore be dis'p'inted. He's liable raise Cain. He's—"

"Get him on the telephone; you know his number. Tell him this place is closed for tonight and for every day and every night until further notice from me. And tell the same thing to everybody else who calls up or stops by during the reunion. Get me?" By her tone she menaced the darky.

"Yassum."

"Then turn that hall light out."

For three days Mr. Braswell abode under that roof. Frequently during that time he remarked that he couldn't remember when he'd had a pleasanter stay anywhere. Nor could it be said that Miss Sissie failed in any possible effort to make the visit pleasant for him.

He limped down to breakfast next morning; to limp was the best he could do. His entertainer gave her household staff a double surprise, first by coming down to join him at the meal instead of taking her coffee and rolls in her room and second by appearing not in negligée but in a plain dark house-gown which accentuated rather than softened the square contours of her face and the sharp lines in it. By daylight the two had better opportunity to study each other than the somewhat hurried meeting of the night before had afforded.

She saw in him a gentle tottery relic of a man with a pair of faded unworldly old eyes looking out from a bland, wrinkly, rather empty face. He saw in her a most kindly and considerate hostess. Privately he decided she must have had plenty of sorrow in her time—something or other about her told him that life had bestowed upon her more than her proper share of hard knocks. He figured that living here alone in such a big house—except for the servants she seemed to be quite alone—must be lonesome for her, too.

As they sat down, just the two of them, he said, not apologetically exactly but a bit timidly:

"I hope, ma'am, you don't mind if I say a grace at your table? I always like to invoke the divine blessing before I break bread—seems like to me it makes the victuals taste better. Or maybe"—he hesitated politely—"maybe it's your custom to ask the blessing your own self?"

"You say it, please," she urged him in a curious strained fashion, which, however, he did not notice, and lowered her head. She lifted it once—to shoot a quick venomous glance at Pansy, who stood to serve, and a convulsive giggle which had formed in Pansy's throat died instantly. Then she bowed it again and kept it bowed while he asked God to sanctify this food to their uses and to be merciful to all within those walls and to all His children everywhere. For Jesus' sake, Amen!

She piled his plate abundantly and, for all his bodily infirmity, he showed her a healthy appetite. He talked freely, she encouraging him by proving a good listener. He was a widower with one married daughter. Since his wife's death he had made his home with this daughter. Her husband was a mighty fine man—not religious, but high-principled and doing very well indeed as a banker, considering that Forks of Hatchie was such a small town. He himself had been in the grain and feed business for most of his life but was retired now. He'd never been much of a hand for gadding over the world. Going to reunions once a year was about the extent of his traveling around. In all the time since the United Confederate Veterans had been formed he'd missed but one reunion—that was the spring when his wife died.

"Minty—that's my daughter, ma'am—Minty, she didn't want me to come to this one," he went on. "She was afraid for me to be putting out alone on such a long trip 'way down here; she kept saying, Minty did, she was afraid the excitement might be too much for me at my age. But I says to her, I says, 'Minty, child, when my time comes for me to go I don't ask anything better than that it should be whilst I'm amongst my old comrades, with the sound of one of our old battle songs ringing in my ears!' I says to her, 'Shucks, but what's the use of talking that way! Nothing's going to happen to me. I can get there and I can get back!' I says to her. 'Going to reunion makes me feel young and spry all over again.' But, ma'am, I'm afraid Minty was right about it, this time anyhow. I actually don't believe I'm going to be able to get back down-town for today's doings—not for the morning's session anyway. I have to own up to you that I feel all kind of let-down and no-account, someway."

So through the forenoon he sat in an easy chair in an inner sitting-room and Miss Sissie, abandoning whatever else she might have had to do, read to him the accounts of the great event which filled column after column of the morning paper. He dozed off occasionally but she kept on reading, her voice droning across the placid quiet. Following the dinner which came at midday, she prevailed on him to take a real nap, and he stretched out on a sofa under a light coverlid which she tucked about him and slept peacefully until four o'clock. Late in the afternoon a closed car containing a couple—a man and a woman—stopped in the alleyway behind the house and the driver came to the back door, but Miss Sissie went out and gave him a message for his passengers and he returned to his car and drove away. There were no other callers that day.

Mr. Braswell fretted a little after supper over his inability to muster up strength for getting to the auditorium, but somewhat was consoled by her assurances that a good night's rest should put him in proper trim for marching in the big parade next morning. By nine o'clock he was in bed and Miss Sissie had a silent idle evening at home and seemed not ungrateful for it.

On the second morning the ancient greeted her in what plainly was his official wardrobe for parading. A frayed and threadbare butternut jacket, absurdly short, with a little peaked tail sticking out behind and a line of tarnished brass buttons spaced down its front, hung grotesquely upon his withered framework. Probably it had fitted him once; now it was acres too loose. Pinned to the left breast was a huge badge, evidently home-made, of yellowed white silk, and lengthwise of it in straggled letters worked with faded red floss ran the number and name of his regiment. In his hand he carried a slouch-hat which had been black once but now was a rusty brown, with a scrap of black ostrich-plume fastened to its band by a brass token.

With trembling fingers he proudly caressed the badge.

"My wife made it for me out of a piece of her own wedding-dress nearly thirty years ago," he explained. "I've worn it to every reunion since then. It's funny how you put me in mind of my wife. Not that you look like her nor talk like her either. She was kind of small and she had a low voice and you're so much taller and your way of speaking is deeper and carries further than hers did. And of course you can't be more than half as old as she'd be if she'd lived. Funny, but you do remind me of her, though. Still, I reckin that's easy to explain. All good women favor each other some way even when they don't look alike. It's something inside of them that does it, I judge—goodness and purity and thinking Christian thoughts."

If she winced at that last his innocent, weakened old eyes missed it. Anyhow the veteran very soon had personal cause for distress. He had to confess that he wasn't up to marching. Leaving the dining-room, he practically collapsed. He was heart-broken.

"Don't you worry," said Miss Sissie, in that masterful way of hers. "Even if you're not able to turn out with the rest of them you're going to see the parade. I can't send you down-town in my own car—it's—it's broken down—and I can't go with you myself—I—I'm going to be busy. But I can send you in a taxicab with a careful man to drive and you can see the parade."

"That's mighty sweet of you—but then, I reckin it's your nature to be sweet and thoughtful for other folks," he said gratefully. "But, ma'am"—and doubt crept into his voice—"but ain't all the public hacks likely to be engaged beforehand for today?"

"I happen to know the manager of the leading taxicab company here," she told him. "He'll do what I say even if he has to take a rig away from somebody else. I'll telephone him."

"But with the streets all crowded the way they'll be, won't it be hard to find a place where I can watch the other boys marching by?" In his eagerness he was childish.

"That'll be arranged, too," she stated. "As it so happens, I also know the chief of police. I'll call him up and give him the number of the taxi you're in and I'll guarantee one of his policemen will be on the special lookout for you at the far end of the Drive to see to it that you get a good place somewhere along the route."

"Seems like to me the most important people in this town must respect you mighty highly!" he exclaimed happily. "Well, I guess it's that same way everywhere—all kinds of people are bound to recognize a real lady when they meet her and look up to her!"

"Oh, yes, there's one thing more." She added this as if by an afterthought. "You needn't tell anybody you meet—any of your old friends or any of the committeemen or anybody—where you're stopping. You see, I didn't arrange to take in any visitors for the reunion—there were reasons why I didn't care to take in anyone—and now that I have you with me I wouldn't care for anybody connected with the local arrangements to know about it. You understand, don't you?—they might think I was presuming on their rights."

"Oh, yes'm, I understand," he said unsuspectingly. "It'll just be a little secret between us if that's the way you'd rather it was. But I couldn't rightly tell anybody anyhow—seeing that you ain't ever told me what your last name is. I'd like to know it, too—I aim to write you a letter after I get home."

"My name is Lamprey," she said. "Cecelia Lamprey. I don't hear it very often myself—at least, not spoken out in full. And now I'd better be ringing up those influential friends of mine—you mustn't be late getting started."

The same taxicab driver who drove him on this day came again on the third day to take Miss Sissie's venerable house guest to his train. It would appear that her car still was out of commission.

She did not accompany him to the station. Domestic cares would hold her, she told him. She did not go to the front of the house to see him off, either. Indeed a more observant person than Mr. Braswell might have marveled that so constantly she had secluded herself indoors during his visit; and not only indoors, but behind windows curtained against the bright, warm Southern sunshine. They exchanged their farewells in her living-room.

"I ain't never going to forget you," he told her. "If you'd been my own daughter you couldn't 'a' treated me any nicer than what you have—and me just an old stove-up spavined country-jake that you never saw before in your life and probably never will see again. You ain't seen fit, ma'am, to tell me much about yourself—seems like you let me do most of the talking, and that suited me—but old as I am I know a perfect lady when I see one and that's what you are, ma'am, and what always you must have been and always will be—good-by and God bless you!"

Saying nothing, she bent in the attitude of one accepting a benediction, and a moment later she was following him to the door and watching him as he crept in his labored, faltering gait along the entrance-hall. Under his arm was his luncheon to be eaten on the train; she had with her own hands prepared and boxed it. She waited there on the threshold until the hooded front door clicked behind him.

"Pansy," she called then toward the back of the house, and now her voice had in it a customary rasping quality which, strangely, had been almost altogether lacking from it these past two or three days. "You, Pansy!"

"Yassum."

"You might call up that party that we turned down the other night and tell him this place has reopened for business as usual."

Approximately two weeks later, Mr. Randolph Embury, president of the Forks of Hatchie People's Bank, wrote as follows to the mayor of that city where the veterans had met:

> "Dear Mr. Mayor: You may possibly recall that we met in 1922 while serving as delegates for our respective states at the Inter-Southern Commercial Congress in Norfolk? I am therefore taking advantage of our slight acquaintance and am trespassing upon your patience to ask a favor which means a great deal to my wife.
>
> "Her aged father, the late Nathan Braswell, attended the recent Confederate Reunion in your city. Almost immediately upon his arrival back at this place he suffered a stroke of paralysis. Within ten days a second stroke resulted fatally to him. The interment took place yesterday, the twenty-ninth inst. His loss in this community is very deeply mourned. He was the last old soldier left here.
>
> "Although rendered completely helpless by the first stroke, he remained almost entirely rational and coherent until the second one occurred. In this stage of his illness he spoke repeatedly of his experiences while at the reunion. He was a guest in the private home of one who must have been a most cultured and charming lady—undoubtedly a lady of position and affluence. By her graciousness and her zealous

care of him and her constant ministrations to his comfort she made a deep impression upon him. He was most anxious that she should know of his gratitude, and repeatedly he charged us to write her, telling how much he appreciated the attentions shown him.

"Naturally, during his illness and until after the interment neither my wife nor myself had much time for letter-writing. But this morning Mrs. Embury wrote to this lady, thanking her in her dead father's name and in ours and telling her that with practically his last conscious breath he spoke affectionately of her and paid tribute to her splendid womanly qualities and even uttered a little prayer for her well-being. He was a very devout man. That letter I enclose with this one, but in an unaddressed envelop. Mrs. Embury, of course, is most anxious that it should reach the intended recipient promptly.

"The reason for not addressing it you will understand when I tell you that my father-in-law could not remember his benefactress's last name except that it began with an 'L' and sounded something like 'Lampey' or 'Lambry.' He referred to her always as 'Miss Sissie,' which I would judge was her familiar name among more intimate friends. He could not remember the name of the street upon which she resided. However, he did describe the residence as being a very large and very handsome one, standing in a somewhat secluded part of the outskirts and not far from where a railroad track and an overhead viaduct were.

"This, then, is the favor I would ask of you: If the lady is as prominently connected as I had reason to believe from Mr. Braswell's statements, I assume you know her already. If not, I take it that it should not be a very difficult matter to locate one whose character and attainments must have given her a high standing among your good citizens. So I am asking you to see to it that the enclosed letter is put at once into her hands.

"Thanking you in advance for any trouble or inconvenience to which you may be put in carrying out our wishes, I remain,

"Yours most sincerely,

"Randolph Embury."

And within four days got back the following reply:

"Mayor's Office, June 2.

"Dear Sir:

"Yours received and contents carefully noted. In reply to same would say that while ready at any time to serve you and your good wife in every way possible, yet in this case I am put in a delicate attitude and fear you also may be put in one should I undertake to fulfill your desire.

"Undoubtedly the person that your late father-in-law had in mind was one Cecelia Lamprey, better known as 'Sis.' But not by the widest stretch of imagination could anyone think of her as a 'lady.' She is the proprietress of a most notorious assignation house located on North Bonaventure Avenue, this city, and according to my best information and belief, has always been a woman of loose morals and bad repute. I might add that having been elected on a reform ticket and being committed to the task of ridding our city of evil, I am at present setting on foot an effort to close up her establishment, which has until lately enjoyed secret 'protection,' and to drive her from our midst.

"Accordingly, I am constrained to believe that, being probably semi-delirious, the lately deceased, your esteemed father-in-law, must have made a mistake. I assume that he had 'Sis' Lamprey's house pointed out to him and in his ravings got it confused with the domicile where he was housed during his sojourn among us. It is not conceivable to me that a man such as you describe would, while in his sober senses, set foot inside an establishment so readily recognizable at a glance as being absolutely disreputable, let alone remain there for any appreciable period of time. It is equally incredible to think of 'Sis' opening her doors to any decent person or for any worthy purpose.

"In view of these facts I am constrained to believe your wife would shrink from any contact or any communication with such an individual. I am therefore taking the liberty of holding her letter on my desk until you and she have had opportunity to consider this embarrassing situation and to decide what you should do. My advice is that you instruct me to return the letter to you at once and consider the incident closed. However, I await your further instruction.

(Signed) "Jason Broderick, Mayor."

To which the following reply was immediately dispatched by wire:

"Nevertheless, on behalf of my wife and myself, kindly be so good as immediately to deliver the letter in question to the lady in question."

The Order of the Bath

IT SEEMED like everything that was happening that week happened to the Gridleys. Substantially, these were Mrs. Gridley's own words in speaking of the phenomena.

To begin with, their waitress quit practically without any warning at all. Afflicted by that strange and sudden migratory impulse which at times affects most of the birds and many of the hired help, she walked out between two suns. In the second place, the water famine reached a point where the board of trustees forbade the use of water for all-over bathing purposes or for wetting-down lawns or washing cars or sprinkling streets or spraying flower-beds even; and Mr. Gridley, as one of the trustees, felt it incumbent upon him to set a proper example before the rest of the community by putting his own household upon the strictest of rations, abluently speaking. In the third place, Mr. Jeffreys Boyce-Upchurch, the eminent English novelist, became their guest. And fourthly, although not occurring in this order, the Gridleys took on a butler of the interesting name of Launcelot Ditto.

To a considerable extent, three of these events were interrelated. The drought which had brought on the shortage in the village reservoir was the isolated exception, a manifestation of freaky nature and of absolutely unprecedented weather conditions. But the others were more or less coordinated. If their old waitress had not quit on them the Gridleys would not have been in the market for a new servant to fill the vacancy, and if Mr. Boyce-Upchurch had not been coming to stay with them it was possible she might not have quit at all. There was a suspicion that she was influenced by a private objection to so much company in the heat of the summer, Mrs. Gridley's mother and sister from Baltimore, the latter bringing her little boy with her, having just concluded a two weeks' stay; and if it had not been Mr. Boyce-Upchurch who was coming, but some less important person, the Gridleys would have been content with hiring for the succession one who also was a female and home-grown, or if not exactly home-grown, one belonging to almost any of the commoner Nordic stocks—say Scandinavian or Celtic—whereas it was felt that the advent of a Boyce-Upchurch called for something of an especially rich and fruity imported nature in the line of butlers. At least, such was the language employed by Mrs. Gridley's brother, Mr. Oliver Braid, in describing, this phase of the issue. He—young Mr. Braid—was the only member of the household who declined to take the situation seriously. In this regard he stood quite alone. Mr. Gridley took it seriously, as, to a more or less degree, did the neighbors also. But Mrs. Gridley took it most seriously of all.

Its seriousness began to lay hold upon her in the morning on a Monday, which proverbially is a bothersome day for housewives anyhow, when Miss Rena Belle Titworthy, the recording secretary of the Ingleglade Woman's Club and its only salaried officer, called to break the news to her, it being that in the judgment of a majority of the active workers in the club Mrs. Gridley should have the distinguished pleasure of entertaining Mr. Boyce-Upchurch on the occasion of his impending visit. In a more vulgar circle of life the same thing has been termed passing the buck.

"But," expostulated Mrs. Gridley, "but—of course I feel flattered and I am sure Henry will, too, when he comes home tonight and hears about it—but I'm afraid we couldn't make such a prominent man comfortable. Our house is rather small and all that, and besides there's Olga having packed up and left only last night and all that. Really, don't you think, Miss Rena Belle, that he would prefer to go to the hotel where he could be—you know—quieter and more to himself? Or to Mrs. Wainwright's? She's the president of the club and she's the madam chairman of the executive committee besides, and naturally the pleasure of having Mr. Boyce-Upchurch should go to her. Her house is a mansion, almost, while we—"

Miss Titworthy caught her up right there.

"No," said Miss Titworthy firmly. Miss Titworthy had authority about her and a considerable distinction. She was large and deep-chested and combined in her manner the magisterial and the managerial and, subtly, the maternal. She had all that a motherly woman should have, except children. And, as just stated, she was large, while on the other hand Mrs. Gridley was slight and, upon the whole, plastic by temperament, not to say bordering on the yielding. And bulk, in such cases, counts.

"Pardon me," said Miss Titworthy still more firmly, "pardon me, my dear, but no. Madam Chairman Wainwright is closing up their place to go to their other place in the Berkshires; you must have known that. Probably you forgot it. And the hotel is quite out of the question. I had a letter only yesterday from Mr. Boyce-Upchurch, written by him personally—it seems he doesn't carry a secretary with him on his tour—saying he preferred stopping at some private home. He mentioned the inconveniences of American hotels and something about their exceedingly high rates. I'm going to keep it as a souvenir. And so, what with Madam Chairman Wainwright closing up and you being the first vice-president—well, there you are, aren't you?" concluded Miss Titworthy with a gesture which was meant to be a death blow to further argument.

"And then the water being shut off—I'm thinking of that, too," said Mrs. Gridley, but in a weakening tone. "Henry had the plumber come and disconnect all three of the bathtubs. He said he wasn't going to put temptation in the way of his own family or himself, either. I know lots of people are doing it on the sly—using a hose, too—but I can't even have a little water in a sprinkling can for my poor withered flowers. Look at them out of that window there—just literally drying up. And we're sending all the wash, even the flat pieces, to the Eagle Laundry. And Henry is going to his club in town for a bath every day, and I'm doing the best I can with the wash-basin and a sponge, and the way Nora—that's my cook's name—and Delia, the waitress—now that Olga has gone, Delia's the only other girl we've got left—the way those two carry on and complain you'd think I was personally responsible for the fact that not a drop of rain has fallen in over two months. And the English being such great hands for their tubs and all, and Mr. Boyce-Upchurch being an Englishman and all, why, I'm honestly afraid, Miss Rena Belle, that he'll be awfully put out."

"I dessay he'll be able to accommodate himself to a condition over which none of us has any control," stated Miss Titworthy. "He'll arrive Wednesday afternoon on the five o'clock boat. He asked that he be met with a car. I dessay you'll be wanting to give a little dinner to him Wednesday evening. I don't know what he'll want to do Thursday morning—be driven around, I imagine. And Thursday afternoon there's the reception at the Woman's Club, and his lecture is that night, and Friday he leaves for Trenton where he has his next date on Saturday. He did write something about preferring to be ridden over to Trenton."

"I could take him over myself," said Mrs. Gridley, her citadel undermined and she rapidly capitulating, "if he doesn't mind going in a two-seated runabout."

"There'll be no trouble about the car," stated Miss Titworthy. "I dessay someone will proffer the use of a touring car."

"Well, that point is settled then," agreed Mrs. Gridley, now entirely committed to the undertaking. "But I must get somebody in and broken in to take Olga's place between now and Wednesday. Really that gives me only today and tomorrow, and help is so hard to get, you've no idea, Miss Titworthy! I suppose I'd better run into town this afternoon and go to the employment agencies. No, I can't,—there's my bridge lesson. And tomorrow is the Fergus' tea. I can't go then, either. I promised Mrs. Fergus I'd pour. I suppose I'll have to get Henry or my brother Oliver to do it. But neither one of them would know how to pick out a girl, provided there's any choice at the agencies to pick from—oh, dear!"

"Had you thought of a butler?" inquired Miss Titworthy.

"A butler?"

"Yes, instead of a maid. You'll pardon the suggestion but I was thinking that Mr. Boyce-Upchurch being a foreigner and accustomed, of course, to butlers, and a butler giving a sort of air—a tone, as it were—to a household, that perhaps—well—"

They had fallen on fertile ground, those seeds. They were sprouting, germinating. Before the massive shoulders of the Ingleglade Woman's Club's efficient recording secretary had vanished down the bowery and winding reaches of Edgecliff Avenue they were putting forth small green speculative shoots through Mrs. Gridley's mind. Always and ever, from the very first days of her married life, Mrs. Gridley had cherished in the back of her mind a picture of an establishment in which the butler, a figure of dignity and poise and gray striped trousers in the daytime but full-dress by night, would be the chief of staff. As what woman has not? And now for the gratifying of that secret ambition she had an excuse and a reason.

Section Two of this narrative brings us to another conversation. At this stage the narrative seems somehow to fall naturally into sections, but one has a premonition that toward the last it will become a thing of cutbacks and close-ups and iris-ins and fade-outs, like a movie. It brings us to this other conversation, which passed over the telephone between Mrs. Gridley and her brother Mr. Oliver Braid.

"Well, Dumplings," said that gentleman, speaking at noon of Tuesday from his office, "the hellish deed is done!"

"You got one then?" she answered eagerly.

"Got one? Madam, you wrong me and you low-rate him. I got the One and only One—the Original One. The only misleading thing about him is his name. Be prepared for a pleasant shock. It's Launcelot Ditto. I ask you to let that soak into your tissues and be absorbed by the system. Only Ditto means more of the same and if I'm any judge, there aren't any more at home like him and there never will be. But the Launcelot part fits like a union suit.

"Oh, girl, I'm telling you he's got everything, including the adenoids. Not the puny domestic brand of our own faulty and deficient land, mind you, but the large, super-extra-fine export, golden-russet adenoid of that favored island whose boast is that Britons never shall be slaves except to catarrh. And he's as solemn as a Masonic funeral. And he stepped right out of a book by way of the stage. He ought to be serving strawberries and Devonshire cream on the terrace to the curate of St. Ives and the dear old Dowager Duchess of What-you-may-call-'em, while the haw-haw blooms in the hedgerow. He ought to be coming on at the beginning of Act One to answer the telephone and pat the sofa pillows smooth and fold up 'The Pink 'Un,' and sigh deeply because the Young Marster is going to the dogs. He ought to be outlining the plot to a housekeeper in rustling black silk named Meadows."

"Ollie Braid, are you delirious?"

"Not at all. I am dazed, dazzled, blinded, but I am not delirious. I can half shut my eyes and see him in his hours of ease sitting in our buttery perusing that sprightly volume with full-page illustrations entitled 'The Stately Homes of Old England.' Sounds pretty good, eh what? Good—hell! He's perfect. He certainly ought to do a lot for us socially over there in Ingleglade. I can half shut 'em again and see the local peasantry turning a lovely pea-green with envy as he issues forth on the front lawn to set up the archery butts so that we may practice up on our butting. That's another place where the buttery will come in handy."

"He was willing to come out, then?"

"Well, at first he did balk a little on the idea of demeaning himself by accepting a position with the lower or commuting classes. The country, yes; the town, perhaps, but the environs—well, hardly. That was his attitude. But with my lilting love-song I won him, he-siren that I am. I told him Ingleglade was not really suburban but merely outlying, if one gets what one means. That wasn't deception, that was diplomacy. Anyhow, haven't we got some of the outlyingest real-estate dealers in the entire state of New Jersey? Do we not combine all the drawbacks of the city with few or none of the advantages of the country? I often sit and wonder whence comes this magic power of mine for bending strong natures to my will. The crowning stroke was when I told him Boyce-Upchurch was so shortly to honor us. That won him. He admires Boyce-Upchurch tremendously. Not his books—

he hasn't read 'em—but it seems he knows Boyce-Upchurch's uncle, who's an archduke or a belted earl or something well up among the face-cards."

"You talk too much, Oliver. You think you're funny and you aren't."

"Oh, but, madam—"

"Shut up a minute! He has references, of course?"

"Fair lady, sweet dame, I plight you my solemn word that with the references he's got from noble British families he could be our ambassador to the Court of St. James the day after he took out his naturalization papers. He's temporarily unattached but that's because he hasn't been able to find anybody worthy of him. He's only taking us on trial. Why hark ye, lass, he used to work for the 'Un'rable 'Urrible 'Ubbs. He's got the documents to prove it."

"The what?"

"I'm merely telling you what he said. It didn't sound like a name to me, either, at first. But now it's beginning to grow on me; I may make a song out of it."

"When will he be out?"

"This very night. I'm chaperoning him personally. We are to meet at the ferry, and I'm to wear a primrose in my buttonhole in case he's forgotten how I look. I'm reading up now on the history of the Norman Conquest. I want to be prepared to meet him on his own ground should he care for conversation."

"Ollie, you always were an idiot."

"Dear wench, 'tis a family failing. I have a sister, a flower-like slip of a thing, but, alas, she suffers from pollen in the pod."

"And what's more, she's going to give you a hard slap the first chance." Over the line her voice took on an uncertain tone. "Of course I know you're exaggerating frightfully but—"

"As regards Launcelot, you couldn't exaggerate. He confounds the powers of description. He baffles the most inventive imagination. He—"

"Oh, do listen! All at once I'm beginning to worry about Norah. I hadn't thought of her until right now."

"What of Norah?"

"Well, from what you say and even making allowances for your romancing, this man must be very English. And Norah's so—so Irish. Delia is, too, for that matter. But especially Norah."

"Strange, but I had noticed that myself about our Norah."

"Notice it?—I should say. She calls the English—what is it she calls them?"

"Black-and-Tans. Also Saxon oppressors. Also a name which is pronounced by hissing first and then gritting the teeth in a bitter manner. I think it's an old Gaelic word signifying Oliver Cromwell. You may recall having heard that Norah has a brother who had some personal misunderstanding with the authorities in Dublin in the year 1916. He became at that time very seriously antagonized toward them. And it looks to me as though Norah was inclined to take sides in the controversy."

"Naturally. But she may make trouble. I hadn't thought of that before. And if he should happen to do anything or say anything to arouse her or if she should take one of her grudges against Mr. Boyce-Upchurch—oh, I'm scared, Oliver!"

"Prithee be blithe and gay. Norah and I understand each other. We have a bond between us or will have one as soon as I tell her privately that I'm contributing to a fund for financing an uprising on the part of those poor down-trodden Hindus. Immediately on my arrival this evening I'll take Norah apart and—"

"You'll do what?"

"Don't worry. I'm going to put her back together again, so you'd never notice it. But I'll take her apart and beg her for my sake to remain calm, cool, and collected. You leave Norah to me."

"I suppose I'll have to; there's nothing else to be done. And, Oliver, you may be a born idiot but just the same you're a dear for going to all this trouble on my account and I do appreciate it. There—I'm throwing you a kiss by wire."

"Kindly confine yourself to appreciating Launcelot—that, God wot, will be reward enough for me, fond heart. And in case either our butler or our guest, or both of them, should desire to call the tenants in from the estate, all to stand and join in singing the Royal Anthem, please remember how it goes—God Save the King until Norah's Brother Can Get at Him!"

Ditto shifted from civilian garb and served dinner that evening. It became a meal that was more than a meal; it became a ceremonial. There was a formalism to it, there was pomp and circumstance. The passing of a dish was invested with a ritualistic essence. Under Ditto's ministrations so simple a dessert as cold rice pudding took on a new meaning. One wondered what Ditto could have done with a fancy ice. One felt that merely with a loaf of bread and a jug of wine and none of the other ingredients of Old Omar's recipe for a pleasant evening, he nevertheless could have fabricated the plausible illusion of a banquet of courses. Mrs. Gridley was thrilled to her marrows—possibly a trifle self-conscious but thrilled.

After dinner and a visit to the service wing, Mr. Braid sought out his sister on the veranda where she was doing what most of her sister-villagers of parched Ingleglade were doing at that same hour—wishing for rain.

"Well, Dumplings," he said, "you may continue to be your own serene self. In me behold a special plenipotentiary doing plenipotenching by the day, week, or job, satisfaction guaranteed or money refunded. I've just had a little heart-to-heart chat with Norah and there isn't a cloud in the sky as large as a man's hand."

"I wish there were—this terrible drought!" she said, her thoughts divided between the two concerns uppermost in her mind. "What did you say to her?"

"I approached the subject with my customary tact. With a significant glance toward the visiting nobleman I reminded Norah that blood was thicker than water, to which she piously responded by thanking God for three thousand miles of the water. Still, I think she's going to keep the peace. For the moment, she's impressed, or shall I say fascinated. Ditto is high-hatting her something scandalous, and she's taking it. For all our Norah's democratic principles she evidently carries in her blood the taint of a lurking admiration for those having an aristocratic bearing, and Ditto is satisfying the treasonable instinct which until now she has had no chance to gratify—at least, not while living with us. As for Delia, that shameless hussy is licking the spoon and begging for more. She's a traitor to United Ireland and the memory of Daniel O'Connell.

"Mind you, I'm not predicting that the spell will endure. The ancient feud may blaze up. We may yet have a race war in our kitchen. For all you know, you may at this moment be sitting pretty on a seething volcano; but unless something unforeseen occurs I think I may safely promise you peace and harmony, during the great event which is about to ensue in our hitherto simple lives.

"For, as I said just now, Norah is under a thrall—temporary perhaps but a thrall just the same. Well, I confess to being all thralled-up myself. That certainly was a high-church dinner—that one tonight was. Several times I was almost overcome by a well-nigh irrepressible temptation to get up and ask Ditto to take my place and let me pass a few things to him."

"I don't believe there ever has been such a drought," said Mrs. Gridley.

"Ho, hum, well, I suppose we'll all get used to this grandeur in time," said Mr. Braid. "I wonder if he is going to put on the full vestments every night no matter whether we have company or not? I wish on nights when we do have very special company he'd loan me his canonicals and wear mine. I expect he'd regard it as presuming if I asked for the address of his tailor? What do you think, Dumplings?"

"I wish it would rain," said Mrs. Gridley. "And I hope and pray Norah doesn't fly off into one of her tantrums. I wonder does Mr. Boyce-Upchurch like Thousand Islands dressing or the Russian better? What were you just saying, Ollie?"

Mr. Braid tapped his skull with his forefinger.

"Ah, the family failing," he murmured, "that dread curse which afflicts our line! With some of the inmates it day by day grows worse. And there's nothing to be done—it's congenital."

"I expect the best thing to do is just to take a chance on the Russian," said Mrs. Gridley. "If he doesn't like it, why he doesn't like it and I can't help myself, I didn't catch what you said just then, Ollie?"

"Abstraction overcomes the victim; the mind wanders; the reason totters," said Mr. Braid. "By the way, I wonder if Ditto would care to have his room brightened with a group view of the Royal Family—the King in shooting costume, the Queen wearing the sort of hat that the King would probably like to shoot; the lesser members grouped about? You know the kind of thing I mean."

"Would you start off tomorrow night with clams or a melon?" asked Mrs. Gridley.

"Or perhaps he'd prefer an equestrian photograph of the Prince of Wales," said Mr. Braid. "I know where I can pick up one second hand.

I'll stop by tomorrow and price it. It's a very unusual pose. Shows the Prince *on* the horse."

"Melon, I guess," said Mrs. Gridley. "Most Englishmen like cantaloups, I hear. They're not so common among them."

"My duty being done I think I shall retire to my chamber to take a slight, not to say sketchy bath in a shaving mug," said Mr. Braid.

"I wish it would rain," said Mrs. Gridley.

Numbers of friendly persons met Mr. Boyce-Upchurch at the boat that Wednesday afternoon. Miss Titworthy inevitably was there and riding herd, so to speak, on a swaying flock of ewes of the Ingleglade Woman's Club. She organized a sort of impromptu welcoming committee at the ferry-house. Mrs. Gridley missed this, though. She had to stay outside with her runabout. Her husband and brother—the latter had escorted Mr. Boyce-Upchurch to One Hundred and Twenty-fifth Street from the University Club where he had been a guest of someone since finishing his New England swing the week before—were with the visiting celebrity. They surrendered him over to Miss Titworthy, who made him run the gantlet of the double receiving line and introduced him to all the ladies. Of these a bolder one would seek to detain him a minute while she told him how much she admired his books and which one of them she admired most, but an awed and timider one would merely say she was *so* glad to meet him, having heard of him *so* often. Practically every timider one said this. It was as though she followed a memorized formula. Now and then was a bolder bold one who breasted forward at him and cooed in the manner of a restrained but secretly amorous hen-pigeon.

Mr. Boyce-Upchurch bore up very well under the strain of it all. Indeed, he seemed rather to expect it, having been in this country for several months now and having lectured as far west as Omaha. He plowed along between the greeters, a rather short and compact figure but very dignified, with his monocle beaming ruddy in the rays of the late afternoon sun and with a set smile on his face, and he murmuring the conventional words.

The ceremonial being concluded, the two gentlemen reclaimed him and led him outside, and there he met Mrs. Gridley, who drove him up the Palisades Road, her husband and brother following in a chartered taxi with Mr. Boyce-Upchurch's luggage. There was quite a good deal of luggage, including a strapped steamer-rug and two very bulging, very rugged-looking kit bags and a leather hat-box and a mysterious flat package in paper wrappings which Mr. Braid told Mr. Gridley he was sure must contain a framed steel engraving of the Death of Nelson.

Mr. Braid pattered on:

"For a truly great and towering giant of literature, our friend seems very easy to control in money matters. Docile—that's the word for it, docile. He let me tip the porter at the club for bringing down these two tons of his detachable belongings, and on the way up Madison Avenue he deigned to let me jump out and go in a shop and buy him an extra strap for his blanket roll, and he graciously suffered me to pay for a telegram he sent from the other side, and also for that shoe-shine and those evening papers he got on the boat. Told me he hadn't learned to distinguish our Yankee small change. Always getting the coins mixed up, he said. Maybe he hasn't had any experience."

"Rather brusk in his way of speaking to a fellow," admitted Mr. Gridley. "You might almost call it short. And rather fussy about getting what he wants, I should say. Still, I suppose he has a great deal on his mind."

"Launcelot will fairly dote on him," said Mr. Braid. "Mark my words, Launcelot is going to fall in love with him on the spot."

Meanwhile, Mrs. Gridley was endeavoring to explain to Mr. Boyce-Upchurch why it was that in a town lying practically on a river so large and so wide as the Hudson there could be a water shortage. He couldn't appear to grasp it. He declared it to be extraordinary.

This matter of a water shortage apparently lingered in his mind, for half an hour later following tea, as he was on the point of going aloft to his room to dress for dinner he called back to his host from half-way up the stairs:

"I say, Gridley, no water in the taps, your wife tells me. Extraordinary, what? Tell you what: I'll be needing a rub-down tonight—stuffy climate here and all that. So later on just let one of your people fetch up a portable tub to my room and bring along lots of water, will you? The water needn't be hot. Like it warm, though. Speak about it, will you, to that slavey of yours."

Mrs. Gridley gave a quick little wincing gasp and a hunted look about her. But Delia had gone to carry Mr. Boyce-Upchurch's waistcoat upstairs. The episode of the waistcoat occurred a few minutes before, immediately after the guest had been ushered into the house.

"Frightfully warm," he remarked on entering the living-room. "Tell me, is America always so frightfully warm in summer?" Then, without waiting for an answer, he said: "Think I must rid myself of the wescut. All over perspiration, you know." So saying, he took off first his coat and next his waistcoat and hung the waistcoat on a chair and then put the coat back on again. Still, as Mr. Braid remarked in an undertone to nobody in particular, it wasn't exactly as though Mr. Boyce-Upchurch had stripped to his shirt-sleeves because, so Mr. Braid pointed out to himself, the waistband of the trousers came up so high, especially at the back, and the suspenders—he caught himself here and mentally used the word "braces" instead—the braces were so nice and broad that you didn't see enough of the shirt really to count.

Dinner was at seven-thirty, with twelve at the table and place cards, and Delia impressed to aid Ditto at serving, and the finest show of flowers that Mrs. Gridley's dusty and famished garden could yield. She had spent two hours that afternoon picking the least wilted of the blossoms and designing the decorative effects. Little things occurred, one or two of them occurring before the dinner got under way.

Ditto approached the lady of the house. "Madame," he said throatily, in the style of one who regally bears yet more regal tidings, "madame, Mr. Boyce-Upchurch doesn't care for cocktails. 'E would prefer a sherry and bittez."

"Oh!" exclaimed Mrs. Gridley in a small panic of dismay. "Oh, I'm so sorry but I'm afraid there isn't any sherry."

"There's cooking sherry out in the kitchen, sis," said Mr. Braid, who stood alongside her smiling happily about nothing apparently. "Tackled it myself the other day when I was feeling daredevilish."

"But the bitters—whatever they are!"

"Give him some of that cooking sherry of yours and he'll never miss the bitters."

"Sh-h-h," she warned, "he might hear you."

He didn't, though. At that moment Mr. Boyce-Upchurch was in conversation with Mrs. Thwaites and her husband from two doors away. He was speaking to them of the hors d'œuvres which had just been passed, following the cocktails. The Thwaites were fellow countrymen of his; their accent had betrayed them. Perhaps he felt since they spoke his language that he could be perfectly frank with them. Frankness appeared to be one of his outstanding virtues.

It now developed that the relish attracted him and at the same time repelled. Undeniably, Norah's fancy ran to the concoction of dishes, notably, appetizers and salads, which one read about in certain standard women's magazines. Her initial offering this night had novelty about it, with a touch of mystery. Its general aspect suggested that Norah had drowned a number of inoffensive anchovies in thick mayonnaise and then, repenting of the crime, had vainly endeavored to resuscitate her victims with grated cheese.

"Messy-looking, eh?" Mr. Boyce-Upchurch was pointing an accusing finger at the coiled remains on a bit of toast which Mrs. Thwaites had accepted, and he was speaking in a fairly clear voice audible to any who might be near at hand. "Glad I didn't take one. Curious fancy, eh what, having the savory before dinner instead of afterwards—that is, if the ghastly thing is meant to be a savory?"

Major Thwaites mumbled briefly in a military way. It might have been an affirmative mumble or almost any other variety of mumble; you could take your choice. Mrs. Thwaites, biting at her lower lip, went over and peered out of a front window. She had an unusually high color, due perhaps to the heat.

That, substantially, was all that happened in the preliminary stages of the dinner party. There was one more trifling incident which perhaps is worthy to be recorded but this did not occur until the second course was brought on. The second course was terrapin. Mrs. Gridley was a Marylander and she had been at pains to order real diamond-backs from down on the Eastern Shore and personally to make the stew according to an old recipe in her family. Besides, the middle of July was not the regular season for terrapin and it had required some generalship to insure prime specimens, and so naturally Mrs. Gridley was proud when the terrapin came on, with the last of her hoarded and now vanishing store of Madeira accompanying it in tiny glasses.

Mr. Boyce-Upchurch sniffed at the fragrance arising from the dish which had been put before him. He sniffed rather with the air of a reluctant patient going under the ether, and with his spoon he stirred up from the bottom fragments of the rubbery black meat and bits of the queer-shaped little bones and then he inquired what this might be. He emphasized the '*this.*'

"It's terrapin," explained Mrs. Gridley, who had been fluttering through a small pause for him to taste the mixture and give his verdict. "One of the special dishes of my own state."

"And what's terrapin?" he pressed. She told him.

"Oh," he said, "sort of turtle, eh? I shan't touch it. Take it away, please," — this to the reverential Ditto hovering in the immediate background.

From this point on, the talk ceased to be general. In spots, the dinner comparatively was silent, then again in other spots conversation abounded. From his seat near the foot, Mr. Braid kept casting interpolations in the direction of the farther end of the table. Repeatedly his sister squelched him. At least, she tried to do so. He seemed to thrive on polite rebuffs, though. He sat between the Thwaites, and Major Thwaites was almost inarticulate, as was usual with him, and Mrs. Thwaites said very little, which was not quite so usual a thing with her, and Mr. Braid apparently felt that he must sow his ill-timed whimsicalities broad-cast rather than bestow them upon the dead eddy of his immediate neighborhood.

For instance, when Miss Rachel Semmes, who was one of Ingleglade's most literary women, bent forward from her favored position almost directly opposite the guest of honor and said, facing eagerly toward him over the table, "Oh, Mr. Boyce-Upchurch, talk to me of English letters," Mr. Braid broke right in:

"Let's all talk about English letters," he suggested. "My favorite one is 'Z.' Well, I like 'H,' too, fairly well. But to me, after all, 'Z' is the most intriguing. What's your favorite, everybody?"

Here, as later, his attempted levity met deservedly the interposed barrier of Miss Semmes' ignoring shoulders. She twisted in her place, turning her back on him, the more forcibly to administer the reproof and with her eyes agleam behind her glasses and her lips making little attentive sucked-in gasping sounds, she harkened while Mr. Boyce-Upchurch discoursed to her of English letters with frequent references to his own contributions in that great field.

As the traveled observer in his own time may have noted, there is a type of cultured Britisher who regards it as stupid to appear smart in strange company, and yet another type who regards it as smart to appear stupid. Mr. Boyce-Upchurch fell into neither grouping. He spoke with a fluency, with an authoritative definiteness, with a finality, which checked all counter-thoughts at their sources. In his criticisms of this one and that one, he was severe or he was commendatory, as the merits of the individual case required. He did not give opinions so much as he rendered judgments. There was about him a convincing firmness. There was never even a trace, a suggestion of doubt. There were passages delivered with such eloquence that almost it seemed to some present as though Mr. Boyce-Upchurch must be quoting from a familiar manuscript. As, if the truth must be known, he was. Still, had not all of intellectual America as far west as Omaha acclaimed "Masters of the Modern English Novel, with Selected Readings from the Author's Own Books" as a noteworthy platform achievement?

Thus the evening passed, and the Gridleys' dinner party. All had adjourned back again to the living-room, where coffee and cigarettes were being handed about, when from without came gusts of a warm swift wind blowing the curtains and bringing a breath of moistness.

"Oh, I believe it's really fixing to rain," declared Mrs. Gridley, hopefully, and on this, as if in confirmation, they all heard a grumble of distant summer thunder off to the northwest.

At that, Mrs. Thwaites said she and the Major really must run home—they'd come away leaving all the windows open. So they bade everybody good night—the first ones to go.

Mr. Braid saw them to the door. In fact he saw them as far as the front porch.

"Coming to the lecture tomorrow night, I suppose," he said. "Rally around a brother Briton, and all that sort of thing?"

"I am not," said little Mrs. Thwaites, with a curious grim twist in her voice. "I heard it tonight."

"Perishing blighter!" said the Major; which was quite a long speech for the Major.

"I'm ashamed!" burst out Mrs. Thwaites in a vehement undertone. "Aren't you ashamed, too, Rolf?"

"Rarther!" stated the Major. He grunted briefly but with passion.

"Fault of any non-conformist country," pleaded young Mr. Braid, finely assuming mortification. "Raw, crude people—that sort of thing. Well-meaning but crude! Appalling ignorance touching on savories. No bitters in the home. No—"

"Don't make fun," said Mrs. Thwaites. "You know I don't mean that."

"Surely, surely you are not referring to our notable guest? Oh, Perfidious Albinos!" He registered profound grief.

"I am not." Her words were like little screws turning. "Why should we be ashamed of him—Rolf and I? He's not typical—the insufferable bounder! Our writing folk aren't like that. He may have been well-bred—I doubt it. But now utterly spoiled."

"Decayed," amended her husband. "Blighting perisher!" he added, becoming, for him, positively oratorical.

"It's you Americans I'm ashamed of," continued this small, outspoken lady. "Do you think we'd let an American, no matter how talented he might be, come over to England to snub us in our own homes and patronize us and preach to us on our shortcomings and make unfair comparisons between his institutions and ours and find fault with our fashion of doing things? We'd jolly well soon put him in his place. But you Americans let him and others like him do it. You bow down and worship before them. You hang on their words. You flock to hear them. You pay them money, lots of it. You stuff them up with food, and they stuff you with insults. This one, now—he's a sponge. He's notorious for his sponging."

"Pardon, please," interjected Mr. Braid. "There you touch my Yankee pride. Sponging is an aquatic pastime not confined to one hemisphere. You perhaps may claim the present international champion but we have our candidates. Gum we may chew, horn-rimmed cheaters we may wear, but despite our many racial defects we, too, have our great spongers. Remember that and have a care lest you boast too soon."

"You won't let me be serious, you do spoof so," said Mrs. Thwaites. "Still, I shall say it again, it's you Americans that I'm ashamed of. But I was proud of you tonight, young man. When you mispronounced the name of Maudlin College by calling it 'Magdeline,' the Yankee way, and he corrected you, and when immediately after that when you mentioned Sinjin Ervine as 'St. John' Ervine and he corrected you again, I knew you must be setting a trap. I held my breath. And then when you asked him about his travels and what he thought of your scenic wonders and he praised some of them, and you brought in Buffalo and he said he had been there and he recalled his trip to Niagara Falls and you said: 'Not Niagara Falls, dear fellow—*Niffls!*' why that was absolutely priceless scoring. Wasn't it absolutely priceless, Rolf?"

"Rarther!" agreed the Major. He seemed to feel that the tribute demanded elaboration, so he thought briefly and then expanded it into "Oh, rarther!"

"We do our feeble best," murmured young Mr. Braid modestly, "and sometimes Heaven rewards us. Heaven was indeed kind tonight.... Speaking of heavenly matters—look!"

As though acting on cue the horizon to the west had split asunder, and the red lightning ran down the skies in zig-zag streaks, like cracks in a hot stove, and lusty big drops spattered on the porch roof above them.

"It's beginning to shower—and thank you once more for 'Niffls.'" Mrs. Thwaites threw the farewell over her shoulder. "We shall have to run for it, Rolf."

In the steeple of the First Baptist Church of Ingleglade, two blocks distant, the clock struck eleven times. Except for the kitchen wing the residence of the Gridleys on Edgecliff Avenue was, as to its lower floor, all dark and shuttered. The rain beat down steadily, no longer in scattered drops but in sheets. It was drunk up by the thirsty earth. It made a sticky compound of a precious wagon-load of stable leavings with which Mrs. Gridley, one week before, had mulched her specimen roses in their bed under the living-room windows. It whipped and it drenched a single overlooked garment dangling on the clothes line between the two cherry trees in the back yard. Daylight, to any discriminating eye, would have revealed it as a garment appertaining to the worthy and broad-beamed Norah; would have proven, too, that Norah was not one who held by these flimsy, new-fangled notions of latter-day times in the details of feminine lingerie. For this was an ample garment, stoutly fashioned, generously cut, intimate, bifurcated, white, fit for a Christian woman to wear. It surreptitiously had been laved that morning in the sink and wrung out and hung for drying upon a lately almost disused rope, and then, in the press of culinary duties, forgotten. Now the rain was more or less having its way with it, making its limp ornamentation of ruffles limper still, making the horn buttons upon its strong waistband slippery. So much for the exterior of this peaceful homestead.

Above in the main guest-room, Mr. Boyce-Upchurch fretted as he undressed for bed. He felt a distinct sense of irritation. He had set forth his desires regarding a portable tub and plenty of water to be made ready against his hour of retiring yet, unaccountably, these had not been provided. His skin called for refreshment; it was beastly annoying.

A thought, an inspirational thought, came to him. He crossed to his front window and drew back the twin sashes. The sashes opened quite down to the floor and immediately outside, and from the same level, just as he remembered having noted it following his arrival, the roof of the veranda sloped away with a gentle slant. The light behind him showed its flat tin covering glistening and smooth, with a myriad of soft warm drops splashing and stippling upon it. Beyond was cloaking impenetrable blackness, a deep and Stygian gloom; the most confirmed Styg could have desired none deeper.

So Mr. Boyce-Upchurch walked back and entered the bathroom. There, from a pitcher, he poured the basin full of water and then stripped to what among athletes is known as the buff, meaning by that the pink, and he dipped an embroidered guest towel in the basin and with it sopped himself from head to feet, then dampened a cake of soap and wielded it until his body and his head and his limbs and members richly had been sudded. This done he recrossed his chamber, pausing only to turn out the lights. He stepped out upon the porch roof, gasping slightly as the downpouring torrent struck him on his bare flesh.

From the head of the stairs Mr. Gridley, in a puzzled way, called down:

"Say, Emaline?"

"In a minute—I'm just making sure everything is locked up down here," answered Mrs. Gridley in a voice oddly strained.

"Say, do you know what?" Mr. Gridley retreated a few steps downward. "He's gone and put his shoes outside his door in the hall. What do you suppose the big idea is?"

"Put out to be cleaned," explained Mr. Braid from the foot of the stairs. "Quaint old custom—William the Conqueror always put his out. But don't call 'em shoes; that's one of those crude Americanisms of yours. The proper word is 'boot.'"

"Well, who in thunder does he expect is going to clean them?—that's what I want to know!" demanded the pestered Mr. Gridley.

"Perhaps the slavey—" began Mr. Braid.

"Ollie, for heaven's sake hush!" snapped Mrs. Gridley. "I warn you my nerves can't stand much more tonight. They're still up out in the kitchen—and suppose Delia heard you. It's a blessing she didn't hear him this afternoon."

"I wonder if he thinks I'm going to shine 'em?" inquired Mr. Gridley, his tone plaintive, querulous, protesting. He strengthened himself with a resolution: "Well, I'm not! Here's one worm that's beginning to turn."

"There's Ditto," speculated Mrs. Gridley. "I wouldn't dare suggest such a thing to either of those other two. But maybe possibly Ditto—"

"Never, except over my dead body," declared Mr. Braid. "I'd as soon ask His Grace the Archbishop of Canterbury to press my pants for me. Fie, for shame, Dumplings!"

"But who—"

"I, gallant Jack Harkaway the volunteer fireman," proclaimed Mr. Braid. "I, Michael Strogoff the Courier of the Czar—I'll shine his doggone shoes—I mean, his doggone boots. I'll slip up and get 'em now. There's a brush and some polish out back somewheres. Only, by rights, I should have some of the genuine Day & Martin to do it with. And I ought to whistle through my teeth. In Dickens they always whistled through their teeth, cleaning shoes."

"Well, for one, I'm going to take a couple of aspirin tablets and go straight to bed," said Mrs. Gridley. "Thank goodness for one thing, anyway—it's just coming down in bucketsful outside!"

On the porch top in the darkness, Mr. Boyce-Upchurch gasped anew but happily. The last of the lather coursed in rivulets down his legs; his grateful pores opened widely and he outstretched his arms, the better to let the soothing cloudburst from on high strike upon his expanded chest.

On the sudsy underfooting his bare soles slipped—first one sole began to slip, then the other began to slip. He gasped once more, but with a different inflection. His spread hands grasped frantically and closed on the void. Involuntarily he sat down, painfully and with great violence. He began to slide: he began to slide faster: he kept on sliding. His curved fingers, still clutching, skittered over stark metal surfaces as he picked up speed. He slid thence, offbound and slantwise, toward the edge. He gave one low muffled cry. He slid faster yet. He slid across the spouting gutter, over the verge, on, out, down, into swallowing space.

Out in the service ell the last of the wastage from the Gridleys' dinner party was being disposed of and the place tidied up against the next gustatory event in this house, which would be breakfast. Along the connecting passage from his butler's pantry where he racked up tableware, Ditto was speaking rearward to the two occupants of the kitchen. He had been speaking practically without cessation for twenty minutes. With the *h*'s it would have taken longer—probably twenty-two to twenty-four minutes.

He was speaking of the habits, customs, and general excellencies of the British upper classes among whom the greater part of his active life congenially had been spent. He was approaching a specific illustration in support and confirmation of his thesis. He reached it:

"Now, you tyke Mr. Boyce-Upchurch, now. Wot pride of bearin' 'e's got! Wot control! Wot a flow of language when the spirit moves 'im! Always the marster of any situation—that's 'im all oaver. Never losin' 'is 'ead. Never jostled out of 'is stride. Never lackin' for a word. Stock of the old bull-dog—that's wot it is!"

Where he stood, so discouraging, he could not see Norah. Perhaps it was just as well he could not see her. For a spell was lifting from Norah. If there is such a word as 'unenglamored' then 'unenglamored' is the proper word for describing what Norah rapidly was becoming.

From Delia the tattle-tale, Norah had but just now heard whispered things. She was sitting at ease, resting after an arduous spell of labors, but about her were signs and portents—small repressed signs but withal significant. The lips tightly were compressed; one toe tapped the floor with an ominous little tattoo; through the clenched teeth she made a low steady wasp-like humming noise; in the eyes smoldered and kindled a hostile bale. It was plain that before long Norah would herself be moved to utterance. She did but bide her time.

However, as stated, Ditto could not see. He proceeded to carry on:

"No nonsense abaht 'im, I tell you. Knows wot 'e wants and speaks up and arsks for it, stryte out."

Several of Mrs. Gridley's specimen rose bushes served somewhat to break the force of Mr. Boyce-Upchurch's crash, though their intertwining barbed fronds sorely scratched him here and there as he plunged through to earth. He struck broadside in something soft and gelatinous. Dazed and shaken, he somehow got upon his feet and first he disentangled himself from the crushed-down thorny covert and then he felt himself all over to make sure no important bones were broken.

Very naturally, the thought next uppermost with him, springing forward in his mind through a swirl of confused emotions, was to reenter the house and return, without detection, to his room. He darted up the front porch steps and tried the front door. It was barred fast. He tried the windows giving upon the porch; their blinds were drawn, latched from within.

Out again in the storm he half circled the main body of the house, fumbling in the cloaking blackness at yet more snugly fastened windows. An unbelievable, an appalling, an incredible conviction began to fasten its horrid talons upon Mr. Boyce-Upchurch. He could not get in without arousing someone and certainly in this, his present state, he dare not arouse anyone in order to get in. Yet he must get in. Desperation, verging already on despair, mounted in his swirling brain.

Past a jog in the side wall he saw, thirty feet on beyond and patterning through some lattice-work, a foggy shaft of light from a rain-washed window. As cautiously he moved toward it a taut obstacle in the nature of a cord or small hawser rasped him just under the nose and, shrinking back, he was aware of a ghostly white article swinging gently within arm-reach of him. Partly by touch, partly by sight, he made out its texture—woven linen or cotton cloth, limp and clammy with wetness—and he made out its contours; divined likewise its customary purposes. At home a few old-fashioned ladies still were addicts; he recognized the pattern; he had an elderly maiden aunt. In emergency it would provide partial covering—of a sort. Most surely this was an emergency. And yet—

As he hesitated, with tentative fingers still pawing the sopping shape of it, and torn between a great loathing and a great and compelling temptation, the sound of a human voice penetrated the clapboards alongside him and caused him to cower down close.

"Doggone it!"

Mr. Braid, bearing in one hand a brace of varnished boots of Regent Street manufacture, tumbled over a sharp-cornered object in the inky darkness of the cuddy behind the living-room and barked his shins, and his cry was wrung with anguish.

"Doggone it!" he repeated. "Who's gone and hid the infernal electric light in this infernal Mammoth Cave of a storeroom? And where in thunder is that box of polish and that blacking brush? I'm sure I saw 'em here the other day on one of these dad-blamed shelves. Ouch!"

His exploring arm had brought what from weight and impact might have been an iron crowbar to clatter down upon his shoulders. As a matter of fact, it was the discarded handle of a patent detachable mop.

"Oh, damn!" soliloquized Mr. Braid. "Everything else in the condemned world is here but what I'm after. And I haven't got any matches and I can't find the light bulb. Maybe Norah or Delia 'll know."

He backed out of the cavernous closet into the hall, heading for the kitchen by way of the intervening pantry.

That vocal threat of peril from within diminished, died out. Mr. Boyce-Upchurch straightened, and in that same instant, piercing the night from a distance but drawing nearer, came to his dripping ears the warning of a real and an acute danger. A dog—a very large and a very fierce dog, to judge by its volume of noise output—was coming toward him from the right and coming very swiftly.

The Thwaites' police dog, born in Germany but always spoken of by its owners as Belgian, was the self-constituted night guard of all premises in the entire block. To her vigilant senses suspicions of a prowler abroad had floated out of the void. Baying, belling, she was now bounding across lots to investigate.

With a frenzied snatch, Mr. Boyce-Upchurch tore the pendent flapping thing free from its clothes-pin moorings and he thrust his two legs into its two legs and convulsively he clutched its hemmed girth about his middle, and forgetting all else save that a menacing monster was almost upon him breathing its hot panted breaths upon his flinching rear, he flung himself headlong toward that sheltering entryway from whence the blurry radiance poured.

Enlarging upon his subject, Ditto stepped into the kitchen.

"As I was syin' a bit ago, tyke Mr. Boyce-Upchurch," he continued. "Look at 'm, I arsk you? Poise, composture, dignity—that's 'im agyne! It's qualities like them 'as mykes the English wot they are the 'ole world over. It's—"

"Saints defind us!" shrieked Norah, starting up.

In through the back door burst Mr. Boyce-Upchurch, and he slammed it to behind him and backed against it, and for a measurable space stood there speechless, transfixed, as it were, being, in a way of speaking, breeched but otherwise completely uncovered excepting for certain clingy smears of compost—compost is the word we will use, please—upon the face and torso.

Delia's accompanying scream was just a plain scream but Norah's further outcry took on the form of articulated words:

"Proud, sez you? Yis, too proud to sup our cocktails but not too proud to be rampagin' around in the rain turnin' somersaults in somebody's cowyard. Dignified, you sez? Yis, too dignified to ate the vittles I was after fixin' fur him, but not too dignified to come lapein' in on two dacint women wearin' nothin' only a pair of somebody's—*Whooroo*, it's me own best Sunday pair he has on him!"

On the linoleum of the butler's pantry behind them Mr. Oliver Braid laid him down, holding in either hand a Regent Street boot, and uttered gurgling sounds denoting a beautiful joy.

From the American of July 22d:

> Among the passengers sailing today on the Mulrovia for Southampton was Mr. Jeffreys Boyce-Upchurch, the well-known English novelist, returning home after suddenly breaking off his lecture tour in this country on account of lameness resulting from a severe fall which he is reported to have had less than a week ago while filling an engagement in New Jersey. Mr. Boyce-Upchurch declined to see the reporters desirous of questioning him regarding the accident. Walking with a pronounced limp, he went aboard early this morning and remained secluded in his stateroom until sailing-time.

From the Telegram, same date, under Situations Wanted:

> BUTLER, English, unimpeachable references, long experience, perfectly qualified, desires employment in cultured household, city preferred. Positively will not accept position where other members of domestic staff are Irish. Address: L. D., General Delivery.

Two of Everything

THERE was no warning. There rarely is in such cases. To be sure, those gophers acted peculiarly a minute before the tremor started, and that whistling marmot did too. But until he felt the first heave, Chaney attached no significance to the behavior of such as these. He was not concerned with the small mammalia of northern Montana. The fishing was what interested him.

He was disentangling a fly from where, on the back cast, it had woven itself into an involved pattern with the adjacent shrubbery, when he became aware that dozens of the little gray ground-squirrels were popping out of the mouths of their burrows and scooting about in all directions, making sharp chirking noises as they went. Through the day he had seen them by the hundreds and usually they were in motion, but this was the only time he heard an outcry from any of them. A fat one popped up out of the dirt crust almost between his toes and caromed off against an ankle. It appeared to be in an especial haste to get somewhere else.

Just about this time the marmot, a much larger animal, scuttled down the hill, whistling steadily and wrinkling up its back like a caterpillar in a hurry. What happened, of course, was that the earth sent along a preliminary notification to the creatures who delve in the earth and live in the earth, telling them their ancient mother was about to have a very hard chill. This is the way a layman might put it; no doubt a geologist would phrase the explanation differently. But it was a warning, all right enough.

While Chaney still was mildly speculating regarding the reasons for the panic among these ground-dwellers, the solid boulder beneath his feet seemed to lift and stir and the scrub aspens behind him all at once began to bend the wrong way, that is, toward the wind instead of from it. So then he knew it must be a quake. Instinctively he slid off the stone and splashed down on the loose shale in the edge of the creek bed. As he half crouched there, up to his shanks in water and suddenly apprehensive, he felt through his boot soles a progressive rippling movement that grew swift and more violent. It was as though the world were flindering its skin on the haunches of these mountains precisely as a pestered horse does to get rid of a horsefly.

Evidently this meant to be quite a shock. It was quite a shock. The newspapers were full of it for a week; the scientists were full of it for months after the newspapers eased up. Over in southern California it shuffled the houses of one coast town like a pack of cards and down in the Wyoming Rockies it blocked a gap through which a river ran, so that a valley of ambitious irrigation projects became a lake while the dispossessed residents were getting their families and their cattle out. But when Chaney looked up and saw the face of the cliff above him starting to come loose, he very naturally jumped to the conclusion that the whole thing had been devised for the main purpose of annihilating him; there was going to be a disaster and he was going to be the chief victim.

The mental process of any normal human being would operate thus in a similar abnormal emergency. Lightning strikes near us and in the moment of escape we give thanks for deliverance from a peril launched expressly at us. Heaven sped its direst artillery bolt with intent for our destruction, but we were too smart for it; we dodged. Probably it is mortal vanity that makes us say that to ourselves—and even believe it. We are forever assuming that nature gets up her principal effects either for our benefit or for our undoing.

Anyhow, that was how it was with Chaney. There he squatted with his pleasant sins all heavy upon him, and the front of Scalded Peak was fetching away from its foundation to coast down and totally abolish Chaney. His bodily reflexes synchronized with his mind's. As his brain recorded the thought his legs bent to jump and set him running off to the left along the shore. But before he could take ten long leaps the slide was finished and over with.

It was miraculous—he marveled over that detail later when he was in a frame fit for sorting out emotions—it really was miraculous that the entire contour of one side of the basin could change while a scared man was traveling thirty yards. Yet that was exactly what took place. In so brief a space of time as this, the façade of the steep, rocky wall had been rent free and shoved off and had descended a thousand feet or so, picking up a million billion bushels of loose stuff on the way, and had stopped and was settling.

In another half-minute the grit clouds were lifting, and Chaney was rising up from where he had flopped over into a tangle of windfall. He was bringing his face slowly out from under the arms which instinctively he had crossed on his head as he stumbled and sprawled and he was wiping his hand across his eyes and taking stock of the accomplished transformation and of his own sensations.

There had been an intolerable numbing, deafening roaring and crashing in his ears, and a great incredible passing before his eyes; he could remember that. There had been a sense that the air about him was filled with sweeping stones as big as court-houses, that tons upon tons of weight were crushing down about him and on him; that something else, which was minute but unutterably dense and thick, was pressing upon him and flattening him to death; that tree tops near at hand overhead were whipping and winnowing in a cyclonic gale that played above all else; and then all definitely he knew for a little while was that his mouth was full of a sour powder and his right cheek was bleeding. Also that the earthquake had passed on to other parts and that the avalanche begotten of it had missed him by a margin of, say, six rods.

He lay almost on the verge of the damage. He turned over, but very cautiously through a foolish momentary fright of jarring to life some poised boulder near by, and sat up in a kind of nest of dead roots and dead boughs and cleared his vision and stared fearsomely to his right. Just over there was a raw gray pyramidal smear, narrow at the top where a new gouge showed in the rim-rock, and broad at the base. It was slick and it was scoured out smoothly up the steep slope, but below, closer to him, the overturned slabs and chunks of stone had a nasty, naked aspect to them, an obscene aspect what with their scraped bare bellies turned uppermost.

In a minute for creation, or put it at fifty years as men measure time, the kindly lichens and mosses would grow out on their gouged shoulders and along their ribs, and the soil and the wood-mold would gather in their seams, and grass would come up between them, and then shrubs and finally evergreens from the crevices; in a few centuries more this scarred place would be of a pattern again with its neighborhood. But now it was artificial looking, like a mine working or the wreckage of a tremendous nitro-glycerine blast.

The stream had turned from steel-blue in its depths and greenish white on the rapids to a roiled muddy gray, but as Chaney rolled his eyes that way it showed signs of clearing. Seemingly there had been only one great splash and wave when the slide came down, and the course of the stream had not materially been changed. Already the dust had gone out of the air; it covered the leaves, though.

He stood up and mastered the trembling in his legs and shrugged the stupefaction out of himself. He was not even bruised. Except for that little scratch on his cheek he had no wound whatsoever. But in certain regards he decidedly was out of luck. His present possessions were reduced to precisely such garments as he stood in and what articles he had in the pockets of those garments, and to one fishing rod which might or might not be smashed.

The guide who had brought him into this country—Hurley was the guide's name—and the camp which he and the guide had made an hour earlier and their two saddle-horses and their one pack-horse and all their joint belongings had vanished with not a single scrap left to show for them. Chaney convinced himself of this tragic fact as soon as he scrambled up on the lowermost breadth of the slide. Presently he balanced himself, so he figured, directly above where the pup-tent had stood and the camp litter had been spread about. He saw then that so far as Hurley and the horses and the dunnage were concerned, this was their tomb for all time.

About four o'clock they had come over the top and on down the steep drop to Cache Creek. They turned the stock loose to graze on the thin pickings among the cottonwoods and willows. He put up the tent and spread the bed-rolls while Hurley was making a fireplace of stones and rustling firewood. He left Hurley at the job of cooking and went a short distance along the creek toward its inlet in the canyon between the west flank of Scalded Peak and the east flank of Sentinel Peak to pick up some cut-throats for their supper. On the second cast he lashed his leader around a springy twig. He climbed a big rock to undo the snarl—and then this old and heretofore dependable earth began to get up and walk.

And now here it was not five o'clock yet, and he was alone among these mountains, and Hurley's crushed body was where neither digging nor dynamite would bring it forth. By his calculation it was hard to say exactly, with everything altered the way it was; but as nearly as he could guess, he was right above where Hurley ought to be—with at least forty feet of piled-up, wedged-in, twisted-together soil and boulders and tree roots between him and Hurley. Probably the poor kid never knew what hit him. He had been right in the path of the slide and now he was beneath the thickest part of it. He had seemed to be a pretty fair sort too, although as to that Chaney couldn't say positively, having hired the boy only the day before at an independent outfitter's near Polebridge on the North Fork, where he had left his car.

For him, the lone survivor of this quick catastrophe, there was nothing to do except to get out. That part of it didn't worry Chaney much. He was at home in this high country. He had hunted and fished and ranged over a good part of it. With the taller peaks to guide him and the water courses to follow—on this side of the Continental Divide they nearly all ran west or southwest—a man could hold to his compass points even through unfamiliar going.

He would scale the wall of the bowl right away. He didn't want darkness to catch up with him before he was over the top; the place already was beginning to be haunted. Except on the eastern slopes night came late in these altitudes; it would be after nine o'clock before the sunset altogether failed him. He would lie down until morning came, then shove ahead, holding to the trail over which he and Hurley had traveled in until it brought him out on the Flathead plateau. To save time and boot-leather, he might even take a short cut down through the timber to the foot-hills; there were ranches and ranger stations and fire-watchers' lookouts scattered at intervals of every few miles along the river flats.

He might be footsore by the time he struck civilization with word of the killing and certainly he would be pretty hungry, but that was all. He wouldn't get cold when the evening chill came on. He had on a coat and it was a heavy blanket coat, which was lucky, and he had matches, plenty of them. He had loose matches in the breast pocket of his shirt and a waterproof box of matches in the fob pocket of his riding-breeches. He even had two knives; a hunting-knife in a sheath on his belt, a penknife in his pocket.

Chaney was a great one for doubling up on the essentials whenever he took to the woods. He'd have a small comb and toothbrush in his folding pocket kit; another comb and another toothbrush tucked away somewhere in his saddle-bags or his blanket roll. He always carried two pairs of boots too.

It was a regular passion with him, this fad for taking along spares and extras on a camping trip or, for that matter, on any sort of trip. People had laughed at him for being so old-maidish, as they put it. Chaney let them laugh; the blamed fools! It was his business, wasn't it, if he chose to be methodical about these small private duplications? More than once his care had been repaid in dividends of comfort. And anyhow the thing had come to be a part of him. He was forty-five, at the age when men turn systematic and set in their ways.

The only salvage left out of the disaster was his rod. He might as well take that along. Uncoupled and with the links tied together, it would not encumber him on the hike. He descended from the cairn and, finding the rod uninjured, was in the act of freeing the leader from its entanglement in the brushy top of an aspen when all at once his nervous hands became idle while his brain became active over a new thought.

It was a big notion and in that same instant he decided to follow after the impulse of it.

Suppose, just suppose now for the sake of argument, that he went away from this spot leaving no trace behind to betray that he had gone away alive and sound? He canvassed the contingency from this angle and that, his imagination busy with one conjecture, one speculation, one eventuality after another, and nowhere found a flaw in the prospect.

This is what would happen—it morally was bound to happen, unless he made a false step: Sooner or later and in all probability before a week was up, a rescue party would come into Cache Creek looking for him and Hurley. They were due out in four days to refit with fresh supplies for another journey down on Pronghorn Lake, twenty miles to the southwest. Within five days or six their prolonged absence, coupled with their failure to send back word of their whereabouts by some passing tourist, would be enough to cause alarm at Polebridge, where Hurley's people lived. Besides, the earthquake surely would make the natives apprehensive of accidents in the mountains.

So the relief force would set out on the hunt for the missing pair. Any seasoned mountaineer could hold to their trail. There was the site where they had camped last night, the place where they had halted at noon today to graze the horses and eat their own luncheon; the cigarette butts and dead matches dropped by them. Eventually, picking up a clue here and a clue there, the searchers would arrive at this spot—to find what? A land-slip covering the only fit camp-ground in the Scalded Peak basin and covering it forty or fifty feet deep at that.

It would take a crew of men with tackles and hoists and explosives six months to explore the lower part of that slide, even if you conceded they could transport their machinery over the range and set it up. Yes, it would take longer than that. Because as fast as they excavated below, the smaller stuff would sift down from above and more or less undo what they had done. So they wouldn't do it; they couldn't.

Besides, what would be the use of trying? So the searchers would argue. Hurley and Chaney were buried in a mighty grave of the mountains' own providing. Let them stay buried. That undoubtedly would be the final conclusion. It had to be.

Well, Hurley eternally would be buried, but as for him, he would be far away, released by the supposition, yes, by the seeming indubitable proof of a violent death, from all present entanglements—his debts, his distasteful obligations, his meager and unprofitable business back in that dull North Dakota town, which he hated. He would have quittance of certain private difficulties more burdensome to bear than any of these. And for good and all he would be done with that wife of his. And this thought was the most delectable of all the thoughts that he shuttled in review through his mind.

Heaven knows how often he had wished he might get clear of the woman, with her naggings and her suspicions and her jealousies. He cared for her not at all; he was sure she cared for him only in the proprietorial sense. She wanted him only because he was somebody to be scolded, somebody to be managed, something to take the blame for what went wrong. And there had been plenty going wrong, at that. She wouldn't miss him; with her talent for dramatizing herself, she would glory in the rôle of widowhood. As for missing her—he grinned.

Let her take the insurance. He carried a policy for five thousand, the annual premium paid up, and sooner or later the insurance company would have to fork over. Five thousand was enough for her and more than she deserved. Let her collect it and save it or blow it in just as she pleased; she was welcome to it and welcome to what few odd dollars she might make from the sale of the shop. The prospect of an insurance company being mulcted for money not honestly owed appealed mightily to a phase of his nature.

Legally speaking, officially speaking, Herb Chaney would be dead and spoiling under these rocks, with his score wiped out and his transgressions atoned for. But the man who had been Herb Chaney would be abroad in the world, foot-loose as a ram, free as a bird, with no past behind him and all the future before him. Independence, irresponsibility, liberty, a fresh start, a good time—golly, but it sounded good!

It remained, though, not to muddle by any slip or miscue what Providence had vouchsafed. There should be more evidence, he decided, to support the plausible theory now provided; but no rebuttal to weaken or upset that evidence. He set about manufacturing this added evidence.

He finished the job of getting his line loose, then broke the second joint of the rod just below the top ferrule, making the fracture clean and straight across so it might appear that a whizzing missile had cut it through. By pounding it with a stone he battered the reel to bits. Where the outflung verge of the slip met the creek he tipped up as heavy a boulder as he could raise with the trunk of a snapped-off lodge-pole pine for a lever, and propped the large boulder with a smaller one. Into the cranny thus provided, he shoved the butt of the rod and the fragments of the reel; then kicked out the prop and eased the main boulder down again into its former place.

The broken second section stuck out, pressed flat upon the gravel in the creek; the stout casting line held fast the rest of that section and the tip, so that they bobbed in the shore ripples, scraping on the wet pebbles. There was the marker plain enough to see. To any trained eye it would be like a signal post. The finders would pry up the big stone, but that was as far as they could go. Behind and beyond, the mass of the slide arose. They must inevitably figure him as dropping his fishing gear when the danger impended and fleeing blindly rearward, not away from but directly into the path of the avalanche.

He satisfied himself that no sign of his handiwork, nothing to suggest human connivance, was left behind at the scene of this artifice. Then the refugee started climbing the wall down which less than an hour before he had descended. The trail was rocky; it would register no tell-tale retreating footprints. Even so, he took pains to leap from stone to stone, avoiding any spots of hard-packed soil.

Two-thirds up he came to a flattish stretch where a vein of fine gravel and coarse quartzy sand was exposed. Coming down, he recalled having noticed that sandy streak. It presented an obstacle, being fully twenty feet broad. Immediately, though, an old Indian device for deceiving a pursuer occurred to him. As a boy in Iowa he had heard it described. So he turned the other way and backed across the strip, lifting his feet high at each step and setting them down again well apart, with the heels pressed deeply in so that the toe impressions would be the lighter. From the farther side he looked back and was well content. Anybody would be willing to swear those prints had been made by a man going down the trail, not by one returning.

After that, until the afterglow faded out and darkness caught up with him, he traveled north, holding to the ridges whenever he could. All along he had a nagging feeling that he had overlooked something or failed in something. Something had been left, something forgotten. But what was it? Or was it anything? This harassment first beset him at the top of the rim when he was crawling over it like a fly out of an empty teacup. He hesitated momentarily and was inclined to turn back and make search but could not muster the will for the effort. His nerves had had a tremendous jolt and that silent void below him, with the shadows sliding up its sides as though to overtake him, already was peopled with ghosts.

It abode with him, this worry did, through his flight in the sunset and the twilight. It walked with him through the dusk, lively as a cricket and ticking like a watch, and bothered him that night where he slept lightly in a gully among clumped huckleberry bushes. It was next day before it left him. He shook it off finally. Anyhow, he couldn't put a finger on it, whatever the darn thing was, and probably it didn't matter anyhow.

He traveled north, as I was just saying. Nobody saw the solitary swift figure of the fugitive when occasionally it appeared against a sky-line. There was nobody within ten miles to see it. That evening, finishing a forced march, he passed the international boundary without knowing it, spending the night in an abandoned shanty on an abandoned coal prospector's claim. He had huckleberries for supper. His dinner and breakfast had been the same.

On the second morning he was dead tired and his stomach gnawed and fretted him, but he resisted a strong yearning to enter a very small town which he saw below him in a wooded valley, with the Canadian flag floating from the peaked roof of a customs agency. He was across the line then; he had hoped he was but until now hadn't been sure.

Having mastered his temptation, Chaney swung wide of the settlement. By good luck the detour took him through a pass in an east-and-west spur of the foot-hills and brought him out on a flatter terrain and presently, to a railroad track. He followed along the track and so he came to a water-tank looming like a squatty watch-tower above an empty, almost treeless plain. This was about the middle of the forenoon.

Chaney had the virtue of patience. He dozed in the shade of the tank until a west-bound freight came across the prairie and stopped to water the locomotive. He had money in his pocket; he might have tried bribing the train crew to let him ride in the caboose. This didn't suit his plan, though. Avoiding detection for as long as possible, his pose after detection did come would be that of a penniless adventurer, a vagrant wandering aimlessly. He found the door of a vacant furniture car open and hopped nimbly in.

Sixty miles farther along, a brakeman booted the supposed tramp off into the outskirts of a sizable British Columbia community. He walked into the municipal center and found a lunch-wagon. He spent a solid hour eating orders of ham and eggs and never missed a stroke. The chain of sequences between the man who dodged the avalanche in Scalded Peak basin and the man, a much thinner and a much dirtier man with half a week's beard on his face, who gulped down food in this owl wagon, now had a wide missing link in it.

Still, to make sure, he journeyed briskly on, paying his way this time, to the coast. In Vancouver he stayed two weeks and accumulated a wardrobe and had some dental work done. He had a different name and a different face, for he let his whiskers grow. At Vancouver, where he lodged in a cheap hotel, he posed as a timber cruiser on a vacation. He had cut timber as a young fellow and knew the jargon.

Feeling perfectly secure of his disguise and his new identity, he presently drifted over to his own side of the line, making a way down the Pacific across Washington and Oregon to California and thence by slow stages into Arizona. En route he earned money at various odd jobs—helping to harvest alfalfa, picking fruit, working in a vineyard, in a cannery. He enjoyed his vagabondage after spending so many uncongenial years in a dead hole of a North Dakota county-seat.

He enjoyed it all the more upon reading in a Los Angeles paper a dispatch from Helena wherein it was set forth that the insurance company after considerable backing and filling, eventually had flinched at the prospect of a lawsuit and had conceded his death and settled in full with his wife. He didn't begrudge her the money. He, the deceased, was having a pretty good time of it himself. A bunch of wise guys, those insurance guys had been, to pay up. They'd saved themselves lawyers' fees and court costs. Juries nearly always sided with a widow. It was a cinch any jury would have sided with his widow. His widow—he liked that. Gee, how he did like that! It meant he was absolutely safe.

So safe did he reckon himself to be that within four months he married the daughter of an Arizona rancher on whose place he had been working as a sheep-hand. Probably the girl liked his sophisticated ways, and his white even teeth, shining through his crisp black beard when he grinned. Probably she didn't know some of the teeth were false teeth until after the marriage. Whether he liked her or not the fact remained that within sixty days he deserted this wife. He knew now that he wasn't cut out to be a husband, at least not for long. He had the gipsy's callus on his heel.

So one night, feeling restless, he just up and went. Next morning his father-in-law's adobe was a hundred miles of desert behind him.

Another night—this was months later, though—he was killing time with some associate loafers in a poolroom in El Paso. His name now was Harper; his Arizona name had been Hayes. Harper wore a mustache but no chin beard. The original owner of the face, away back yonder, had been smooth-shaven. It was a great convenience to be able to take on a new personality either by using a razor or by letting it be. Harper owned a brace of razors.

This night in the poolroom a heavy-set, sort of countrified guy, a guy who didn't look at all as a detective should look, came in and flashed a badge and a warrant on him and called him Chaney—Herbert H. Chaney, that way, in full, to prove there was no mistake, and told him he was under arrest.

Chaney was never the one to start a jam; the stranger had shown the butt of an automatic when he was showing the badge. There was no trouble whatsoever. With an admirable docility he submitted to being pinched. His captor escorted him to a second-rate American-plan hotel and took him up to a room on the third floor. Here after Chaney had stripped to his undershirt and drawers, the other man handcuffed him by the left wrist to the iron side-rail of one of the twin beds that were in the room and Chaney lay down; then the officer took off his coat and vest and collar and took a chair and sat down to talk the thing over with him.

Almost the talk ran through a friendly groove; really across stretches of it you might call it downright friendly. The stranger was jubilant over his coup, having made the arrest so deftly with no mussiness or cutting up. It seemed that there had been a long stern chase leading up to this present culmination and he wanted a breathing space in which to get his wind back, so to speak, and congratulate himself.

For his part, Chaney was inclined to accept the inevitable without crabbing. Something the heavy-set man said now at the outset bent him strongly to that course. It stilled a sudden fear in him. What charge could these insurance people bring against him except breach of trust, or whichever fancy name it was they called it by when a fellow kept his mouth shut and let somebody else pay over coin that wasn't exactly owing?

Of course, having rounded him up this way, they would have to go through the forms of getting him extradited to Montana and getting him indicted and then bringing him to trial or something; but from what he knew about the law, he judged it would be more like a civil proceeding than a criminal one. It wasn't as though he had profited in a money way by his own duplicity. An innocent party to the transaction had the spending of that five thousand. All along Chaney had viewed his behavior under this head in more or less a heroic light—standing aside and not saying a word while a dependent woman came into a mighty snug little fortune.

And wife-desertion was no felony; he had looked that point up. Even if Mrs. Chaney were inclined to be spiteful, they couldn't stick you away for sliding out and leaving a woman. Thank heaven, a husband had a few rights left in this country. Chaney even abandoned a notion he had of denying that he was Chaney and fighting it out on that line. What would be the good? He settled on the hillocky mattress to hear what this hick-looking bull might have further to say about it all.

"I guess maybe you're wondering in your own mind how I come to get into the case to begin with," the latter had said a minute or two earlier. "Well, you might as well know it—I've been on the payroll of the Equity and Warranty Company from back when this thing first broke. Yes, sir, from the start back up there in Montana. It was them sent me out with orders to keep on goin' till I'd turned you up. When you monkey with those folks you're monkeyin' with a buzzsaw. They don't ever quit, not that outfit don't. That's why they paid up when your wife pushed her claim—to throw you off the track, case you heard about it. They'd rather see you nailed than have the money back. That's them!"

He lighted a cheap cigar and then as an afterthought offered Chaney its mate. But Chaney didn't want to smoke just then. All Chaney wanted to do was just to listen.

"Come to think about it, though, I guess the thing you're wonderin' about the most is how us insurance people come to figger out that you wasn't dead but 'live and kickin'," continued the smoker. "I know good and well that if I was in your fix that's what I would be interested in the most. That's right, ain't it?"

Chaney raised his head from the pillow and nodded, and was, as the saying is, all ears.

"Well, sir, I got to take the compliments for that part of it all by myself. You might not believe it, but if it hadn't been for me they or nobody else would probably never have suspicioned anything out of the way about you bein' squashed out nice and flat under that landslide. The way it come up was this way: I live at Kalispel, out in the Flathead valley, you know. I'm the resident agent there for the Equity and Warranty Company and on the side I'm a deputy sheriff for Flathead County, or the other way around, whichever way you want to put it. And it so happened I was the second human bein' to get into that Scalded Creek basin after the quake last year. But this boy Hurley's brother was the first.

"Just as soon as they felt the quake down on the river, this here brother, name Sherman Hurley, he took a notion into his head that something was wrong up in the mountains with his brother, the one that had hired out to guide you. It was almost like as if he'd got a message from his brother's spirit. So nothin' would do but what he must start right in and make sure, one way or the other. So he lit out and he traveled all that night, him knowin' all the trails and the lay of the land, and by movin' about as fast over them ridges as his pony could take him he made the trip in four or five hours less time than 'twould take doin' it the regular easy way.

"By daylight next mornin' he was there and he took one look around him and didn't see hide nor hair of you two nor of the horses, but he did see that slide where it had come down right square on top of the camp-ground along the creek, and he decided to himself, the same as anybody else with good sense would, that the whole outfit of you was under that mess of truck. He didn't waste no time foolin' around. If he went in there fast, he came out still faster. It wasn't noon yet when he got back to Polebridge with the news. His pony had went lame and he'd finished the trip, jumpin' and runnin'.

"Well, they telephoned down to Kalispel and the sheriff sent me on up by automobile to sort of represent the county, and he sent word on ahead for the gang that was goin' in to wait till I got there. Well, I burnt up the road gettin' through. They had quite a posse organized when I pulled in— rangers and several kinfolks of the Hurleys and some neighbors and part of a road crew out of the Park. This young Sherm Hurley was practically all in from what he'd been through with and mighty near grieved to death besides—he took on worse than any of his family did—but he was still bent and determined on goin' back the second time. He just would go, takin' the lead, tired as he was.

"Somehow him and me was ahead of the rest when we hit the rim and purty soon after that I seen somethin' that set me to thinkin'. I always did have kind of a turn for the detectin' business; that was partly what induced me to be a deputy sheriff. Yes, sir, I seen something. Guess what it was I seen?"

Chaney shook his head.

"Tracks, that's what. But I seen something a heap more significant right shortly after that. But these first things were tracks. I didn't tell nobody what was sproutin' in my mind, but I motioned everybody to stay where they was for a minute and then I got down off the plug I was ridin' and made one or two rough measurements and sized up things. Then I holloed back to the others to come ahead and we went on down.

"So in a few minutes more we was all down there together in that basin. But while the crowd was prowlin' round, with young Hurley beggin' 'em to fix up some way of gettin' his brother's body out from under those jagged rocks and them all keepin' on tellin' him it looked to them like it was goin' to be an impossible job, I was doin' some prowlin' on my own hook. Inside of three minutes I'd run onto something else that set me to thinkin' harder than ever. Try guessin' what that was."

"Was it—was it the fishing rod?" asked Chaney. The question popped out of him of its own accord.

"Nope—you're gettin' warm though. It was something right close by. Say"—he raised his voice admiringly—"say, plantin' that busted bamboo pole there wasn't such a bad idea on your part. I've said that to myself often since then and I still say so. It showed you two had been there before the slide and it made it look like you'd been took by surprise when the big disturbance started. But the thing I'm speakin' about now wasn't anything you'd fixed up for a plant. It was something you must have overlooked in the excitement. Well, nobody could have blamed you much for that. It must have been pretty squally times down in that deep hole when the earth began to rock and the cliffs began to crumble. You bet!

"Try to think of something besides the pole," he prompted. "Go on and try!"

His prisoner, who was sitting up now, made a gesture to indicate that he still was entirely at a loss.

"I'll give you a hint to help tip you off. What was you doin' just before the hell-raisin' broke loose?"

showin' there to give you away, and no doubt you sayin to yourself how smart you was all the time you was makin' 'em! Why, say, listen, the only way it could 'a' been possible for you to make 'em honest would for you to be twins.

"Well, later on when I found out more about you, I wouldn't been much surprised to hear you was twins and carried the other twin hid on your person somewheres and trotted him out when you wanted to use him. Because by all accounts you certainly are a great one, Chaney, for havin' an extry supply of everything in your war bags. Well, maybe that is good medicine—I won't say; but it certainly turned out bad for you this one time.

"Well, anyhow, I kept my mouth shut, not takin' nobody in my confidence, on the trip back to Polebridge. As soon as I could get a minute to myself I called up Kalispel—and say, talk about your coincidences! The news of you and young Hurley bein' missin' had been given out the day before by the sheriff and it was telegraphed all over the country to the newspapers, and the home office of our company in New Haven, Connecticut, had seen the dispatch and wired to the district agency at Helena sayin' you carried a policy with us and for them to start an inquiry into the circumstances and get confirmation and all; and the district agency had wired to me sayin' the same thing.

"Maybe them home-office folks wasn't astonished when the word came right back to 'em that their local representative was already on the job and smellin' a rat. Just to show you, they thought so well of me on account of what I'd already nosed out they didn't send no special investigator out from headquarters to handle the matter. They turned it over to me, with an expense account and a drawin' account and all; just told me to drop everything else and stick to this case till I found you. So I got a leave of absence from the sheriff's office, and, buddy, I've been on your trail ever since, and that's goin' on eleven months.

"Sometimes I'd think I was right close up behind you and then again there'd be times when I'd lose the scent altogether and have to scout round on the loose till I crossed it again. There's been gaps and breaks to your movements where I just had to take a chance and bridge over the jump and bulge ahead. Why, I'd lose sign of you and your probable whereabouts for weeks and months hand-runnin'. But I didn't quit you, not for a single minute, never, at no time."

Having achieved the somewhat difficult feat of incorporating four separate negatives into one positive sentence, the pleased man-hunter contemplated his legs outstretched before him with a gloating, reminiscent smile.

"Well, that's about all of the yarn," he added after a short pause. "No, it ain't quite all, neither. There was the way I first came to come to get you spotted definite. Startin' off, I says to myself: 'He wouldn't go east or south; if he did, he'd run into one of the Park hotels or a bunch of dude tourists on one of the main trails. He couldn't come back out at the west side because that's where people who saw him when he went into the mountains would be sure to meet him and remember him. So, if he's got any gumption at all, he's went north.' That's what I says, dopin' things out.

"So I goes north my own self. About all I had to go on for a spell was a photograph of you that the home-office people dug up—that and a pretty complete schedule of your ways and your habits. I banked on them more'n I did on the picture—a fellow can change the way he looks, but he ain't so apt to change the way he does. As it turned out, I was right. Because when I'd worked along as far as Vancouver and made a canvass of all the dentists in the telephone directory, and run across one dentist over on a back street that had only just lately finished makin' an extra upper plate for a feller answering to your general plans and specification—a feller, by gee, that already had a perfectly good plate in his top jaw—why, then I knowed I was on the right track.

"When you come right down to it, old-timer, that was what finally fixed your clock for you. Say, you certainly are a great hand, ain't you, for havin' two of everything? Yes, sir, you bet, two of everything!"

Seeming to like the phrase, he repeated it again and once again. All at once then it flashed to Chaney's brain that in the drawled and deliberate repetition was a special emphasis, the hint and the menace of a special meaning. What was this guy driving at, anyhow? What revelation as yet unmentioned was impending? Then, with the next words from his captor it came—the realization.

"I gotta hand it to you there, yes, sir. Two of everything for you, includin' aliases—*and wives*. Whoa! Stiddy, boy! Stand hitched!"

For the bigamist, with a vision of state's prison before his eyes, had jerked so hard in his scrambling leap that he almost dislocated his shackled wrist and did rack the frail bed down.

We of the Old South

JUST as he was, Captain Ransom Teal might have stepped right out of the pages of some story book. He looked like a refugee from a list of illustrations. Still, and with all that, there was on his part no conscious striving for effect. He looked that way because that was the way he looked. And his general walk and conversation matched in. He moved in the gentle prismatic shimmer of his own local color. He was the genuine article, absolutely.

On the other hand, Miss Blossom Lamar Clayton was what you might call self-assembled.

Hers was a synthetic blend, the name being borrowed in these quarters, the accent in those. As for the spare parts, such as mannerisms and tricks of gesture and the fashion of dressing the hair, they had been picked up here, there and elsewhere, as the lady went along. Almost the only honest thing about her was the original background of an inconsequential little personality. She was so persistent a cadger, though, that only once in a while did the primary tints show through those pilfered, piled-on coats of overglazing.

She was living proof of what petty larceny will do for a practitioner who keeps it up long enough and gets away with it most of the time. She was guilty on twenty counts but the trouble was you couldn't convict her. Not with the evidence on hand, anyhow.

They met—the escaped frontispiece and the human loan collection—in Hollywood, hard by one of the larger moving-picture plants. It was a first-rate site for such a meeting between two such specimens to take place, and highly suitable, because out there so many of the fictions are dressed up as facts and nearly every fact has a foundation of fiction which lies under it and lies and lies and lies. Almost anything can happen in Hollywood. And almost everything does, if you believe what you read in the Sunday supplements.

To be exact, the trails of these two first crossed in the dining-room of Mrs. H. Spicer. They crossed there and shortly thereafter became more or less interwoven.

Miss Clayton had been a guest at Mrs. H. Spicer's for some weeks past now, long enough to be able to describe beforehand what would be served for dinner on any given day. In the matter of her menus Mrs. H. Spicer was very High-church; she followed after ritual. This saved mental fag, which is a thing to be avoided when one is conducting a high-grade boarding-house mainly patronized by temperamental ladies and gentlemen who either are connected with, or who hope ultimately to be connected with, what used to be the largest single amusement industry in the United States before bootlegging crowded it back down into second place.

A tapeworm would have some advantage over a surviving sojourner beneath Mrs. H. Spicer's roof because the tapeworm never can tell in advance what it is going to have for its chief meal for the day, whereas if you were hardy and lasted through the second week at Spicer's, you knew that Monday's dinner would be based on the solid buttresses of corned beef and cabbage, and Tuesday's on lamb stew with cole-slaw on the side, and Wednesday's on liver and bacon, and so on through to Sunday's crowning feast, which was signalized by chicken fricassee accompanied by a very durable variety of flour dumpling with fig ice-cream for dessert; then repeat again in serial order, as named.

It was Mrs. Spicer's brag that she ran a homelike establishment. She said it really was more like one big happy family than a mere boarding house; to make it such was her constant aim, she said. But Tobe Daly said—behind her back, of course—that if this was home he knew now why so many girls left it. Tobe was always pulling some comical line.

This, being a Friday, was fish day with rice pudding to follow. Miss Clayton, having finished her rice pudding, was in the act of rising from her chair to go out and join this same Mr. Tobe Daly on the porch when Mrs. H. Spicer brought in a strange old gentleman. With the air which she always wore when presenting a fresh recruit to the other members of her constantly changing family groups—a kind of soothing yet a fluttering air—the landlady piloted him to the small table for four over in the far corner and presented him to the pair who still lingered at it—Miss Clayton and a Mrs. Scofield—and assigned him to the one vacant place there and told Katie, the second dining-room girl, to bring him some dinner.

Immediately there was something about the newcomer to catch the fancy and set the mind to work. There was more than a something, there was a great deal. It was not so much that he wore white whiskers and wore his white hair rather long. Hollywood is one spot where whiskers—a vast number of them—command favorable attention and have a money value.

The reckless partisan who swore never to trim until William Jennings Bryan had been elected president comes into his belated own there. After all these long and cumbered years he has at last his place in the sun—as a benevolent uncle, or a veteran mining prospector, or the shaggy but kind-hearted keeper of the lighthouse on the coast where the little child drifts ashore in the storm, lashed to a mast, or the aged wanderer of the waste-lands who in Reel Three turns up and in Reel Six turns out to be the long-lost father of the heroine. Or what not.

So it was not this new boarder's whiskers and his long hair which centered the collective eye of the dining-room so much as it was his tall, slim, almost straight old figure, his ruddy and distinguished but rather vacuous face, his high white collar and black string tie, his black frock coat with the three upper buttons of the waistcoat unfastened so that the genteel white pleated shirt bosom ballooned out of the vent, his slim "low quarter" shoes. More than these it was his bearing, so courtly, which meant so old-fashioned, and most of all it was the sweeping low salute he rendered to Mrs. Scofield and to Miss Clayton before he sat down and drew up. It was as though he said: "As examples of fair womanhood I render tribute to you both. Through you I honor all the gracious sex of which you two are such shining ornaments."

You almost could hear him saying it; your imagination told you this was precisely the sort of high-flown, hifalutin language he would use, and use it naturally, too. For here was a type come to life, a character bit in the flesh. And that's a rare bird to find even in Hollywood where types do so freely abound.

He asked Miss Clayton a question or two, and she made hurried and, one might have thought, confused answers before she escaped to the veranda where Tobe Daly, that canny squire of dames, was holding space for her alongside him on the top step.

"Gee," began Tobe, "did you make it?"

"Make what?" she asked, settling and smoothing her skirts.

"The old pappy guy, who else?"

"He's nice," said Miss Clayton, still engaged in the business of drawing the skirt down over her knees.

"He's a freak," said Mr. Daly. He cocked a shrewd appraising squint at her side face. "Say, I was piping it off through the front window when the old battle-ax towed him in and interduced him to you gals, and the way it

Ladies and Gentlemen | 67

looked to me you kind of ducked soon as he began shooting conversation at you."

"Never mind that part of it," she countered. "Who is he and where did he come from? Or, don't you know? All I caught was his name. Teal, something like that."

"Teal, huh? Swell name for an old duck, I'll claim. Jimmy Hoster yonder was just giving me the low-down on him. It seems like Chief Gillespie—you know, director with the Lobel outfit—well, Gillespie he piped him off down there in Alabama or wherever it was down South that he's had his bunch on location, shooting stuff for that new costume picture that Winifred Desiree and Basil Derby are being featured in. So Gil brought him along with 'em when they got back this morning, figuring, I guess, on using him in that picture or else in something else.

"They had him over on the Lobel lot this afternoon and they tell me he went big just on his looks. Well, you got to hand it to that Gillespie—he's some picker. If that old boy only had one of these here white goatees on his chin instead of those mountain-goat drapes, he'd be the most perfect Southern Colonel ever I saw in the fillums or on the talking stage, either one. But he's the first one ever I saw—you know what I mean, O. K. in every touch—outside of a book or a show shop. I figure quite a lot of 'em around here will be wanting him."

"I wish somebody would decide they wanted me," she said. "This just hanging round and hanging round gets on my nerves—not to speak of other reasons."

"Well, ain't I told you I'm on the look-out for something for you? Ain't I told you all about what I been doing 'specially on your account? But with a million of these janes from all over the country swarming in here and fighting for every chance that turns up, it's kind of hard making an opening for a new hand."

"If I could just get on once, even as an extra, I'd show 'em something."

"If you'd listen to reason, kid, and be good to me"—he sank his voice—"you know, be a real little cozy pal, I'll guarantee you'll be something better than an extra. A fella likes to be a good fella and a good sport and all, and go through for somebody, but what I say is he's due his reward. Now, ain't he?"

The girl seemed not to have heard him.

"He's nice," she said, as though to herself. "I'll bet anything he's awfully nice."

"Who? Oh, you mean old Uncle Whiskers. Forget him—think about me a spell. Why not be reasonable now, like I was just now saying?" He scrooged in closer.

She edged away, keeping distance between them. Mr. Daly caught a flash of her quick grimace. From wheedling, his tone changed to a rasping one of rising temper. "Maybe he's nice," he said, "but even so I noticed you sort of run out on him a while ago." He let a little grit of satire sift into the next sentence: "What's the matter—don't you real Southerners like to get together when you get a chance and hold hands and sing Dixie Land? Or is it you was scared of something?"

"Say, look her-r-r-e, you lay off that stuff." If the truth must be known Miss Clayton was a child of Pittsburgh. And in Pittsburgh to r-r-r is human, to forgive almost impossible—if you're a purist in the matter of phonetics. And in moments of stress this native was prone to forget things which laboriously she had learned, and revert to the native idioms.

"Well, then, all I got to say is that if you're Southern I'm a Swede watchmaker." He shrugged, then got on his legs. "Say, little one, if you want to get huffy and act standoffish I'm pretty well up on the huff stuff myself. But stick around here awhile longer and you'll see how far a head of taffy hair and a doll-baby face will get you without you got somebody on the inside of one of the big plants to plug your game." Young Mr. Daly, camera-man by profession and skirt-chaser on the side, tipped his hat brim the fractional part of an inch. "So long; and think it over."

The dusk gathering under the pepper trees along the sidewalk absorbed his runty but swaggering shape. Left alone, Miss Clayton put her elbows on her knees and her chin on her fisted hands and thought it over. She took stock of herself and her prospects, social and artistic, also financial. On the whole she didn't have such a very cheerful evening sitting there all by herself.

It was next morning when the California pathways of those two Southerners—the seventy-nine-year-old regular and the twenty-year-old volunteer—really met and joined. It started at the breakfast table, which they had now to themselves. The disgruntled Mr. Daly had come down earlier. Mrs. Scofield would come down later. Between engagements in small mother rôles—not necessarily small mothers but nearly always small rôles—she was resting, which is a professional term signifying restlessness.

Captain Teal had eaten his prunes—Native Sons, Tobe would have called them—and was waiting for his bacon with an egg, when Miss Clayton entered. At sight of her he instantly was on his feet, much to the surprise of Katie, the other dining-room girl, who thought she knew boarding-house manners but was always willing to learn something; and he made a featly bow of greeting in which the paternal was blended with a court chamberlain's best flourish, and drew out Miss Clayton's chair for her. Katie perceived that the old gentleman was not welcoming his fellow lodger to a place at Mrs. H. Spicer's board so much as he seemed to be welcoming her to his own. For the moment, he was the entertainer, Miss Clayton his honored guest. There was a trick about it, someway.

He waited in a silence which throbbed with the pulse of a considerate gallantry until the lady had stated her wishes to Katie, she choosing the apple sauce in preference to the prunes. Then he took up at the point where he had left off on the interruption of her flight the evening before.

"I hardly dared hope I should have the esteemed pleasure of meeting a fellow Southerner—and one so charming—so soon after my advent into this far Western city," he said. "When our delightful hostess mentioned the fact I was agreeably surprised, most agreeably. You will pardon me the liberty I take in paying you compliments at so early a stage of our mutual acquaintance. But between Southerners meeting so far from home there is bound to be a bond, as you know." His antique stilted language had a pleasant flavor for the show girl. She wanted to giggle and yet she was flattered. "I was on the point of putting more questions last evening when something intervened—I believe you were called away. Pardon me again, but might I inquire from what part of our beloved South you hail?"

"From Georgia," she answered, more or less on a venture. Back in New York it usually had sufficed when she announced that she was a Southerner.

"Why, then, that does indeed strengthen the tie between us," he said. "By birth I am a Carolinian but my dear mother was a Georgian of the Georgians. She was a Colquit—one of the Savannah Colquits." So, in another century, a descendant of a Tudor or a Percy might have spoken. "From what part of that noble old state do you come?"

"Well, not from any place in particular," she parried desperately. "I mean, not from any regular town, you understand. I was born out in the country, on a kind of a country place—a farm, sort of."

"Ah, a plantation," he corrected her gently. "In our country we call them plantations. But near where? And in what county?"

To gain time she spooned her mouth full of apple sauce. This was like filling in a blank for a census taker, only worse. In a panic she cast about in that corner of her mind where her knowledge of geography should have been. She thought of Columbus. There ought to be a Columbus in Georgia; there just must be. There was one in Ohio, she remembered: she played it once with a Shubert road show. And one in Indiana, too. She knew a fellow from there, a chorus man in the Follies. So she took a chance:

"I was born out from a town called Columbus—about twenty miles out, I think."

"Oh, Columbus—a lovely and a thriving little city," he said, and she breathed easier but only for an instant. "I know it well; I know many of the older families there. If you are from near Columbus you must know the—"

She broke in on him. These waters grew steadily deeper.

"Well, you see, I left there when I was only just a little thing. All I can remember is a big white house and a lot of colored peop—" she caught herself—"a lot of darkies. My parents both died and my—my aunt took me. That is to say, she wasn't my real aunt; just a close friend of the family." Swiftly she continued to improvise. "But I always called her Auntie. She moved up North to live and brought me along with her. Her name was Smith." (That much was pure inspiration, Smith being such a good safe common name.) "So that's where I've lived most of my life—in the North. I don't know scarcely anything about my relatives. But at heart I've always been a very intense Southerner."

"I can well understand that," he said, and the badgered fictionist hoped she had steered him back into safer shallows. "A real Southerner never ceases to be one. But I might have guessed that you had been reared among Northern influences and Northern surroundings. Your voice, in speaking, seems to betray the fact."

She experienced a disconcerting shock. Until now, she had thought practice had made perfect. Besides, she had studied under what she regarded as first-rate schooling. At the outset of her stage career, when she first decided to be a Southern girl because being a Southern girl was popular and somehow had romance in it, she had copied her dialectics from a leading lady in a musical production, who in turn had copied the intonations of a stage director who once had been a successful black-face comedian. And if a man who had been an end man in a minstrel show for years didn't know how Southerners talked, who did? For months, now, barring only that nosey Tobe Daly, nobody had shown suspicion. Possibly Captain Teal read the flustered look on her face and mistook its purport, for he hastened to add:

"I mean to say that the North has contaminated—or perhaps I should say, affected—your Southern pronunciation. My hearing is not the best in the world but, as well as I may hear, it would seem that you speak certain words with—shall we say, an alien inflection. Pardon me again—the fault lies with my partial deafness—but I am afraid I did not quite catch your name last evening?"

She told him.

He bent toward her across the slopped breakfast dishes. He was as eager and happy as a child with a bright new toy. That was what he would have put you in mind of—a bearded octogenarian débutante in that pitiable state we call second childhood, but for the moment tremendously uplifted by a disclosure held to be of the utmost importance.

"Why, my dear child," he said, "you don't mean to tell me! Where did you get your middle name? Was Lamar, by any chance, your mother's maiden name."

She nodded dubiously. As well be hanged for a sheep as a lamb. But she had not hanged herself; in another minute she was to find that out. She had soundly strengthened herself.

"Then we are related, you and I, my dear. Not closely related, but even so, there is a relationship. I suppose you might say we are very distant cousins. Now—"

"I never was the one to bother much about family."

"Ah, but you would have bothered, as you call it, had you but known. Why, my dear child, you are related to some of the finest and oldest families in the South. Let me tell you who you are."

They sat there then, she listening and secretly amused at first and on the whole rather pleased with herself, and he all afire with the enthusiasm which the aging so often give to trivialities. While his bacon grew stiffer and his egg grew limper, each according to its own special chemistry, in the nest of their pooled cold greases, he ramified a luxuriant family tree, trunk, branch and twig, dowering her with a vast wealth of kinspeople whose names she knew she never would be able to remember—Waltours, Bullochs, Gordons, Telfairs, Hustouns.

It seemed that among her forbears commonplace persons had found mighty few places. They had been statesmen, educators, railroad builders, gracious belles, warriors, orators, noble mothers, racers of fast horses, owners of broad fertile acres, kindly masters and mistresses of hundreds of black slaves, and their memories were a noble inheritance for her to carry onward with her. Just trying to keep track of the main lines almost made her head ache.

"My dear young lady," he was saying as they got up together to quit the dining-room, emptied now of all except them, "we must see more of each other while we both are in this strange city. We who are of the old South will never lack for a congenial topic of conversation when we are thrown together. Northerners might not understand it, but you, with the legacy of blood that is in your veins—you will understand. After you, my dear; after you, please." This was when they had gone as far as the door into the hallway. "And now then," he was saying, as they passed along the hall, "let me tell you something more about your Grandfather Lamar's estate and domestic establishment. The house itself I remember very clearly, as a youth. The Yankee general, Sherman, burnt it. It was white with...."

That was the proper beginning of as freakish a companionship as that habitat for curious intimacies and spiteful enmities, Mrs. H. Spicer's, had ever seen. Of a younger man, of a man who had been indubitable flesh and blood, Tobe Daly might have felt, in a way of speaking, jealous. At least he would have been annoyed that an interloper should all of a sudden come between him and his desires upon this casual little Doll Tearsheet of the theater who called herself Blossom Lamar Clayton. But of a man old enough to be the kid's grandfather, almost old enough to be her great-grandfather— furthermore a pompous, stilted, stupid, toploftical old dodo who behaved more like something out of one of these old-timey before-the-war novels than a regular honest-to-gracious human being—well, to be jealous of such a man would be just plain downright foolish, that's all. For Tobe an attitude of contemptuousness appeared to be the indicated mood. So he rode, as the saying goes, the high horse, and only once did he take advantage of a favoring opportunity openly to twit the girl regarding her choice of beaux.

"That will be about all from you," she snapped at him, using back-stage language. "I'm picking my own friends these days. And you lay off from handing out your little digs at him across the table meal-times. He may not be on to you—he's too decent and polite himself to suspect anybody else of trying to razz him on the sly—but I'm on. So I'm serving notice on you to quit it because if you don't, the first thing you know you'll be in a jam with me. I know how to handle your kind. I was raised that way. I guess it's a kind of a tip-off on the way I was raised that I had to wait until I met a man who'll be eighty his next birthday before I met somebody who knows how to treat a girl like she was a lady."

Tobe, drawing off, flung a parting retort at her.

"Say, kiddo, how did you find out what it feels like to be a lady?"

"I never found out," she said. "I never knew before. But I'm taking lessons now."

That precisely was what she was doing—taking lessons. For her it was a new experience to be on terms of confidence with a man holding her in somewhat the affectionate regard which he might have bestowed upon a daughter, did he have one. Most of the men with whom she had come in contact before this coveted to possess her. Here at last was a relationship in which the carnal played no part; she somehow sensed that had he been in his prime instead of, as he was, teetering toward an onrushing senility, Captain Teal, believing her virginal—she grimaced bitterly to herself at that—yet would have shown her no fleshly side to his nature. In these present environments he was as much out of place as Sir Roger de Coverley would be at a Tammany clambake, but the thing she liked about him was that for all his age and mental creakiness he nevertheless created out of himself an atmosphere of innate chivalry in which he moved and by which he went insulated against all unchaste and vulgarizing contacts. Not that she put this conception of him in any such words as these. But she was a woman reared in a business where observation counts, and she could feel things which she might not always express.

Toward him her own attitude rapidly became more and more protecting as a thwarted maternal complex in her—that same mothering instinct which in one shape or another expresses itself in every woman—was roused and quickened. She was pleased now that she had not obeyed an impulse which had come to her more than once in that first week of their acquaintance to confess to him that she was an imposter masquerading under false colors, making believe to be something she had never been. Confessing might have eased her conscience, but it would have wrecked his faith in her and surely it would have marred their partnership, might even have smashed it up entirely. And she didn't want that to happen. Oddly, she felt that with each passing day she was going deeper and deeper into debt to the Captain.

The obligation, though, was mutual; it fell both ways. If from him she was absorbing a belated respect for the moralities and a desire to put on certain small grace-notes of culture, she in return was giving the antiquarian company for long hours which otherwise would have been his hours of homesickness and loneliness. Probably he was used to loneliness. He never had married—a fact which he had confided to her in their first prolonged talk. But beyond question he would, lacking her companionship, have been most woefully homesick. So she let him bore her with interminable stories of a time which was to her more ancient that the Stone Age, to the end that he should not be bored. It cost her an effort, but from some heretofore unused reservoir of her shallow being she pumped up the patience to lend a seemingly attentive ear while he discoursed unendingly and with almost an infantile vanity upon the glories of the stock from which he sprang. These repetitive tales of grandeur were pitched in the past tense; she took due note of that. She fully understood that his time of affluence was behind him. He didn't tell her so. There was about him no guile. At seventy-nine he was as innocent a babe as ever strayed in the Hollywood woods. Nevertheless it would appear that by his code a gentleman did not plead his poverty. Honorable achievement might be mentioned; but adversity, even honorable adversity, was not a subject for conversation. But she saw how threadbare his black frock coat had become and how shiny along the seams, and how fragile and ready to fall apart his linen was. A woman would see those things. Adversity was spreading over him like a mold. But it was a clean mold. Soon, unless his fortunes mended, he would be downright shabby; but never would he be squalid or careless of the small niceties. That much was to be sensed as a certainty.

For sake of his peace of mind she secretly was glad that she had never let him see her smoking cigarettes. It seemed that in his day ladies had not smoked cigarettes. She sat up through most of one night letting out hems in her skirts. She concealed from him that she used a lip-stick and face paint. She derived a tardy satisfaction from the circumstance that in a feminine world almost universally barbered and bobbed she, months before she met him, had elected to keep her curls unshorn. Then her intent had been to conform to the image she was assuming. Flappers were common among the juveniles and some who could not be rated among the juveniles likewise flapped; but who knew when a casting director might require an old-fashioned type of girl for a costume piece. Her present reward was the old Captain's praise for her tawny poll. He was much given to saying that a woman's crowning glory was her hair and deploring the tendency of the newer generation to shear and shingle until the average woman's head was like the average boy's.

When he chid her for some slip not in keeping with his venerated ideals of womanhood on a pedestal he did it so gently that the reproof never hurt.

Frequently it helped. Besides, he never put the fault on her; always he put it on the accident of her Northern upbringing.

There were lesser things that she learned from him. For instance, that it was a crime against a noble foodstuff to put sweetening in corn bread; that it was an even worse offense to the palate when one ate boiled rice with sugar and milk on it; that a cantaloup never should be regarded as a dessert but always as an appetizer; that hot biscuit should be served while hot, not after the cold clamminess of *rigor mortis* had set in; that Robert E. Lee was the noblest figure American life ever had produced or conceivably ever would.

To the Captain this last, though, was not to be numbered among the lesser verities. It was a very great and outstanding fact and a fact indisputable by any person inclined to be in the least degree fair-minded. He had served four years as a soldier under General Lee—a private at eighteen, a company commander at twenty-one. To have been a Confederate soldier was a more splendid and a more gallant thing even than being a member of one of the old families. He told her that half a dozen times a day. He told her many men of her family had been Confederate soldiers, too; some of them officers of high rank. She began, without conscious effort, to think of them as members of her family who belonged to her and to whom, through the binder of blood ties, she belonged.

By virtue of a certain adaptability of temperament she did more than this. That flexible mimetic quality which enabled her to slip easily into any given rôle lent itself to the putting on of a passable semblance to a full-flowered creation which might never have existed at all excepting in Captain Teal's fancy, and one which we know probably doesn't exist at all nowadays but which all the same was to him very real, as being the typical well-bred Southern woman of all days and all times—a sprigged-muslin, long-ringletted, soft-voiced, ultra-maidenly vision. Physically she differed from this purely abstract picture; concretely she strove to fit herself into the frame of that canvas. To herself she had an acceptable excuse for the deception. For one thing, it was good business. Her venerable admirer should know if anybody did what real old-fashioned Southern girls were like. And to one who had modeled after his pet pattern there must, sooner or later, come an opportunity to play the rôle before the camera.

So, through three weeks of that Hollywood autumn, they waited, each of them, for the call to work; and while their funds shrank, they met regularly for meals and they took strolls together and she gave to him most of her evenings. He spun his droning reminiscences of dusty years and deplored the changes worked by a devastating modernism, and she postured and posed and, bit by bit, built up and rounded out her amended characterization—a self-adopted daughter of the Lamars and Claytons—and constantly did her level best to look and act and be the part.

This went on until the end of the third week, at which point Destiny, operating through the agency of Mr. Andrew Gillespie, took a hand in their commingled affairs.

Gillespie, coming in off the lot to the head offices, was pleasantly excited over his new notion. He revealed it with no preamble:

"Say, you two, I've got an idea for livening up that big fight scene a little bit."

The executive head gave a grunt which terminated in a groan. He craved to swear; but not even Mr. M. Lobel, of Lobel's Superfilms, Inc., dared swear now. Employees whose salaries ranged above a certain figure might be groaned at but could not, with impunity, be sworn at. The ethics forbade it; also such indulgence might result in the loss of a desired director or a popular star. And Gillespie appertained to the polar list of the high salaried. So Mr. Lobel merely groaned.

"What's the matter?" asked Gillespie sharply.

"Nothing, nothing at all, only I am thinking," rejoined Mr. Lobel, with sorrowful resignation. "I am thinking that only two days ago right here in this very room you promised me that positively without a question you would keep down the expensives from now on on this here dam' costume production which already it has run up into money something frightful."

"Who said I was going to spend any more money?"

"An idea you just mentioned, Gillespie," stated Mr. Lobel, "and with you I got to say it that ideas are usually always expensive."

"This thing won't cost anything—it won't cost a cent over a couple of hundred for salary, costumes, props and all, if it costs that much. And it'll put a little note of newness, a kind of different touch into that battle scene; that's what I'm counting on."

"Oh, well, Gillespie, in that case—" The grief was lifting from Mr. Lobel. He turned to his second in command. "Wasn't I only just now saying to you, Milton, that Gillespie is the one always for novelties?"

The director chose to disregard the compliment.

"Do you recall that handsome-looking old scout that I brought back with me here last month from the Southern trip?"

"Like a skinny Santa Claus, huh? Sure, I seen him," said Mr. Lobel, "and wondered what you was maybe going to do with him."

"Me, too," said Mr. Liebermann, affectionately known among lesser members of the staff as "Oh-yes-yes Milton." "The one with the w'ite w'iskez, you mean. Also I wondered about him."

"Well, then, here's the answer," explained Gillespie. "Just a few minutes ago it came to me. I'm going to give him a bit to play in the Gettysburg stuff. Did either of you two ever happen to hear of John Burns?"

"Let me think—the name comes familiar," said Mr. Lobel; "wasn't he a middle-weight prize-fighter here some few years back? Let's see, who was it licked that sucker?"

"No, no, no," Gillespie broke in on the revery. "I mean the John Burns of the poem."

"Sure," assented Mr. Liebermann, who prided himself that although somewhat handicapped by lack of education in his earlier days he had broadened his acquaintance with literary subjects after he quit dress findings and tailors' accessories. "What Gillespie means, Lobel, is the notorious poet, John Burns."

"Are you, by any chance, referring to Robert Burns, of Scotland?" demanded Gillespie with a burr of rising indignation in his voice. Gillespie had been born in the land of cakes and haggis.

"Robert or John or Henry, what's the odds?" countered Mr. Liebermann, and shrugged. "Are you, anyhow, so sure it was Robert? Seems to me—"

"Am I sure? Oh, Lord!" With an effort Mr. Gillespie regained control of his feelings. "The poet I am thinking of was the American poet, Bret Harte. And Harte wrote a poem about old John Burns of Gettysburg. I don't believe that even you ever read that particular poem, Milt." His elaborated sarcasm was lost, though, on Mr. Liebermann. "Anyhow, I'm going to introduce the character of John Burns into the main battle-shots. And this old-timer of mine is going to play him. We can use extracts from the poem for the sub-titles. That's what I came over to tell you, Lobel, not to discuss with our cultured friend here whether the noblest poet that ever lived—a genius that every school child in this country should be familiar with—was named Robert Burns or Oscar Burns or Isadore Burns. By the way, have either of you seen Herzog this morning? He hasn't been on the set, or if he has I missed him. I want to send him in to Hollywood to the address where the old boy's stopping."

Herzog may have been a capable assistant-director—the film world so acclaimed him—but as an emissary his performances might be open to criticism as lacking in some of the subtler shadings of diplomacy.

All went smoothly at the meeting in Mrs. H. Spicer's parlor until after he delivered the purport of his superior's message, Captain Teal harkening attentively.

"Very well, sir," said the Captain. "I am indebted to you, sir, for bringing me this summons. Kindly present my compliments to Mr. Gillespie and inform him that I shall report for duty tomorrow morning promptly on the hour named."

"He ain't waiting for any compliments, I guess," said Herzog. "What he wants is for you to be there on time so's we can give you the dope on the bit you're going to play and get you measured for the clothes and all. Did I mention to you that you're cast for a battle scene? Well, you are. Possibly you seen some of this here war-stuff in your day, eh?"

"Sir," said the Captain stiffly, "I had four years of service in a heroic struggle such as this world never before had seen. Permit me to ask you a question: Possibly—I say possibly—you may have heard of the War Between the Sections for the Southern Confederacy?"

"Well, if I did, it wasn't by that name," confessed the tactless Mr. Herzog. "What's the diff', if I did or I didn't?"

"None whatsoever, sir, to you," stated Captain Teal. "The difference to me is that I took part in that great conflict." But his irony was lost and spent itself on the soft California air. By clamping his hat, which he had worn throughout the interview, more firmly down upon his head, Mr. Herzog, still all tolerant affability, now indicated that he was about to take his departure.

"One moment, if you please," added Captain Teal. "There is another matter which I desire may be brought to the attention of my worthy friend, Mr. Gillespie." He spoke as one conferring favors rather than as one who just had been made the recipient of a favor. "Stopping here in this same establishment is a most gifted young Southern lady—a Miss Blossom Lamar Clayton. She has had experience of the dramatic profession; I would say she has undoubted gifts. But as yet she has been unable, through lack of suitable opportunity, to demonstrate her abilities in the local field. Personally, I am most deeply interested in her future—"

"Why, Foxy Grandpa, you old son of a gun!" exclaimed the edified Mr. Herzog. With a jovial thumb he harpooned the Captain in the ribs. "What do you mean, you old rascal, hooking up with a skirt at your age?"

"Sir," said Captain Teal, in an awful, withering voice, "it pleases you to be offensive. The young lady in question not only is my protégée, in a way of speaking, but I have the very great honor to be distantly related to her family. Do I make myself sufficiently plain to your understanding? And kindly remember also that my name to you, sir, and all your ilk is Teal, Captain Rodney Teal, sir."

But Mr. Herzog declined to wither.

"No offense," he said. "Just let me see if I get the big idea? I suppose you want Gillespie to give the gal the once-over and see whether he can use her?"

"In other words than those you use, that, sir, was the concern I had in mind," said Captain Teal.

"Well, then, why not bring her along with you in the morning?" suggested Mr. Herzog, with a placating gesture, he being now vaguely contrite over having in some utterly inexplicable way given offense to this touchy old party, and somehow impressed by the other's tremendous show of outraged dignity. "I suppose there's no harm in that. If Gillespie likes her looks he might give her a show at some little thing or other; you never can tell. And he's a great hand for making his own finds. And if he don't fall for her you pass her along to me for a screen test, and if she comes clean there I might work her in among the extras and let her pick up a little money that way to carry her along. Get me?"

Which generous avowal so mollified the old Captain that, in token of his forgiveness and his gratitude, he bestowed upon Mr. Herzog a most ceremonious handshake at parting.

As it turned out, here was one beginner who needed no rehearsals. Noting how aptly the aged novice seemed to slip into the personality of the part as soon as he had put on the costume, with its saffron vest, its curl-brimmed, bell-crowned high hat, its blue coat that was swallow-tailed and tall in the collar, "and large gilt buttons size of a dollar"—see the poem for further details—Gillespie decided that a rehearsal might be a mistake. It might make this eleventh hour addition to the cast self-conscious, which of course was what Gillespie above all things desired to avoid. He didn't want Captain Teal to try to act. As he repeatedly emphasized, he just wanted him to be himself.

Nor did it occur to Gillespie, any more than it occurred to Herzog, assisting him in the day's job, to take the old man into their confidence touching on what of theme and development had gone before in the making of this masterpiece of an historical production, or on what would follow after. Players of character bits are not supposed to know what the thing's about. Indeed, there are times when the patron of the silent drama, going to his favorite theater and viewing the completed work, is inclined to believe that some of the principal performers could have had but a hazy conception of what it was all about. Nobody, one figures, ever explained the whys and wherefores to them, either. However, that is neither here nor there, this being no critique of the technique of the motion-picture art but merely an attempt to describe an incident in the filming of one particular scene in one particular motion-picture, namely the epic entitled "Two Lovers of War-Time."

There should have been a broad sea of ripening wheat rolling upward along a hillside slope to a broken stone wall. Gillespie, usually a stickler for the lesser verities, was compelled to forego the ripening wheat because, while outdoor stagecraft has gone far in these later times and studio stagecraft has gone still farther, you cannot, in California in the fall of the year, months after the standing crop has been cut, artificially produce a plausible semblance of many acres of nodding grain all ready for the reaper. So he contented himself with a stubble field, and privately hoped no caption observer would record the error. But the traditional stone fence, which is so famous in song and story, was there. And thither the Captain was presently escorted.

"Now, here's the layout," specified Herzog, who actively was in charge of this phase of the undertaking. "You're supposed to be the only civilian"— Herzog pronounced it *civil-an*—"the only civilian in the whole town that didn't beat it when the enemy came along. All the rest of 'em took it on the run to the woods but you stuck because you ain't scared of nobody. You're one of these game old patr'ots, see? So you just loaded up your old rifle and you declared yourself in. So that makes you the hero of the whole outfit, for the time being. Get me?... Good! Well, then—now follow me clos't, because this is where the real action starts—the very next morning you happen to be out here on the edge of the town and right over yonder is where the big doings bust out. The book that the chief got the notion for these shots out of don't say how you got here in the first place but we're taking it for granted, me and Gillespie are, that you're just fiddling around looking for trouble on your own hook. The book does say, though—it's a poetry book—that your gang get a slant at you when you show up and they start in making funny cracks and asking you where you got them funny clothes you got on and asking you what you think you're going to do anyhow with that there big old musket you're lugging with you.

"But I figure that would kind of slow up the action, so I've changed it around some from the way the book's got it. The way it's going to be is the battle gets going good before you join in. One gang—one army, I mean—is behind that fence and the other army comes running up towards 'em from down at the foot of that hill yonder, whooping and yelling and shooting and all. And with that, you cut in right between 'em, all by your lonesome, and take a hand. That brings you out prominent because you're the only guy in sight that's dressed different from everybody else. All the rest of these guys are in soldier's clothes. So this gives you your chance to hog the picture for a w'ile. It's good and fat for you along here.

"Well, then, that other army that I've just been telling you about comes charging on right up to the wall and there's close-in fighting back and forth—hand-to-hand stuff, what I mean—for two or three minutes before the break comes and the gang that is due to be licked decide they've had enough and start retreating. And all this time you're right in the thick of it, shooting first, and then when your gun's empty you club it by the barrel and fight with it that way. Don't be afraid of being too rough, neither. These extras are under orders to go at one another raw, so it'll be more like a battle ought to be. Them that puts the most steam into it will get a finnuf slipped to 'em. They know that, and I wouldn't be surprised but what probably a couple of dozen of 'em should get laid out in earnest; so you needn't feel backward about wading in and doing your share. Just put yourself right into it, that's the idea, and cut loose regardless. I'll be off to one side cueing you through my megaphone which way to go when they first pick you up for the long shots, but after that it's all up to you. Don't think about the camera nor nothing else. Don't look at a camera. Don't look around, even to see where any of the cameras are. But then, seeing you told me yourself only last week about having fought in one of them regular wars, I guess I don't need to tell you how to go to it. It'll all come back to you in less than a minute, I'll bet you.... Now then, come on over here and let me get you set."

Herzog's optimistic prediction was justified. In less than a minute it did come back to Captain Teal. The first preliminary crackle of musketry fire brought it back to him with a mighty surge of clamoring, swirling memories. The first whiff of acrid powder smoke in his nostrils, the first sight of those ragged gray uniforms, those dusty blue uniforms, changed the memories into actualities. The weight of sixty years slipped off his shoulders; the rich saps of youth mounted for a little passing time into his pithy marrows, giving swiftness to his rickety legs and strength to his withered arms. It was proof of what an imagination fired by vivid reminders of clanging bygone things could do for an ancient's body.

Headlong once more into battle went Captain Teal, and as he did he uttered sundry long-drawn wolfish yells, one yell right behind another, until you would have thought, had you been there to listen, that his throat surely must split itself wide open.

In he went, and he took sides. He took the wrong side. That is to say, and speaking from strictly a technical standpoint, he took the wrong side. But from Captain Teal's standpoint he took the right side and the only side which with honor he might take. To be sure, no one beforehand had advised him specifically in this matter of taking sides. It had been Herzog's oversight that he had not dwelt more clearly upon this highly important point, which he had assumed his venerable pupil would understand. And now it was Herzog's handicap, as the Captain's intention became plain, that Herzog's hoarsely bellowed commands—commands at the outset but merging swiftly into harsh and agonized outcries—should fall upon that ear of Captain Teal which was his deafer ear.

Not that it would have made any difference to Captain Teal had he been able to hear. With his head back and his parted white whiskers flowing rearward over his shoulders, with the Rebel yell still shrilly and constantly issuing from him, he went in and he took command of those onrushing supernumeraries who wore the gray, and he bade them go with him and give the Yankees hell, and he led them on up the hill to where the blue-clad forces held its crest. Theirs not to question why, theirs but to do or die; which, as may be recalled, was once upon a time precisely and identically the case with other doughty warriors taking part in an earlier onslaught upon the serried field of battle. If, at the last moment their overlords chose to amend the preordained course of events, so be it. Since confusion and chaos were to rule the hour, why then in that case might the best man win. Behold, now, how all drilled plans had suddenly been tossed aside; but at least they had a fit commander to follow after. And at least they knew the purport of that most dwelt-upon and salient order—to smite and spare not. They were lusty lads, these extras, no lustier perhaps than the Unionists yonder awaiting the clash and grapple, but better captained.

And so, while the obedient camera-men kept on grinding, and while Herzog shrieked and impotently danced and finally, casting his megaphone from him, stood and profaned his Maker's name, Long John Burns led Pickett's charge, and Gettysburg, after sanguinary losses on both sides, was a Confederate victory, and American history most wondrously was remade.

"Ow!" Mr. Lobel heaved the sorrowful expletive up from his lower stomach spaces. "All them extras to pay for all over again! All them re-takes to be retook. All that money wasted because a crazy old loafer must run—must run—" He grasped for the proper word.

"Run amuck," supplied Liebermann, proud of his erudition.

"—Must run a regular muck. Yes, if you should ask me, one of the worst mucks ever I have seen in my whole life," continued Mr. Lobel. "And you it was, Gillespie, that stood right here in this office only last Toosday of this week and promised me you should keep down expensives. Who's a man going to believe in this picture business? I ask you!"

"What of it?" said Gillespie. "It was worth a little money to let the old laddy-boy get the smoke of battle in his nose once more before he dies and have a thrill. I didn't think so awhile ago when he was rampaging through that flock of extras, but I'm beginning to think so now. We'll tell him he's just a trifle too notionate for this game and pay him off—with a wee something on the side for a bonus. If you won't do it I'll do it myself out of my own pocket. And then we'll ship him back to that sleepy little town where he came from. Anyhow, it's not a total loss, Lobel, remember that. We're going to salvage something out of the wreck. And we owe the old boy for that."

"What do you mean, salve something out of it?" inquired Mr. Lobel.

"We grab off that little Clayton girl—the one I tried out in those interior shots yesterday. She's got it in her, that kid has. I don't mean brains, although at that I guess she's about as smart as the average fluffy-head that's doing ingénues along this coast. But she's got the stuff in her to put it over. Tell her a thing once and she's got it. And she screens well. And she's naturally camera-wise. She'll go a good way, I predict. And if it hadn't been for the old man we wouldn't have her. He practically rammed her down my throat. It seems she's his cousin, eight or ten times removed, and nothing would do him but that I must hitch her onto the payroll. To get him in the proper humor I had to take her on. But now I'm glad of it. I'll be wanting a little contract soon for this Clayton, Lobel, so we'll have her tied up before somebody else begins to want her. Because, sooner or later, somebody else will."

Traffic swirled past the two Southerners where they stood in a side eddy in the train shed. They were saying good-by, and now all at once the girl felt a curious weakness in her knees as though she were losing a dependable prop.

"I must get aboard," he said, looking down at her from his greater height. "We'll be leaving in a minute or so. You need not distress yourself about me, my dear. I could never have been happy for very long in this place—it's not like our country. These Northern people mean well no doubt; but after all they're not our people, are they? And this avocation was not suited for one of my years and—and antecedents; that I also realize. I have no regrets. In fact"—a flare lit in his faded old eyes—"in fact, I greatly enjoyed the momentary excitement of once more facing the enemies of our beloved land—even in make-believe. Indeed, I enjoyed it more than I can tell. I shall have that to look back on always—that and the very great pleasure of having known you, my dear."

He lifted her hand and kissed it and started away, and she saw him going—a picture out of a picture book—through a sudden mist of tears. But he came back for one more farewell passage:

"Remember, my dear," he said, "that we—you and I—are of the Old South—the land of real gentlemen and real ladies. You'll remember that always, won't you?"

And now, with both her arms around him and her lips pressed hard against his ruddy old cheek, she promised him she would.

She meant it, too, at the moment. And perhaps she did and then again perhaps she didn't. The world she lived in is so full of Tobe Dalys. As the brethren of the leathern pants and the silken neckerchiefs of Hollywood are so fond of saying—those mail-order movie cow-punchers who provide living backgrounds for the Westerns—"*Quien sabe?*"

Killed with Kindness

NEEDLES and pins, needles and pins, when a man's married his trouble begins. That's the way the old application goes. But in the case of Jerome Bracken it didn't go. After he married, life ran for him on very smooth rollers and there were neither needles nor pins to prick him. Possibly that was because he chose for his wife a virtuous and well-meaning woman, one a bit narrow in her views perhaps and rather stiffly opinionated, as a good many good women are who protect their own tepid moralities behind a quill-work of sharp-pointed prejudices. They are the female porcupines of the human race, being colorless and lethargic in their mentalities but acute and eager when they take a dislike. Still, the porcupine rates high among the animals. While generally not beloved, it generally is respected. And undoubtedly this lady who became Mrs. Jerome Bracken was well-meaning and remained straitly so until the end of all regulated things.

Or then on the other hand, possibly Jerome Bracken's marriage was a success because he picked precisely the sort of woman who had the qualifications for being a suitable wife to an up-and-coming man, a man who kept on up and kept on coming until he had arrived, with both feet planted on how firm a foundation! But then Jerome always had been, as the phrase is, a clever picker. He proved that when as a very young man he moved to Dyketon and picked Queen Sears for his girl. He kept on proving it—by picking the right business, the right code of deportment before the eyes of mankind, the right church to belong to, and precisely the right father-in-law.

This Queenie Sears, now; she was not the one he married, naturally not. Queenie Sears was not the sort any man in his sane senses would marry, she being what used to be called a fancy woman. She was an inmate of Madam Carrie Rupert's house when he first met her and it was there, under that hospitable but disreputable roof, down on Front Street in Dyketon's red-light district, that the meeting took place.

About this first meeting there was nothing significant. He called, a stranger, and she entertained him, it being her business to entertain callers. He at this time was a shrewd but countrified youth of twenty or thereabouts.

She was a little older than that, blonde, simple-minded, easy-going, rather pretty in an insipid way, with a weak, self-indulgent mouth. Already she was plump, with the certainty before her that, barring ill health to pull her down, the succeeding years would enhance her plumpness into rolls and cushions of fat. Probably, if the truth were known, she deliberately elected to take on this life she was leading. However, and be that as it may, she had the customary story to account for her present vocation when somebody who was maudlin with a sympathy based on alcohol asked her how she came to be what she was.

Hers was a stock story lacking novelty as well as sincerity—a sentimental fiction dealing with a trusting and ignorant maiden's downfall in an orange grove vaguely described as being "away down South," and then discovery and disgrace and a traditional proud father whose heart could be flinty and yet broken, and a shamed girl's flight in the night and all the rest of the stage props. But sometimes it was a plantation instead of an orange grove; or if the inquirer happened to be a Southerner, it might be a ranch in the far West. Queenie was taking no chances on getting herself checked up.

As for Jerome, his tale was a short one, not particularly interesting but having the merit, as hers did not, of a background of fact. Raised on a farm in the central part of the state; poor parents; common school education; lately landed in Dyketon; stopping now at a second-rate boarding-house out on Ninth Street; working for eighteen a week as a bookkeeper at Stout & Furst's clothing store; ambitious to better himself in both these latter regards—that, brought up to date, was young Bracken.

Nor was there any special significance in the intimacy which followed between these two. He visited her at more or less regular intervals. Thus early he was shaping his days into a calculated and orderly routine which remained a part of him forever after. She liked him, being at heart kindly and, considering her trade, susceptible to affectionate impulses; he liked her, being lonely, and that substantially was all there was to it.

At the end of a year he began his journey up in the world. Mr. Gus Ralph, president of the Ralph State Bank, took him on as an assistant receiving teller at a hundred a month and prospects. Unknown to the newcomer, Mr. Ralph had had his eye on him for some time—a young man of good manners and presumably of good habits, bright, dignified, industrious, discreet, honest—in short, a hustler. Mr. Ralph was on the lookout for that kind. He made a place for the young man, and from the hour when he walked into the counting-house and hung up his hat Jerome was justifying the confidence Mr. Ralph put in him. If he was continuing to sow his wild oats—and privately he was—at least he sowed none during banking hours, nor did any part of his harvesting in public, which was sufficient for his new boss. Mr. Ralph often said he had been a youngster once himself, saying it with an air which indicated that he had been very much of a youngster indeed.

At the end of six months more, which would make it about eighteen months in all, young Jerome ceased his sowing operations altogether. He didn't fray the rope; he cut it clean through at a single decisive stroke.

"Queenie," he said to her one night, "this is going to be the last time I'm ever coming down here to see you."

"Well, Jerry," she answered, "that'll be all right with me unless you start going to see some other girl in some other house along the row here."

"It's not that," he explained. "I'm going to quit going down the line altogether. I'm through"—he made a gesture with his hands—"through with the whole thing from now on."

"I see," she said, after a moment or two. "Been getting yourself engaged to some nice girl—is that the way it is, Jerry?"

"Yes," he told her, "that's the way it is, Queenie."

She did not ask who the nice girl might be nor did he offer to tell her. In that ancient age—the latter decades of the last century before this one—there was a code for which nearly everybody of whatsoever station had the proper reverence. In some places—bar-rooms, for example, and certain other places—a gentleman did not bring up the name of a young lady. It was never the thing to do.

"Here, Jerry," she said next. "I'll be kind of sorry to say good-by, but I want you to know I wish you mighty well. Not that you need my good wishes—you're going ahead and you'll keep on going—but I want you to have them. Because, Jerry, if it was my dying words I was speaking I'd still say it just the same—you've always been on the square with me, and that's what counts with a girl like me. You never came down here drunk, you never used rough language before me, you never tried to bilk me or take advantage of me any kind of way. Yes, sir, that's what counts. Even if I don't never see you face to face again I won't forget how kind and pleasant you've been towards me. And I'd die before I'd make any trouble for you, ever. You go your way and I'll go mine, such as it is, and that'll be all there is to it so far as I'm concerned.

"Now then, you've told me some news; I'll tell you some. I'm fixing to buy out Miss Carrie. She wants to quit this business and go over to Chicago and live decent. She's got a married daughter there, going straight, and anyhow she's made her pile out of this drum and can afford to quit, and I don't blame her any, at her age, for wanting to quit. But me, it's different with. I've got a little money saved up of my own and she's willing to take that much down and take a mortgage on the furniture and trust me for the rest of the payments as they fall due. And just yesterday we closed up the bargain, and next week the lease and the telephone number and all go in my name. So you see I'm trying to get along, too, the best way I can." She lifted the glass of beer that she was holding in her hand. "Here's good luck!"

She took the draught down greedily. Her full lips had the drooping at their corners which advertises the potential dipsomaniac.

Face to face, through the rest of her life he never did speak to her. To be sure, there were at irregular intervals telephone conversations between them. I'll come to that part of it later. Anyhow, they were not social conversations, but purely business.

He saw her, of course—Dyketon was a small place then; it was afterwards that it grew into a city—but always at a distance, always across the wide gulf that little-town etiquette digs for encounters in public between the godly and the ungodly. Once in a while she would pass him on the street, she usually riding in a hack and he usually afoot, with no sign of recognition, of course, on the part of either. Then again, some evening at the theater, he, sitting with his wife down-stairs, would happen to glance up toward the "white" gallery and she would be perched, as one of a line of her sisters of transgression, on the front row there. The Dyketon theater management practiced the principle of segregation for prostitutes just as the city government practically enforced it in the matter of their set-apart living-quarters. These communal taboos were as old as the community itself was. Probably they still endure.

With time, even the occasional sight of his old light-o'-love failed to revive in his mind pictures of the house where he once had knowledge of her. The memories of that interior faded into a conglomerate blur. One memory did persist. Long after the rest was a faint jumble he recalled quite sharply the landlady's two pets—her asthmatic pug-dog with its broody cocked eyes, and her wicked talking parrot with its yellow head and its vice for gnawing woodwork and its favorite shrieked refrain: "Ladies, gent'men in the parlor!"

He remembered them long after he forgot how the place had smelled of bottled beer and cheap perfumery and unaired sofa-stuffing; and how always on the lower floor there had prevailed in daytime a sort of dusky gloom by reason of the shutters being tightly closed and barred fast against sunlight and small boys or other Peeping Toms who might come venturing on forbidden ground; and how, night-times, above the piano-playing of the resident "professor" and the clamor of many voices there would cut through the shrill squeals of an artificial joy—the laughter forced from the sorry souls of those forlorn practitioners at the oldest and the very saddest of human trades.

The one he married was the only daughter of his employer, Mr. Gus Ralph; a passionless, circumspect young woman three or four years his senior. The father approved heartily of the engagement and in testimony thereof promptly promoted Jerome to a place of more responsibility and larger salary; the best families likewise gave to this match their approval. Even so, Mr. Ralph never would have advanced the future son-in-law had not the latter been deserving of it. The elder man's foresight had been good, very, very good. Jerome was cut out for the banking business. He proved that from the start. He knew when to say no, and prospective borrowers learned that his no meant no. Personally he was frugal without being miserly and, in the earlier days at least, he had firmness without arrogance; and if personally he was one of the most selfish creatures ever created, he had for public affairs a fine, broad spirit.

He had been brought up a Baptist but almost on the heels of his wedding he joined his wife's congregation. She was a strict Presbyterian, and in Dyketon the Presbyterians, next after the Episcopalians, constituted the most aristocratic department of piety. This step also pleased old Mr. Ralph exceedingly.

It wasn't very long before Mr. Bracken, as everybody nearly except his intimates called him, was chief of staff down at the bank, closest adviser and right-hand-man to the owner. In another five years he was junior partner and vice-president. Five years more, and he, still on the sunny side of thirty-five, was president. Mr. Ralph had died and among the directors no other name was considered for the vacancy. His election merely was a matter of form. With his wife's holdings and his own and his widowed mother-in-law's, he controlled a heavy majority of the stock.

Jerome Bracken was a model to all young men growing up. Look at the way his earthly affairs were prospering! Look at his tithes to religion and to charity—one-tenth of all he made bestowed on good causes and in good deeds; a sober man laying up treasures not only in this world but for the world to come. Look how the Lord was multiplying his profits unto him! Mothers and fathers enjoined their sons' notice upon these proofs. Jerome Bracken's life was like a motto on a wall, like a burning torch in the night-time.

Still, there were those—a few only, be it said—who claimed that with increasing years and increasing powers Mr. Bracken took on a temper which made him hard and high-handed and greedy for yet more authority. This hardness does come often to those who sit in lofty seats and rule over the small destinies of the smaller fry. On the other hand, though, anyone who notably succeeds is sure to have his detractors; success breeds envy and envy breeds criticism. That fierce light which beats upon a throne brings out in clean relief any imperfections of the illumined one, and people are bound to notice them and some people are bound to comment on them.

Take, for instance, the time when that young fellow, Quinn, was caught dead to rights pilfering from the petty cash. It seemed he had been speculating in a small way at bucket-shops and, what was worse, betting on the races. It further seemed to quite a number of citizens that Mr. Bracken might have found it in his heart to be pitiful to the sinner. Not much more than a boy and his father and mother hard-working, decent people and his older brother a priest and all—these were the somewhat indirect arguments they offered in condonement. And besides, wasn't old man Quinn ready to sell his cottage and use the money from the sale to make good the shortage? Then why not let the whole messy business drop where it was? Least said soonest mended. And so on and so forth.

Mr. Bracken couldn't see the situation in any such light. He felt sorry enough for the lad and sorrier for the lad's family, and so stated when a sort of unofficial delegation of the pleaders waited on him. Nor was it the amount of the theft that counted with him; he said that, too. But in his position he had a duty to the commonweal and topping that, an obligation to his depositors and his patrons. He refused to consent that the thing be hushed up. He went himself and swore out the warrant, and that night young Quinn's wayward head tossed on a cot in the county jail. Mr. Bracken went before the grand jury likewise and pressed for the indictment; and at the trial in circuit court he was the prosecution's chief witness, relating with a regretful but painstaking fidelity the language of the defendant's confession to him.

Young Quinn accordingly departed to state's prison for two years of hard labor, becoming what frequently is spoken of as a warning and an example. While there he learned to make chair-bottoms but so far as might be learned never made any after his release. When last heard of he was a hobo and presumably an associate of members of the criminal classes. By all current standards of righteous men the example was now a perfected one.

Persons who found fault with the attitude Mr. Bracken had taken in the case naturally did not know of any offsetting acts of kindliness performed by him behind closed doors. Regarding these acts there was no way for them to know. Had they known, perhaps they might have altered their judgments. Or perhaps not. Behind his back they probably would have gone right on picking him to pieces. A main point, though, was that nobody berated him to his face; nobody would dare. He passed through his maturing years shielded by an insulation of expressed approval for what he said and what he thought and what he did.

This was true of the home circle, which a fine and gracious flavor of domestic harmony perfumed; and it was true of his life locally and abroad. When you get to be a little tin god on wheels, the crowd is glad to trail along and grease the wheels for you with words of praise and admiring looks. And when everybody is saying yes, yes, oh yes, to you, why, you get out of the habit ever of saying no, emphatically no, to yourself. That's only human nature, which is one of the few things that the automobile and the radio have not materially altered.

So much, for the moment, for this man who was a model to young men growing up. It is necessary to turn temporarily to one who went down, down, down, as that first one, in the estimation of a vast majority of his fellow beings was going up and up and ever higher up.

Queenie Sears was the one whose straying feet took hold on hell. Presently her establishment had a booze-artist for a proprietor and a hard and aggravating name among the police force. They called it the toughest joint in the First Ward. City court warrants were sworn out against her— for plain drunkenness, for disorderly conduct along with drunkenness, for fighting with other women of her sort, for suffering gaming and dope-peddling on her premises.

When an inmate of her house killed herself under peculiarly distressing circumstances, sermons were preached about her from at least two city pulpits, the ministers speaking of depravity and viciousness and the debauching of youth and plaguish blots on the fair burnished face of the civic shield. When she took the Keeley Cure—and speedily relapsed—those who frequented her neighborhood of ill repute had a hearty laugh over the joke of it. She was gross of size and waddled when she walked, and her big earrings of flawed diamonds rested against jowls of quivering, unwholesome bloat.

But dissipation did not destroy the beldame's faculties for earning money—if money got that way could be said to be earned—and for putting it by. Mr. Jerome Bracken, who had known her back in those long bygone days of her comeliness, was in position to give evidence, had he been so minded, regarding her facility at saving it up. This was how he came to have such information:

Once or twice a year, say, she would call him on the telephone at his office in the bank. Across the wire to him her eaten-out voice would come, hoarse and flattened—a hoarseness and a flatness which increased as the years rolled by.

"Jerry," she would say, following almost a set pattern, "you know who this is, don't you—Queenie?"

"Yes," he would answer; "what can I do for you now?"

"Same as you done the last time," she would say. "I've got a few more iron men tucked away and I'm looking for a little suggestion about a place to put 'em. And, Jerry, I hope you don't mind my calling you up. There ain't nobody else I could depend on like I can on you."

She never told him, in dollars and cents, how much she had for investment nor did he ever ask. If inwardly he guessed at the possible total his guess did not run to large figures. But just as he might have done in the case of any individual seeking his counsel in this regard, he would recommend to her this or that bond or such-and-such standard stock, and she would repeat the name after him until she had memorized it and then she would thank him.

"I'm mighty much obliged to you, Jerry," she would say. "I ain't ever lost any money yet by following after your advice. It's awful good of you, helping me out this way, and I appreciate it—I certainly do."

"That's all right, Queenie," he would tell her, in his precise manner of speech. "I'm glad to be able to serve you. You are free to call on me—by telephone—whenever you care to."

"I won't never forget it," she would reply. "Well, good-by, Jerry."

It never happened more than twice a year, sometimes only once in a year as they—these years—kept on mounting up.

They mounted up until Dyketon had increased herself from a sprawled-out county-seat into a city of the second class. She had 100,000 inhabitants now—only 83,000 according to the notoriously inadequate federal census figures, but fully 100,000 by the most conservative estimates of the Board of Trade—and old inhabitants were deploring that whereas once they knew by name or face everybody they met, now a fellow could take a stroll on almost every street and about every other person he ran into would be a total stranger to him.

New blood was quick and rampant in Dyketon's commercial arteries and new leaders had risen up in this quarter or that, but two outstanding figures of the former times still were outstanding. On all customary counts Mr. Jerome Bracken was the best man in town and old Queenie Sears the worst woman. He led all in eminence, she distanced the field in iniquity. By every standard he was at the very top. Nobody disputed her evil hold on the bottommost place of all. Between those heights of his gentility and those depths of her indecency there was a space of a million miles that seemed to any imagination unbridgeable; at least that seemed so to Dyketon's moralists, provided they ever had coupled the honored president of the State Bankers' Association and the abandoned strumpet of Front Street in the same thought, which was improbable.

A certain day was a great day for him who was used to great days. But this one, by reason of two things, was really a day above other great days. In the same issue of the Dyketon Morning Sun appeared, at the top of the social notes, an announcement of his daughter's engagement to Mr. Thomas H. Scopes III, a distinguished member of one of the oldest families in town, and, on the front page, his own announcement as an aspirant for the Republican nomination for United States Senator.

Until now he had put by all active political ambitions. From time to time, tempting prospects of office-holding had come to him; he had waved them aside. But now, his private fortune having passed the mark of two millions, and his business being geared to run practically on its own momentum and smoothly, he felt, and his formal card to the voters so stated, that he might with possible profit to the commonwealth devote the energies of his seasoned years to public service as a public servant. Quote: If the people by the expression of their will at the approaching primaries indicated him as the choice of his party for this high position, then so be it; his opponent would find him ready for the issue. End quote.

All the morning and all the afternoon until he left his office he was receiving the congratulations of associates and well-wishers upon Miss Bracken's engagement and likewise upon his own decision to run for Senator. His desk telephone was jingling constantly. He stopped in at his club on the way home—the Metropolis Club it was, and the most exclusive one in town—and there he held a sort of levee. Whole-hearted support was promised him by scores, literally. The most substantial men in the whole city gathered about him, endorsing him for the step he had taken and pledging themselves to work for him and predicting his easy nomination and his equally easy election. The state generally went Republican—not always, but three times out of four on an average. Under this barrage of applause he unbent somewhat, showing more warmth, more geniality, than he had shown anywhere for a good long while. He did not unbend too far, though, but just far enough.

The club cynic, an aged and petulant retired physician, watching the scene in the club library from his regular seat by the tall marble fireplace, remarked under his voice to the first deputy club cynic, who now bore him company and who would succeed him on his death:

"Haughty as hell, even now, ain't he? Notice this, Ike—he's not acknowledging the enthusiasm of that flock of bootlickers that are swarming around him yonder, he's merely accepting it as his proper due. What does the man think he is anyhow—God Almighty?"

"Humph!" answered the deputy. "You rate our budding statesman too low. Down in that Calvinistic soul of his he may sometimes question the workings of the Divine Scheme, but you bet he never has questioned his own omnipotence—the derned money-changing pouter pigeon. Look at him, all reared back there with one hand on his heart and the other under his coat-tails—like a steel engraving of Daniel Webster!"

"Not on his heart, Ike," corrected the chief cynic grimly; "merely on the place where his heart would be if he had any heart. He had one once, I guess, but from disuse it's withered up and been absorbed into the system. Remember, don't you, how just here the other week he clamped down on poor old Hank Needham and squeezed the last cent out of him? He'll win, though, mark my words on it. He always has had his way and he'll keep on having it. Lord, Lord, and I can remember when we used to send real men to Washington from this state—human he-men, not glorified dollar-grabbers always looking for the main chance. Given half a show, Hank Needham could have come back; now he's flat busted and he'll be dead in six months, or I miss my guess."

These isolated two—the official crab and his understudy—were the only men in the room, barring club servants, who remained aloof from the circle surrounding the candidate. They bided on where they were, eyeing him from under their drooped eyelids when, at the end of a happy hour, he passed out, a strong, erect, soldierly man in his ripening fifties. Then, together, they both grunted eloquently.

In a fine glow of contentment Jerome Bracken walked to his house. He wanted the exercise, he wanted to be alone for a little while with his optimism.

He was almost home when a city hospital ambulance hurried past him, its gong clanging for passage in the traffic of early evening. Just after it got by he saw a white-coated interne and a policeman wrestling with somebody who seemed to be fastened down to a stretcher in the interior of the motor, and from that struggling somebody he heard delirious sobbing outcries in a voice that was feminine and yet almost too coarsened and thick to be feminine.

Vaguely it irked him that even for a passing moment this interruption should break in on his thoughts. But no untoward thing disturbed the household rhapsody that night. There, as at the office, the bell on the telephone kept ringing almost constantly, and, being answered, the telephone yielded only felicitating words from all and sundry who had called up.

A man who had no shadow of earthly doubt touching on his destinies slept that night in Jerome Bracken's bed. And if he dreamed we may be well assured that his dreams were untroubled by specters of any who had besought him for mercy and had found it not. A conscience that is lapped in eider-down is nearly always an easy conscience.

It was the fifth day after the next day when, with no warning whatsoever, Jerome Bracken got smashed all to flinders. He was in his office at the rear of the bank going over the morning mail—it mostly was letters written by friendly partisans over the state, including one from the powerful national committeeman for the state—when without knocking, his lawyer, Mr. Richard Griffin, opened the door and walked in followed by his local political manager, who also happened to be the local political boss. The faces of both wore looks of a grave uneasiness, the manners of both were concerned and unhappy.

"Morning, gentlemen," said Mr. Bracken. "What is pressing down on your minds this fine day?"

Yankee-fashion, Mr. Griffin answered the question by putting another.

"Bracken," he said, "how long have you been knowing this woman, Queenie Sears?"

"What do you mean?" demanded Mr. Bracken sharply.

"What I say. How long have you known her? And how well?"

"I don't understand you, Dick." The other's tone was angry. "And by what right do you assume—"

"Bracken," snapped Griffin sharply, "I'm here as a man who's been your lifelong friend—you must know that. And Dorgan here has come with me in the same capacity—as a friend of yours. This thing is serious. It's damned serious. It's likely to be about the most serious thing that ever happened to you. I'll repeat the question and I'm entitled to a fair, frank answer: How long have you been acquainted with Queenie Sears?"

In his irate bewilderment Mr. Bracken could think of but one plausible explanation for this incredible inquiry. He started up from his chair, his hands gripping into fists. He almost shouted it.

"Has that dirty, libelous, scandal-mongering rag of an afternoon paper down the street had the effrontery this early in the campaign to attempt to besmirch my character? If it has I'll—"

"Not yet!" For the first time the politician was taking a hand in the talk. "But it will—before sundown tonight. Catch a Democrat outfit passing up a bet like this! Sweet chance!" He looked toward the lawyer. "You better tell him, Griffin," he said with a certain gloomy decision. "Then when you're through I'll have my little say-so."

"Probably that would be best," agreed Griffin resignedly. "Sit down, won't you, Bracken? I'm going to hand you a pretty hard blow right in the face."

His amazement growing, Mr. Bracken sat down. Through what painfully followed, the other two continued to stand.

"Bracken," stated Griffin, "I'll start at the beginning. Something like a week ago Queenie Sears was taken from her dive down on the river shore to the municipal infirmary. She had delirium tremens—was raving crazy. She'd had them before, it appears, but this attack was the last one she'll ever have. Because it killed her—that and a weak heart and bad kidneys and a few other complications, so the doctors say. Anyhow, she's dead. She died about an hour ago.

"Well, early this morning her mind cleared up for a little while. They told her she was going, which she probably knew for herself, and advised her to put her worldly affairs—if she had any—in order. It seems she had considerable worldly affairs to put in order, which was a surprise. It seems from what she said that she had upwards of a hundred and fifty thousand dollars, all in gilt-edged securities, all tucked away in a safe-deposit box, and all of it, every red cent of it, coined from the blood and the sweat and the degradations of fallen women. No need for us to go into that now. God knows, enough people will be only too glad to go into it when the news leaks out!

"As I say, they told her at the hospital that she was dying. So she asked for a lawyer and they got one—a young fellow named Dean that's lately opened up an office. And he came and she made her will and it was signed in the presence of witnesses and will be offered for probate without delay. Trust some of our friends of the opposition to attend promptly to that detail. And, Bracken—take it steady, man—Bracken, she left every last miserable cent of that foul, tainted one hundred and fifty thousand dollars to you."

"What!" The cry issued from Bracken's throat in a gulping shriek.

"I'm saying she left it all to you. I've just seen the will. So has Dorgan. I sent for him as soon as the word reached me about half an hour ago and we went together and read the infernal thing. It says—I can almost quote it verbatim—that she's leaving it to you because for thirty-six years you've been her best friend and really her only friend and her one disinterested adviser. And furthermore because—with almost her dying breath she said it—because you were solely instrumental in helping her to save and preserve her earnings.... God, but that's been hard! Now then, Dorgan, it's your turn to speak."

So Dorgan spoke, but briefly. Five minutes later, from the door on the point of departure, he was repeating with patience, in almost the soothing parental tone one might use to an ailing and unreasonable child, what already he had said at least twice over to that stricken figure slumped in the swivel chair at the big flat desk.

"Sure," he was saying, "I'll believe you, and Griffin here, he'll believe you—ain't he just promised you he would?—and there's maybe five or six others'll believe you—but who else is goin' to take your word against what it says in black and white on that paper? And her lookin' into the open grave when she told 'em to set it down? Nope, Bracken, you're through, and it's only a mercy to you that I'm comin' here to be the first one to tell you you are. You can explain till you're black in the face and you can refuse to touch that dough till the end of time, or you can give it to charity—if you're lucky enough to find a charity that'll take it—but, Bracken, it's been hung around your neck like a grindstone and it was a dead woman's hands that hung it there and it makes you altogether too heavy a load for any political organization to carry—you see that yourself, don't you? And so, Bracken, you're through!"

But to Bracken's ears now the words came dimly, meaning little. Where he was huddled, he foresaw as with an eye for prophecy things coming to pass much as they truly did come to pass. He saw his wife—how well he knew that lukewarm lady who was not lukewarm in her animosities nor yet in her suspicions!—saw her closing a door of enduring contempt forever between them; he saw the breaking off of his daughter's engagement to that young Scopes, who was the third bearer of an honored name, and his daughter despising him as the cause for her humiliation and her wrecked happiness; he saw himself thrown out of his church, thrown out of his bank, thrown out of all those pleasant concerns in which he had joyed and from which he had rendered the sweet savors of achievement and of creation. He saw himself being cut, being ignored, by those who had been glad to kowtow before him for his favor, being elbowed aside as though he were a thing unclean and leprous.

He heard, not Dorgan passing a compassionate but relentless sentence on him and his dearest of all hopes, but rather he seemed to hear the scornful laughter of unregenerate elderly libertines, rejoicing at the downfall of an offending brother exposed at his secret sins; and he seemed to hear derisive voices speaking—"Walking so straight up he reared backwards, and all the time—" "Well, well, well, the church is certainly the place for a hypocrite to hide himself in, ain't it?" "Acting like butter wouldn't melt in his mouth, but now just look at him!" "His life was an open book till they found out where the dark pages were stuck together, he, he, he!" Thus and so he heard the scoffing voices speaking. He heard aright too, and as his head went down into his hands, he tasted in anticipation a draft too bitter for human strength to bear.

Griffin was another who did not hear the third repetition of Dorgan's judgment. He had gone on ahead like a man anxious to quit a noisome sickroom and to one of the assistant cashiers in the outer office he was saying: "I advise you to get your chief to go home and lie down awhile. It might also be a good idea to call up his family doctor and get him to drop over here right away. From the looks of him, Mr. Bracken's not a well man. He's had a shock—a profound shock. His nerves might give way, I'd say, any minute. I'm afraid he's in for a very, very hard time!"

Peace on Earth

THIS Christmas was going to be different. So far as Mr. and Mrs. Bugbee were concerned the Christmas before had been a total failure, disillusioning, disappointing, fraught with heart-burnings. But this coming one—well, just let everybody wait and see. They'd show them.

"It's going to be so dog-goned different you'd be surprised!" said Mr. Bugbee. He said it after the plan had taken on shape and substance and, so saying, raised a hand in the manner of a man who plights a solemn troth.

But first the plan had to be born. It was born on a day in October when Mr. Bugbee came into the living-room of their light-housekeeping apartment on West Ninth Street just around the corner from Washington Square. The living-room was done in Early Byzantine or something—a connoisseur would know, probably—and Mrs. Bugbee was dressed to match the furnishings. She was pretty, though. Her friends said she reminded them of a Pre-Raphaelite Madonna, which either was or was not a compliment dependent on what privately the speaker thought about the Pre-Raphaelite school. Still, most of her friends liked it, being themselves expertly artistic. She had the tea things out—the hammered Russian set. This was her customary afternoon for receiving and presently there would be people dropping in. She lifted her nose and sniffed.

"Whew!" she exclaimed. "Where have you been? You smell like a rancid peppermint lozenge."

"Been down in the storeroom in the basement getting out my winter suits," he said. "Messy job. I broke up a party."

"Whose?" she asked.

"Mr. and Mrs. Moth were celebrating their woolen wedding," he explained. "They furnished the guests and I did the catering. You ought to see that heavy sweater of mine. It's not heavy any more. I'm going to write a chapter to be added to that sterling work 'Advice to an Expectant Moth-er.'"

"Oh dear!" she said. "That's the trouble with living in one of these old converted houses."

"This one has backslid," he interjected. "Insectivorous, I call it. There were enough roaches down there to last a reasonable frugal roach-collector for at least five years. Any entomologist could have enjoyed himself for a week just classifying species."

"And I fairly saturated your clothes with that spraying stuff before I packed them away," she lamented. "And as for camphor balls—well, if I used up one camphor ball I used ten pounds."

"You must have been a poor marksman. So far as I can judge you never hit a single one of 'em. And so all summer, while we flitted from place to place, gay butterflies of fashion that we are, they've been down there intent on family duties, multiplying and replenishing my flannel underwear, as the Scriptures so aptly put it. Devoted little creatures, moths! They have their faults but they have their domestic virtues, too. I wish they didn't have so much of my golf sweater. It looked like drawn-work."

"What did you do with it?"

"Gave it back to them. All or none—that's my motto. But I piled the rest of the duds on my bed. By prompt relief work much of it may be salvaged."

"Then for heaven's sake close the door before I choke."

He closed the door and came and sat down near her and lighted a cigarette. He wore the conventional flowing Windsor tie to prove how unconventional he was. But he did not wear the velveteen jacket; he drew the line there, having a sense of humor. Nor were his trousers baggy and unpressed. They were unbagged and impressive. Mr. Bugbee was a writer, also a painter. He was always getting ready to write something important and then at the last minute deciding to paint instead, or the other way around. What between being so clever at the two crafts he rarely prosecuted either.

But then as regards finances this pair did not have to worry. There was money on both sides, which among our native bohemians is a rare coincidence. He had inherited some and Mrs. Bugbee had inherited a good deal. So they could gratify a taste for period furniture and practice their small philanthropies and generally make a pleasant thing of living this life without the necessity of stinting.

It was agreed that they had such happy names—names to match their natures. His was Clement and hers was Felicia. It was as if, infants at the baptismal font though they were, they had been christened and at the same time destined for each other. Persons who knew them remarked this. Persons also made a play on their last name. While these twain were buzzing about enjoying themselves, their intimates often called them the Busy Bugbees. But when an idealistic impulse swept them off their feet, as occasionally it did, the first syllable was the one that was accented. It was really a trick name and provided some small entertainment for light-hearted members of the favored circle in which the couple mainly moved. It doesn't take much to amuse some people.

"Just to think!" mused Mrs. Bugbee. "It seems only a week or two ago since we were wondering where we'd go to spend the summer. Time certainly does fly."

"And what a small world it is," amended Mr. Bugbee. "Why, we were sitting right here in this room when that subject first came up and, lo and behold, only five short months afterward we meet again on the very same spot. Where do they get that stuff about a fellow so rarely running into an old friend in New York?"

"You'd better save that cheap wit of yours for somebody who'll appreciate it," said Mrs. Bugbee, but she smiled an indulgent wifely smile as she said it. "Yes, indeed, time does fly! And here winter is almost upon us." She lifted her voice and trilled a quotation: "'And what will poor robin do then, poor thing?'" Mrs. Bugbee loved to sing. She sang rather well, too. About once in so often she thought seriously of taking up grand opera. Something always happened, though. With the Bugbees something always did.

"Don't you be worrying your head about him," said Mr. Bugbee. "Being a wise old bird, the robin will be down in Georgia dragging those long stretchy worms out of the ground. I wish they'd put as good a grade of rubber into elastic garters as they do into those Southern worms. It's what we'll be doing ourselves, poor things, that gives me pause."

"First thing anybody knows Thanksgiving will be here." She went on as though she had not heard him. "And then right away I'll have to begin thinking about Christmas. Oh dear!" She finished with a sigh.

"Damn Christmas!" Mr. Bugbee was fervent.

"Why, Clem Bugbee, aren't you ashamed of yourself?"

So he altered it: "Well, then, damn the kind of Christmas they have in this vast and presumably intellectual city! Giving other people things they don't want that cost more money than you can afford to spend, because they are going to give you things you don't want that cost more than they can afford to spend. Every retail shop turned into a madhouse with the inmates all running wild. Handing out money on all sides to people who hate you because it's not more and you hating them right back because you're being held up this way. Everybody and everything going stark raving crazy on Christmas Eve. Nervous prostrations. Jams in the streets. Sordidness, greed, ostentation, foolish extravagance. Postmen and clerks and expressmen dying on their feet. Truck-drivers spilling the sort of language that's still regarded as improper except when spoken on the stage. Then it becomes realism, but the truck-driver, not being artistic but just a poor overworked slob of a vulgarian, he's maybe arrested for using obscenity.

"Christmas Day, and you go around with 'Merry Christmas' on your lips and murder in your heart. And drink egg-nogs made out of amateur whisky. And eat too much. And go to fool parties where you're bored stiff. Then the bills piling in. And the worthless junk piling up around the flat. And everything. Do I seem bitter? I do? Well, I am!"

"It's easy enough to talk—goodness knows every rational human being deplores the commercialism and the—the mercenaryism—"

"Where did you get that word?"

"Made it up. It's a good word and it's mine and I like it. And don't interrupt. As I was saying, we all deplore the mercenaryism and the materialism and the senseless display that's crept into Christmas, and a lot of people spout about it just as you're doing, but nobody does anything to try to reform it. At least nobody has since they started the custom of sending Christmas cards instead of gifts. But that was a mistake; it's been overdone into an evil. There's a passion to see who can buy the most expensive cards; and you spend weeks beforehand making up the lists and addressing the envelops, and the cards cost as much as the presents used to cost and make ever so much more bother getting them out. Look at what happened to us last Christmas! Look at what's sure to happen this Christmas! And all you do is stand there—sit there, I mean—and spout at me as though I were to blame. Suggest a way out, why don't you? I'd be only too delighted if you would."

"I will," proclaimed the challenged party. He thought hard. "We'll run away from it—that's what we'll do."

"Where do we run?"

"That's a mere detail. I'm working out the main project. In advance we'll circulate the word that we're escaping from the civilized brand of

Christmas; that on December twenty-fifth we're going to be far, far beyond the reach of long-distance telephones, telegraph lines, wireless, radio, mental telepathy, rural free delivery routes, janitors with their paws out for ten-dollar bills and other well-wishers; that we're not going to send any presents to our well-to-do friends and are not expecting any from them; that we're not even figuring on mailing out a single, solitary, dad-busted greetings card. There's plenty of time ahead of us for putting the campaign through. We'll remember our immediate relatives and your pet charities and any worth-while dependents we can think of. And then we'll just dust out and forget to leave any forwarding address."

"We could try Florida again," suggested Mrs. Bugbee.

"The land of the sap and the sapodilla—we will not! What's Florida now except New York with a pair of white duck pants on?"

"Well, the climate there is—"

"It is not! It's all cluttered up with real-estate agents, the climate is. Besides I never could see the advantages of traveling eighteen hundred miles in mid-winter to get into the same kind of weather that you travel eighteen hundred miles in midsummer to get out of."

"Well, then, we might run up to Lake Placid or the Berkshires. Of course it'll be too early at either place for the regular season, but I suppose there'll be a few people we know—"

"You don't grasp the big theory at all. This is not to be an excursion, it's an exploring expedition. We're not a couple of tourists out for winter sports and chilblains on our toes. We're pioneers. We're going forth to rediscover the old Christmas spirit that's sane and simple and friendly. If there is a neighborhood left anywhere in this country where the children still believe in Santa Claus we're going to find it. And we'll bring the word back when we come home and next year thousands of others will follow our examples, and generations yet unborn will rise up and bless us as benefactors of the human race. I shouldn't be surprised if they put up monuments to us in the market-place."

"You might as well be serious about it. And not quite so oratorical."

"I am serious about it—I was never more serious in my life. Beneath this care-free exterior a great and palpitating but practical idea has sprouted to life."

"Well, since you're so practical, kindly sprout the name of the spot where we're to spend Christmas. I'm perfectly willing to try anything once, even against my better judgment, but you can't expect me to get on a train with you without at least a general notion as to the name of the station where we get off."

Mr. Bugbee's brow furrowed; then magically it unwrinkled. "I have it!" he said. "We'll take the Rousseau cottage up at Pleasant Cove. The Rousseaus are sailing next Tuesday for Europe to be gone until spring. Only yesterday Rousseau offered me the use of his camp any time I wanted it and for as long as I pleased. I'll see him tomorrow and ask him to notify his caretaker that we'll be along about the second week in December."

"But it's eight miles from the railroad." Her tone was dubious.

"So much the better. I wish it was eighty miles from one."

"And right in the middle of the mountains."

"You bet it is. I want to be right in the heart of the everlasting peaks. I hope to get snowed in. I crave an old-fashioned white Christmas. I'm fed up on these spangled green, blue, red, pink, purple and blind ones. I want to mingle with hardy kindly souls who have absorbed within them the majesty and the nobility of their own towering hills. I want to meet a few of the real rugged American types once more. I'm weary of these foreigners you see in the subway reading newspapers which seem to be made up exclusively of typographical errors. I yearn to hear the idioms of my native tongue spoken. You remember that gorgeous week we spent with the Rousseaus six summers ago, or was it seven? Anyhow you must remember it—those quaint ruralists, those straightforward sturdy honest old mountaineer types, those characters redolent of the soil, those laughing rosy-cheeked children?"

"I seem to recall that some of them were sallow, not to say sickly-looking."

"December's winds will remedy that. December's eager winds will—"

"How about servants? We'll need somebody surely. And I doubt whether Emile and Eva would be willing to go."

"Gladly would I leave behind those two whom you have heard me, in sportive moments, refer to as our Dull Domestic Finnish. Being aliens, they wouldn't match the surroundings. No doubt some sturdy country lass would be glad to serve us." Mr. Bugbee reverted again to the elocutionary.

"We'll throw ourselves into the Yuletide joy of the community. We'll get up a Christmas tree. We'll hang up our stockings. We'll finance a holiday festival for the grown folks—it won't cost much. You can organize a band of singers and teach them carols and Christmas waits. We'll live and revel, woman, I tell you we'll live."

Before his persuasive eloquence the lingering traces of Mrs. Bugbee's misgivings melted away. Herself, within the hour, she called up Mrs. Rousseau to inquire regarding housekeeping details in the bungalow on the slopes behind Pleasant Cove.

Their train got in at six-ten A. M., which in December is generally regarded as being very A. M. indeed. But the Bugbees didn't much mind having to quit their berths at five-thirty. The sunrise repaid them. There was an eastern heaven that shimmered with alternating, merging, flowing bands of tender pinks and tenderer greens. Mrs. Bugbee said right off it reminded her of changeable silk. Mr. Bugbee said it reminded him of stewed rhubarb. He also said that when he reflected on the pleasing prospect that by coming up here they would miss the Baxters' annual costume ball on Christmas night he felt like halting about once in so often and giving three rousing cheers.

He furthermore said he could do with a little breakfast. He did with a very little. Mrs. Bugbee had brought along a vacuum bottle of coffee and four sandwiches but they were rather small—sandwiches of the pattern usually described in cook-books as dainty; and the stopper of the vacuum bottle could not have been quite air-tight, for the coffee had turned lukewarm during the night.

They emerged from the smelly sleeper into a nipping morning. There was snow on the ground, not a great deal of snow but enough. The two adventurers rather had counted on a sleigh-ride through the woods but here they suffered a disappointment. A muffled figure of a man clunked in rubber boots toward them from the platform of the locked-up station. This was the only person in sight. The stranger introduced himself with a broad yawn and a fine outgushing of frosty breath.

"Name's Talbot," he stated when the yawn had run its course. "I look after the Rousseau camp winters. Boss writ me word to meet you folks. Huh, got quite a jag of baggage, ain't you? I could go round the world twice't with less than that. Well, let's be joggin'."

He relieved Mrs. Bugbee of her two hand-bags and led the way to a bespattered flivver which crouched apprehensively in a maze of frozen wheel tracks behind the shuttered building, Mr. Bugbee following with a heavy suitcase in either hand and a blanket-roll swung over his shoulder by its strap.

"Likely you'll be a mite crowded, but that's your own fault, fetchin' so much dunnage with you," stated their guide. "You two had better ride in the back there and hold a couple of them biggest grips on your laps. I guess I kin wedge the rest of it into the front seat alongside of me. All set?" he asked. "Let's move then."

The car slewed on its tires, then settled deeply into the frozen ruts, jouncing and jerking.

"Wouldn't it have been easier traveling with a sleigh?" inquired Mr. Bugbee, speaking rather brokenly between jolts.

"Don't do much sleddin' in this country any more—not till later, anyway, when the weather gits set," vouchsafed Mr. Talbot. "A thaw's liable to come and then where would you be with your sled runners? Besides, purty near ever'body up here keeps an ottermobile. Set tight!" he commanded. "We're about to hit a rough place."

But by the time he had uttered his warning they had hit it.

"Yes, indeed," went on Mr. Talbot, "ottermobiles is come into quite general use. You folks ever been here before? Yes? Then prob'ly you remember the old Turnbull Tavern that used to stand at the forks over to the Cove? Well, it's gone. Tore it away to put up a fillin' station. We got two fillin' stations—that one and one other one—and they's talk of a third one in the spring."

Above the obstruction of a suitcase which he balanced precariously upon his knees, Mr. Bugbee peered across a landscape which so far as the immediate foreground was concerned mainly consisted of vistas and aisles of stumps, with puddles of ice and spindly evergreens interspersed and a final garnishing of slashed-off faded limbs.

"My recollection is that the wilderness used to come right down to the tracks," he said.

"Ef by wilderness you mean standin' spruce timber, then your recollection is right," answered Mr. Talbot over his shoulder and through the folds of a woolen throat comforter. "But it's mostly been lumbered off for pulp. They're figgerin' some on strippin' the ridges of the hard woods next," he added with a touch of local pride for local enterprise.

The car took the first steep rise into the range, buck-jumping and slewing like a skittish colt. Frequently it seemed to shy from bump to bump. The task of steering engaged Mr. Talbot. He addressed his vibrating passengers but rarely.

"Got a party booked to chore for you," he told Mrs. Bugbee over his shoulder. "Name of Anna Rapley. Widder woman. Had quite a job of it gittin' her to agree to do it. She told me to tell you her wages would be twenty-five a week fur ez long ez you stay."

"Twenty-five a week?" echoed Mrs. Bugbee rather blankly.

"That's whut she says. Says it's her reg'lar price fur a special job like this one is. Says to tell you to take it or leave it, just ez you please. Says it don't make a bit of difference to her either way. Independent, that's her."

"Oh, I'm sure we won't quarrel over the wages!" Mrs. Bugbee hastened to explain. "Of course she's competent?"

"Oh, spry enough so fur ez that goes, but strictly between you and me, watch her!" He twisted his head and punctuated the speech with a slow, significant wink.

"Watch her for what?"

"I ain't sayin'. I ain't even hintin' at nothin'. All I'm tellin' you in confidence is—watch her. She's a good friend of my folks so mebbe I shouldn't 'a' said that much. Just keep your eyes open, that's all."

On through to their destination there was silence between the visitors—the silence of two persons engrossed in inner contemplations. As for Mr. Talbot, he was concerned with restraining his mettlesome conveyance.

At their journey's end, the bungalow where it nestled against a background of mountains half a mile on beyond the clumping of small houses that was the village, made a gladdening sight for the Bugbees, what with its broad front windows shining redly in the clear cold and a slender spindle of smoke rising straight up the air from the mouth of its big stone chimney. Mrs. Bugbee hurried inside to establish liaison with the widow who was a friend to the Talbot family. Her husband tarried on the snow-piled veranda with his belongings piled about him.

"Let's see, now," Mr. Talbot said speculatively. "There's your fare over from the depot—we'll call that six dollars even for the two of you. And two dollars more fur your valises, I guess that'd be fair, considerin'. That comes to eight. Then there was some odds and ends I done myself fur you yistiddy ez an accommodation—shovelin' out this path here and so forth. That'll be about six dollars, I sh'd say."

Mr. Bugbee unpocketed a fold of bills.

"Hold on," bade Mr. Talbot. "Then I got you in three cords of firewood at ten dollars a cord; that mounts up to thirty more. You're lucky I ain't chargin' you full city prices," he continued, studying Mr. Bugbee's expression. "There's some around here would, namin' no names. But you folks bein' sent on by Mr. Rousseau I'm makin' you a rate on that firewood. Thanky."

He accepted payment.

"Oh, yes, there's an order of provisions in the house, too, but the account fur them'll be rendered in your reg'lar weekly bills. I'll make the deliveries without extry cost," he promised generously. "Just call freely fur more stuff ez you need it. I run the leadin' grocery down below, you understand. There's an opposition grocery but I wouldn't recommend no stranger to do his tradin' there unlessen he checked off the statements mighty close. Well, good-by and see you later."

Mr. Bugbee, mechanically holding a depleted roll in his numbed grasp, watched the flivver as it lurched back down the highway. "But at least the sunrise was an unqualified success," he remarked softly to himself. He further comforted himself with the philosophies that first impressions did not necessarily count and that a poor beginning often made a good ending and that to all rules there were exceptions, et cetera, et cetera.

Lack of space forbids that we should trace our two sojourners step by step and day by day through the ensuing fortnight. A few vignettes, a few small thumb-nail views of them, taken in the privacy of their fireside, will suffice, this chronicler hopes, progressively to suggest the course of developments in pursuance of their ambitions for the happiness of the dwellers in that isolated hamlet of Pleasant Cove.

For example, an intimate little scene was enacted before the hearthstone on the second evening but one following their arrival.

Mr. Bugbee was wrestling manfully with a cigar of an exceedingly formidable aspect. That morning he had made a lamentable discovery. It was that he had forgotten to bring along two boxes of his favorite brand of specially cured Havanas which were purchased expressly with that intent. His pocket case was almost empty when he became aware of the oversight. He looked upon it in the light of a tragedy; a confirmed smoker will appreciate how laden with tragic possibilities such a situation might become. He had wired for a supply to be forwarded immediately, but in these parts immediately might be a relative term. So to bridge over the emergency he had procured some substitutes from Mr. Talbot's somewhat restricted stock.

It was with one of the substitutes that now he contended. He freed an intake of smoke and choked slightly, then coughed fretfully.

"It is called 'Jake's Choice,'" he said. "I read it on the box. It was an exceedingly beautiful box—a regular whited sepulcher of a box. I wonder who Jake was? Probably a friend of the manufacturer. But I'll say this much for him—he was no customer! It may have its good qualities. It's certainly very durable and it has splendid powers of resistance—fights back every inch of the way. But for smoking purposes it is open to the same criticisms that a rag carpet is."

"Why don't you throw it in the fire, then?" suggested Mrs. Bugbee. "When I came in here a minute ago I thought for a second the flue must be defective."

"I'd have you know I'm not to be daunted by an enemy that I could crush—maybe—in the palm of my hand. Besides, it's easy enough for you to give such advice—you with plenty of your favorite cigarettes on hand. But cigarettes are not for me—I'm what they call a man's man."

"Speaking of cigarettes—" began Mrs. Bugbee, but got no further. It would seem that Mr. Bugbee was not to be diverted from his present morbid mood.

"Now you take Jake's peculiar Choice," he went on. "I wish I'd had the job of christening this article. I'd have labeled it the 'R. C. N. W. M. P.'"

"What does that stand for?"

"Royal Canadian Northwestern Mounted Police—to give the full title."

"I don't see the application."

"You would if you knew the motto of that magnificent force—'Always Gets Its Man.'" Again he coughed.

"Speaking of names, Anna—"

"You were speaking of cigarettes a moment ago."

"I tried to but you interrupted. Anyhow, cigarettes and Anna are all mixed up with what I wanted to say in the first place."

"You refer to our culinary goddess?"

"Of course."

"Does she smoke?"

"No—never."

"Then why drag in Anna's cigarettes, if she doesn't use 'em?"

"I didn't. It's my cigarettes."

"Well, why then Anna as a factor in this discussion?"

"I'm coming to that. Speaking of names—"

"We are not speaking of names any more. Pray be coherent."

"We are—at least I am. Speaking of names, do you know what she calls me? She calls me 'Miss Fleeceyou,' like that."

"In view of the salary Anna is drawing down I'd call that a touch of subtle irony," stated Mr. Bugbee. "But I see no reason why she should address me as 'Mr. Clammy.' I'm not clammy—I leave it to any impartial judge. I'll not start complaining yet, though. I have a foreboding of worse things to follow. I foresee that when the feeling of formality wears off and we get on an easier social footing she'll call me 'Clam.' I decline to be just plain Clam to Anna or anybody else. If I've got to be a clam I'm going to be a fancy one."

"You drift about so! What I've been trying for the last five minutes to tell you was that Anna has been confiding to me that some of the older inhabitants are taking exception to us—to me, rather. It seems they've already found out that I smoke cigarettes. They regard that as sinful or at least highly improper. There's been talk. She told me so."

"I wonder how they learned of your secret vice!" mused Mr. Bugbee. "It can't be that Anna is a gossip—heaven forbid! Have you been detected in any other shameful practice?"

"Not exactly detected—but, well, criticized. She tells me that certain persons, including one of the two ministers—the Reverend Mr. Peters is the one—have been discussing my costume." She glanced down at her trim riding-breeches and her smart high-laced boots, which with her soft flannel shirt gave her the look of a graceful, good-looking boy. "And I thought I was dressed so appropriately!"

"I believe there is still a prejudice in certain remote districts against the human female leg," said her husband. "Just what fault do the merry villagers find with your get-up?"

"One man at the post-office spoke of these"—she touched a slender Bedford-corded thigh—"of these as choke-bore pants. He said there ought to be a law against a woman parading the public streets with a pair of choke-bore pants on. He said it this afternoon and Anna heard about it and came right straight and told me."

"Strong language for a minister of the Gospel to be using," commented Mr. Bugbee. "Still, the comparison is apt. Choke-bore, eh? Not so bad for a backwoods preacher. The man has traveled and seen the world."

"It wasn't the minister, stupid! It was another man. At that the minister—I mean the Reverend Mr. Peters, not the other one—glared at me today as though he were thinking unutterable things. I thought then he might be miffed because I'd been to see the other minister first. He behaved so—so stand-offish and sort of hostile when I told him about our plan for having a joint Christmas tree for both Sunday Schools. But since I talked with Anna I'm pretty sure it must have been my clothes he didn't like. I'm afraid some of these people are going to be rather difficult, really I am!"

"I'm going to be a trifle difficult myself unless those cigars get here soon," said Mr. Bugbee. "Say, they seem to be having unusually long and silent nights up here this winter, don't they?" he added. "I never thought I'd become so city-broke that I'd miss the plaintive call of the taxicab mooing for its first-born. Gee—it's nearly nine o'clock. If the lights in this house aren't turned out pretty soon some unacquainted passers-by—if any such there be—will suspect the presence of burglars on the premises."

It was on Friday afternoon of that week that a female villager called. She had a keen and searching gaze—that was the first thing to be noticed when the door had been opened in response to her knock. And the second striking thing about her was that on taking a seat she seemed to sink into herself sectionally rather in the style of certain nautical instruments.

The collapsible-looking lady stayed on for upwards of an hour. Upon leaving, she uncoupled joint by joint, as it were, becoming again a person of above the average height. Mr. Bugbee, who after a mumbled introduction and a swift appraisal of the visitor had betaken himself to another part of the house, reentered the living-room upon her departure.

"Who," he asked, "who is yon gentle stranger with the telescopic eye and the self-folding figure? I failed to catch the name."

"Miss Teasdale—a Miss Henny Teasdale."

"Did you say Henny—or do my ears deceive me?"

"Yes; it's short for Henrietta, I think."

"And long for Hen. I'll think that, if you don't mind. If I'm not too inquisitive, might I make so bold as to inquire what brought her hither?"

"She came to tell me some—well, some things. She said she felt it to be her Christian duty to walk up here and tell me these things."

"For example, what?"

"For one thing she thinks we make a mistake in——" Mrs. Bugbee, who appeared slightly flustered, left this sentence uncompleted and built a second one of fresh materials: "Clem, why is it that people have to be so narrow and so critical of other people's motives and so everything?"

"I give it up. But to return to the lady whose fighting name is Henny?"

"Oh, yes! Well, she told me that quite a good many of the members of one of the congregations here rather resent the fact that the pastor of the other congregation is the chairman of my committee that's getting up the Christmas entertainment. And they aren't going to cooperate or let their children come either. There are two cliques, it seems, and they're both awfully cliquey."

"A common fault of cliques, I believe. And what else?"

"And she says some of the young people think our celebration is going to be too tame for them. So they're planning to import special music from over at the junction and throw a jazz party, as they put it, on the same night. It seems there's a barber over at the junction who plays the saxophone and he has an orchestra of four pieces; that's the one they're going to hire."

"Every junction has a barber who plays the saxophone. But formerly the favored instrument was the guitar, though in exceptional cases the harmonica or mouth-organ might be preferred. Proceed, please; you interest me deeply."

"And she says that there's a good deal of curiosity—*curiosity* was the word she used—about our private lives. There actually seems to be a suspicion that we're some sort of refugees or fugitives or something, and that we're trying to ingratiate ourselves with the residents here in order to work some scheme on them later. At least she hinted that much. But this Miss Teasdale doesn't share in this sentiment at all. She said so several times. She said she only came up as a friend to let me know what was going on. She hasn't any ax to grind herself, she says. She doesn't believe in all this envy and jealousy, she says."

"I don't believe the ax is her favorite weapon. I seem to picture her in the privacy of the home circle brewing a great jorum of poison-ivy tea. Perchance she revealed more?"

"Quite a lot more. She says we're being imposed on shamefully in regard to the prices we're paying for things. She says we picked the wrong people to deal with and that if we'd just come to her first she could have saved us money. She says that Anna is charging us about three times what she'd expect from a neighbor for the same services. Still, I gather that there's a sort of feud between her and Anna, so she may be biased. And she says that this man Talbot—"

"All of which reminds me. I had to order more firewood this morning. Due, I take it, to post-war conditions in Europe the price is now twelve dollars a cord. The egg market also shows an advance, influenced no doubt by disquieting advices from Morocco. Well, if we will meddle in world affairs we must pay the price."

"I believe that practically was about all she said," wound up Mrs. Bugbee. "Where's my fur coat and muffler? I've got to hurry down to the Masonic Hall. I called a rehearsal for three o'clock and I'll probably be late as it is." Mrs. Bugbee lost her worried look. "I'm certain of one thing: I'm not going to be disappointed in my Christmas carols. Not that they have such good voices. But such enthusiasm as all eight of them show! And how they're looking forward to midnight of Christmas Eve! And how willing they are to practice!"

As the festival drew nearer, unforeseen complications ensued. Inspired by an affection which the holiday spirit had quickened, various persons back in New York chose to disregard the advertised views of the Bugbees touching on the overworked custom of exchanging gifts. Their hiding-place was known too, as now developed. By express and by parcel-post came packages done up in gay wrappings and bearing cards and sprigs of holly and inevitably containing the conventional remembrances, the customary loving messages. The opening of each box served to enhance an atmosphere of homesickness which was beginning to fill the Rousseau bungalow.

"Well, I've done the best I could," wailed Mrs. Bugbee despairingly. "Of course we have to make some return for all this." She indicated a litter of brilliant paper and parti-colored ribbon bindings on the floor about her.

"Why do we?" he countered, he having just returned from the settlement. "Those darned fools knew how we felt about this business."

"Because we just do, that's why! They'd never forgive us. So while you were gone I wrote out a telegram to Aunt Bessie and telephoned it down to the junction. I gave Aunt Bessie the names of everybody who'd sent us something and told her what stores we have charge accounts at and begged her as a tremendous favor to get each one of them something, no matter what, and send it around to them. It wouldn't have done any good to wire the stores direct—they're too rushed to pay any attention. And poor Aunt Bessie will be up to her ears in her own Christmas shopping and of course it's a dreadful imposition on her and of course she won't have time to pick out suitable presents or anything. But what could I do?"

"I'll tell you what you could have done," said Mr. Bugbee, fixing an accusing eye upon his wife. "You could have dissuaded me from this mad folly, this wild impulse to flee to the wildwood for Christmas. Back there in October had you but done this our associates might even now be saying: 'Poor Bugbee had a brain-storm but what did Bugbee's little woman do? She saved him from himself, that's what Bugbee's little woman did!' But no, woman-like, you fed the flames of my delusion. And now it's too late to turn back. Madam, you have but yourself to blame, I refuse to offer you my pity. Anyhow, I need it all for personal use."

"What else has happened now?" she asked in the resigned tone of one who is prepared for any tidings however grievous and hard to bear.

"I decline to furnish the harrowing details," he replied. "Suffice it to say that one rift shows in the encompassing clouds. In certain local quarters our intentions may be misinterpreted, that I grant you; it would be wasting words to claim otherwise. But today, mark you, I struck the trail of at least one prospective beneficiary who'll surely respond to our overtures with gratitude. He's going to be our reward—perhaps our only one—for making this trip."

"After certain recent experiences I'd love to meet him."

"Your desire shall be gratified. Let me tell you about him: You remember that starved-looking shabby chap that we've seen several times plowing past here through the drifts on his way to the village or back again? And always alone?"

"Yes, I do. We were speaking of him yesterday, saying how forlorn he seemed and how solitary."

"That's our candidate. The name is Sisson. He came into the post-office an hour ago and I got a good look at him—at close range he's even more melancholy than he is viewed from a distance—and after he was gone I asked a few discreet questions about him. He's a mystery. About six weeks ago he moved into a tumble-down cabin about a mile up the mountain behind this clearing and he leads a sort of solitary hermit existence up there. Nobody ever goes to see him and he never comes to see anybody and nobody knows anything about him except that occasionally he gets an official-looking letter from Washington. The postmistress told me that much."

"I believe I can guess." Mrs. Bugbee's voice warmed sympathetically. "He's probably a poor shell-shocked veteran that has hid himself away on account of his nervous condition. And he's been writing to the Government trying to get it to do something about his pension or his disability allowance or something—poor neglected hero! I just feel it that I'm right about him. You know yourself, Clem, how my intuition works sometimes?"

"Well, in a way I rather jumped at that conclusion too," said Mr. Bugbee. "So I dusted out and overtook the nominee and introduced myself and walked along with him. As a matter of fact I just left him. I invited him in but he declined. He behaved as though he distrusted me, but before I quit I succeeded in getting him to promise faithfully that he'd drop in on us late on Christmas Eve. I realized that he wouldn't care to show himself among the crowd down at the hall."

"I think that's a splendid arrangement," applauded Mrs. Bugbee. "Just perfectly splendid! And the next thing is, what are we going to give him?"

"Not too much. We don't want him to get the idea that we look on him as an object of charity. Just one timely, suitable small present—a token, if you get what I mean; that would be my notion."

"Mine, too," chorused Mrs. Bugbee. "But the question is, what?"

They had quite a little dispute over it. She voted first for a pair of military hair-brushes, the Herbert Ryders, of East Sixty-ninth Street, having sent Mr. Bugbee a pair and he being already the possessor of two other pairs. But as Mr. Bugbee pointed out, an offering even remotely suggestive of the military life possibly might recall unpleasant memories in the mind of one who had suffered in the Great War. So then she suggested that a box containing one-half dozen cakes of imported and scented violet soap might be acceptable; there was such a box among the gifts accumulating about the room. But, as Mr. Bugbee said, suppose he was sensitive? Suppose he took it as a personal reflection? They argued back and forth. Eventually Mr. Bugbee found an answer to the problem.

"I'm going to hand him my last full quart of old Scotch," he announced with a gesture of broad generosity. "He'll appreciate that, or I miss my guess."

He had the comforting feeling of having made a self-sacrifice for the sake of a stranger. He had the redeemed feeling of one who means to go the absolute limit on behalf of his fellow man. For Mr. Bugbee had brought with him but three bottles of his treasured pre-Prohibition Scotch. And the first bottle was emptied and the second had been broached and half emptied and only the third precious survivor remained intact.

It was a lovely yet a poignant feeling to have.

On the night before Christmas it was raining. By morning probably the underfooting would be all one nice icy slickery glare but now everything was melting and running. As the Bugbees, man and wife, slopped along up the gentle slope leading from the highway to their front door they were exchanging remarks which had been uttered several times already on the homeward journey but each, with variations, was still repeating his, or as the case was, her contributions to the dialogue, just as persons will do when a subject for conversation happens to be one that lies close to the speakers' heart.

"The little ones," she was saying, "they almost repaid me for all the trouble we've been to and all the pains we've taken. Their glee was genuine. Sometimes, Clem, I think there ought to be a law against anybody celebrating Christmas who's more than twelve years old—I mean celebrating it with gifts."

"Second the motion!" His tone was grim. One might even say it was bitter.

"But some of these older ones—turning up their noses right before our eyes at the little presents that we'd bought for them. What did they expect— diamond bracelets? Do they think we're made out of money?"

"Well, I'm not, for one. I settled Brother Talbot's account for the past two weeks this afternoon. That man's talents are wasted here. He ought to be operating a fleet of pirate ships."

"There was one thing that I haven't had the courage to tell you about yet." She blurted the rest in a gulped staccato: "With me it was absolutely the last straw. And I'm ashamed of myself. But my heart was so set on the singing! That's my only excuse for being so weak."

"Go on. I'm listening."

"Well, you know yourself, Clem, how hard I've worked at drilling those eight men and boys for my Christmas carols? And how I've explained to them over and over again about the meanings of all those beautiful Old World customs such as the English have? And I thought they'd caught the spirit—from the very first they seemed so inspired. But tonight—just a little while ago when you were busy with the tree—they took me aside. They said they wanted to tell me something. And Clem—they—they struck!"

"Struck for what?"

"For money. Said they wouldn't sing a note unless I paid them for their back time."

"And what did you do?"

"I paid them," she confessed. "Five dollars apiece. That is, all but the leader. He—he got ten."

Mr. Bugbee made no comment on this disclosure. But his silence fairly screamed at her. "Wipe your feet before you come into the house," he said. He kicked the muddied snow off his boots and opened the door.

They entered where efforts had been made to create a showing of holiday cheer. There were greens about and a sprig of synthetic mistletoe dangled above the lintel, and on the mantel was a composition statuette of good Saint Nicholas, rotund and rosy and smiling a painted smile. In the act of crossing the threshold they were aware of the presence of a visitor. Very rigidly and rather with the air of being peevish for some reason, a lantern-jawed person stood in the middle of the floor.

"Oh," said Mrs. Bugbee advancing to make the stranger welcome. "How do you do? It's Mr. Sisson, isn't it? My husband told me you were coming."

"He said eleven o'clock." Mr. Sisson's voice was condemnatory. "It's nearly twenty past."

"I'm so sorry—we are a trifle late, aren't we? Detained down in the Cove, you know."

"Personally I alluz make it a point to be on time, myself." Mr. Sisson accepted the outstretched hand of his hostess and shook it stiffly but he did not unbend. He aimed a sternly interrogative glance at Mr. Bugbee: "Whut business did you want to have with me?"

"No business," explained that gentleman. "Pleasure, I hope. We asked you here so that we might wish you a Merry Christmas and a Happy New Year."

"And to offer you a small remembrance," supplemented Mrs. Bugbee. "And here it is—with our very best compliments." She took from a side table a longish, roundish parcel enclosed in white tissue with ribbon bindings and a bit of imitation holly caught in the bow-knot at the top. She put it in his somewhat limp grasp.

Immediately though, his clutch on the object tightened. He fingered its contours. "Feels to me sort of like a bottle," he opined.

"It is," said the jovial Mr. Bugbee. "Open it and see."

The recipient opened it. He tore away the festal wrappings, and held the contents to the light. His eye seemed to kindle. "Looks to me sort of like licker," he said.

"That's what it is."

Mrs. Bugbee was hovering alongside awaiting the expected outburst of gratitude, puzzled though that it should be so long delayed.

"Mind ef I taste it right here?"

"Not at all."

"Got a corkscrew handy?"

"I think I can locate one."

"And a glass?"

Mrs. Bugbee brought a tumbler. Mr. Bugbee found a corkscrew.

Deftly Mr. Sisson unstoppered the bottle. Into the glass he poured a taste of the liquid. He did not invite them to share with him. There was about him no suggestion that he meant to make a loving-cup of it. He sipped briefly. "That's sufficient—I jest wanted to make sure," he stated. "This here is a stimilent containing' more'n one-half of one percent alcohol by volume."

"I should say it is. That Scotch was made back in—" He checked, for Mr. Sisson was behaving very peculiarly indeed.

Mr. Sisson was recorking the bottle and sliding it carefully into a side pocket of his overcoat. From other pockets he brought forth a revolver, a folded document of an official and formidable appearance, it having a seal upon its outermost side, and finally a clanking pair of very new looking, very shiny handcuffs. He laid these one by one upon a convenient table-top and next he cast a determined and confounding stare upon the startled faces of Mr. and Mrs. Bugbee.

The lady's fascinated eyes were fixed for the moment upon the horrifying steeliness of those glinting cuffs, and spasmodically she thrust her hands wrist deep in her ulster pockets. It was evident that, be this daunting intruder's purposes what they might, Mrs. Bugbee did not mean to be manacled without a struggle. But Mr. Bugbee stood unresistingly and blinked like a man coming out of a distressful trance and not sure yet that he is out.

"You're both under arrest," expounded Mr. Sisson. "Fur endeavorin' to ply a third party with alcoholic stimilents."

"But—but we gave it to you—of our own free will!" faltered Mrs. Bugbee.

"Givin', sellin' outright or barterin', the law don't recognize no difference. Anything you say further kin be used ag'inst you. Still, I guess there's evidence aplenty to convict. Prob'ly it'll go the worse with you fur offerin' it to an officer of the law. That's whut I am—an officer of the law. Here's my credentials to prove it. And ef you don't believe me, here's my badge." He flipped back a lapel to display a large and silverish decoration pinned under the flap.

"You can't do this outrageous thing to us," declaimed Mr. Bugbee, now fully emerging from coma. His cheeks were blazing. "It's incredible!"

"It's done done," said their accuser calmly. His manner became more menacing, his tone more emphatic. "Don't think, young man, jest because I'm kind of a new hand at this line that you kin work any bluff on me. I've been studyin' to go into the detective business fur quite some time, havin' took a full course in the Unsleepin' Eye Correspondence Detective College, Dayton, Ohio. After I got my diplomy I came on up here to perfect myself in my callin'. Then a new notion come over me and I took it up with the Government about gittin' onto the revenue enforcement department." He spoke on in the proud yet unboastful way of one who is sure his hearers will be interested in following the successive steps of a brilliant career. "I been writin' back and forth fur quite a spell with them Washington authorities."

"Oh!" The understanding exclamation popped from Mrs. Bugbee of its own accord.

"Whut's that?" demanded Mr. Sisson.

"I—I only just said 'oh,'" explained Mrs. Bugbee weakly.

"I thought so." It was as though Mr. Sisson made a mental note of this admission to be incorporated into the testimony. "But it seems like the Government force is all full up at present. So only last week I got a commission from the county to do shadderin' and hunt down these here Prohibition violators and I been workin' on hidden clues ever since. I'm whut they call an independent secret operative. Ez it happens, though, you're my first case—my first two cases I should say.

"Point is that now I've got you I don't know whut to do with you. Can't git you over to the county-seat tonight, late as 'tis and the roads the way they are. And tomorrer bein' Christmas the judge won't want to set to hold you fur trial. Prob'ly"—he caressed the handcuffs tentatively—"prob'ly I'll have to keep you ez prisoners right here under guard fur the next forty-eight hours or so. Prob'ly that would be the best way. Whut do you think?"

Mr. Bugbee made a sign to Mrs. Bugbee that she should withdraw. She did so with backward apprehensive glances.

"My wife's not trying to escape," explained Mr. Bugbee. "She's only going into the next room for a few minutes. She's had a shock—in fact she's had several shocks this evening."

He waited until the latch clicked, then to their captor he said simply: "How much?"

"Which?"

"I think you got my meaning the first time. How much?"

"Looky here," cried Mr. Sisson indignantly, "ef you're aimin' to question my honor lemme tell you I got a sacred reputation at stake."

"That is exactly my aim. What is the current quotation on honor in this vicinity?"

"Oh, well, if you're willin' to talk reasonable, come on over here closer so's nobody can't overhear us."

Five minutes later Mr. Bugbee went over and opened the hall door. "You can come out now," he said. "Our Christmas guest has gone. And all is well."

Mrs. Bugbee came out. She still was pale. "What—what did you do with him?" She asked it tremulously.

"I have just corrupted the noble soul of the only truly unselfish individual we have met to date in these mountains. I might add that corruption comes high hereabouts. City prices prevail." He took her in his arms and kissed her. "Let us now give thanks for deliverance from a great peril. We ought to do more than just give thanks. How about a little Christmas gift from each to the other?"

"But we decided that this year we'd spend that money up here." She winced.

"Circumstances warrant a redecision. Besides, I'm thinking of useful presents—presents which will bring joy to both of us. A couple of those lovely light green railroad tickets back to New York! You give me one; I'll give you one."

"Oh, Clem!" She hugged him.

"Oh, Felice!" He hugged her. "Where's that time-table? I saw a folder around here the other day. If we caught a morning train out of the junction tomorrow we might get in in time for the Baxters' party tomorrow night. Everybody we know—and like—will be there."

"But you know it's a costume party—fancy dress. And we haven't any costumes."

Airily he gestured away her quavering objections. "Say, do you know one thing?" he said. "This place is incomplete. It needs a motto. If I had time to spare I'd write one out and stick it up as a souvenir of our visit. I'd write on it the words 'E Pluribus Your'n,' meaning: 'It's all for you, dear Rousseau, the Bugbees have had enough.'... Now then, if I could just find that time card? Oh, there it is, yonder behind the clock. We can put in the rest of the night packing, and bright and early tomor—"

He broke off, listening. From without came the advancing sound of slushy foot-treads in a considerable number.

The tramping drew nearer and ended just outside. Masculine voices were uplifted in song:

"Hark-k, the herald angels sing,
 Glor-y to the—"

"That ain't right—wrong key!" they heard a dominating voice cutting in to check the vocal flow. "Git set fur a fresh start."

"My Christmas minstrels," said Mrs. Bugbee.

"Our little band of strikers," murmured Mr. Bugbee. He hurried to the mantel, plucked something from it, then leaped nimbly thence to a front window and crouched behind its curtains, his posture tense. "Here's where I also join the last-straw club," said Mr. Bugbee softly to nobody in particular.

Once again the unseen troubadours essayed the opening measures of their serenade:

"Hark-k the herald angels sing,
 Glor-y to the new-born king,
 Peace on earth—"

Mr. Bugbee snatched a sash up and made a movement as of hurling a heavy object into the drizzling night. It was a heavy object, too, judging by the yelp of pain which followed its outward flight. "I'll peace-on-earth you!" he said, closing the window.

A confusion of noises betokening a retreat died away in the distance.

"Did you throw something?" asked Mrs. Bugbee.

"I did," said Mr. Bugbee. "What's more, I hit something—something in the nature of a solid ivory dome. My darling, congratulate me not only on my accuracy but on my choice of a missile. I am pleased to inform you that I have just beaned the inspired leader of your coterie of private Christmas choristers with a heavy plaster image of dear old Santa Claus.... Let me have a look at this schedule.... Ah, here it is. We can catch a through train at ten-five and—by Jove, look, that's luck!—it will put us into Grand Central in ample time to make the Baxters' Christmas party."

"But we've nothing to go in—it's fancy dress. I told you that five minutes ago," protested Mrs. Bugbee.

"Don't worry," said Mr. Bugbee. "We'll go just as we are—as a couple of All-Day Suckers!"

Three Wise Men of the East Side

WHILE he was in the death-house Tony Scarra did a lot of thinking. You couldn't imagine a better place for thinking; it goes on practically all the time there and intensively. But no matter where the thoughts range and no matter what elements enter into them—hope or despair, rebellion or resignation, or whatever—sooner or later they fly back, like dark homing pigeons, to a small iron door opening upon a room in which, bolted to the floor, there is a chair with straps dangling from its arms and from its legs and its head-rest—in short, the Chair. This picture is the beginning and the end of all the thinking that is done in the death-house.

Such were the facts with regard to Tony Scarra. As nearly as might be judged, he felt no remorse for the murdering which had brought him to his present trapped estate. But he did have a deep regret for the entanglement of circumstances responsible for his capture and conviction. And constantly he had a profound sense of injustice. It seemed to him that in his case the law had been most terribly unreasonable. Statistics showed that for every seventy-four homicides committed in this state only one person actually went to the Chair. He'd read that in a paper during the trial. It had been of some comfort to him. Now he brooded on these figures. Over and over and over again, brooding on them, he asked himself about it.

Why should he have to be the unlucky one of seventy-four? Was it fair to let seventy-three other guys go free or let them off with prison sentences and then shoot the whole works to him? Was that a square deal? Why did it have to be that way, anyhow? What was the sense of it? Why pick on him? Why must he go through with it? Why—that was just it—why? The question-marks were so many sharp fishhooks all pricking down into his brain and hanging on.

His calling had made a sort of fatalist out of Tony Scarra. His present position was in a fair way to make a sort of anarchist out of him.

All the way through, his lawyer kept trying to explain to him touching on the lamentable rule of averages. He was not concerned with averages though. He was concerned with the great central idea of saving his life. To that extent his mind had become a lop-sided mind. Its slants all ran the same way, like shingles on a roof that slopes.

At length there came a morning when the death-house seemed to close in on him, tighter and tighter. It no longer was a steel box to enclose him; it became a steel vise and pinched him. This Scarra was not what you would call an emotional animal, nor a particularly imaginative one. Even so, and suddenly, he saw those bolt-heads in the ironwork as staring unmerciful eyes all vigilantly cocked to see how he took the news. And his thinking, instead of being scattered, now came to a focus upon a contingency which through weeks past he had carried in the back lobe.

"I'm just as sore about this as you are, Tony," the lawyer said. "It hurts me almost as much as it hurts you. Why, look here, yours is the first case I ever lost—the first capital case, I mean. All the others, I got 'em off somehow—acquittal or a hung jury or a mistrial or a retrial or, if it looked bad, we took a plea in the second degree and the fellow went up the road for a stretch. It's my reputation that's at stake in this thing; this thing is bound to hurt my record—the conviction standing and all. So naturally, not only on my own account but on yours, I've done everything I could—claiming reversible errors and taking an appeal and now this last scheme of asking the judges to reopen the case on the ground of newly discovered evidence. We've fought it along with stays and delays for nearly eight months now, going all the way up to the highest court in the state, and here today I have to come and tell you we've been turned down there. It's hard on me, don't forget that, Tony. It'll hurt me in New York. You know what your crowd call me there—the Technicality Kid?"

"You was recommended to me as one swell mouthpiece and I sent for you and you came up and I hired you," answered Scarra in a recapitulation of vain grievances, "and you took my jack and you kept on taking it till you milked me clean, pretty near it, and now you stand there and tell me you're through!"

"No, I'm not through either," the lawyer made haste to say. "There's still the chance the governor might commute the sentence. You know how often that happens—men being repreived right at the very last minute, as you might say. Oh, I'm going to the governor next. We've still got nearly a month left, Tony, and a lot could happen in a month."

"Swell chance I've got with this governor, and you know it. He's a politician, ain't he? Can't you see these here rube papers riding him if he should let off the 'Big City Gunman'? Ain't that their gentlest name for me? No, you quit stalling and listen to me a minute."

There was a tight iron grille between them; they talked with each other through the meshes, and as they talked a keeper watched them, keeping beyond earshot, though. Even in the death-house the sanctity of the professional relation as between a convicted man and his legal adviser was preserved. So the sentry must watch but he might not listen; the meeting partook of the nature of a confessional. All the same, Scarra followed the quite unnecessary precaution of sinking his voice before saying what next he had to say. Saying it, he kept shifting his eyes away from Attorney Finburg's face to look this way and that—first this way, toward the heedful but unhearing keeper, then that way toward the part of the building where, behind soundproof walls, the Chair stood.

"Finburg," he whispered, "I ain't going to let these guys cook me. I'm going to beat their game yet—and you're going to help me." He twisted his mouth into the stiffened shape of a grin; the embalmed corpse of a grin. "Get that? You're going to help me."

Counselor Finburg had eloquent shoulders. Often in debate he used those shoulders of his to help out his pleading hands. He lifted both of them in a shrug of confessed helplessness. Nevertheless his expression invited further confidences. It was as much as to say that this was a poor unfortunate friend who, having a delusion, must be humored in it.

"Don't start that stuff with me," went on Scarra, correctly interpreting the look; "not till you've heard what I got to tell you. Finburg, if I got to croak, I got to croak, that's all. I took plenty chances in my time on getting bumped off and I've seen more'n one guy getting his—what I mean, more'n one besides that hick cop that I fixed his clock for him. If it hadn't been for him I wouldn't been here. But that ain't the thing. The thing is that I ain't going to let 'em make cold meat out of me in that kitchen of theirs out there. They ain't going to fry me on one side like an egg. I'll beat 'em to it, that's all. I couldn't stand it, that's all."

"They say it's absolutely—you know"—Mr. Finburg's lips were reluctant to form the word—"well, painless—and, of course, instantaneous."

"Who says so? A bunch of wise-cracking doctors, that's who. What do they know about it? Any of them ever try it to find out? Finburg, I had a brother and he knew about electricity—was a lineman for a high-tension power company. I've heard him tell about being caught in them currents, heard him tell what other guys went through that took a big jolt of the juice.

The first shock don't always put a guy out. He may look to be dead but he ain't—he's stuck there waiting for the next shot—waiting, waiting. Well, not for me—I'm going to do my own croaking—with a little help from outside. That's where you figure in."

Involuntarily, Finburg made as if to back away. His body shrank back but his feet rooted him fast. A fascination held him.

"You ain't going to lose anything by it," maintained the caged man, pressing his point. "You're going to make by it."

"No, no, no!" Finburg strove to make his dissent emphatic. "Oh, no, Scarra, I'd like to do you any favor in my power but I couldn't do that. Why, man, it's against the law. It's conniving at a suicide. It makes the man who does it an accessory."

"Swell law that wants to croak a poor guy and yet calls it a crime if somebody helps him croak himself!" commented Scarra. "Still, I know about that part of it already. What if I tell you you ain't running any risk? And what if you clean up on the deal yourself? You've been knocking holes in the law ever since you got your license. Why're you weakening now?"

"But—but if you're determined to go this way, why not use something in your cell—some utensil, say?" suggested the nervous Finburg. Already he felt guilty. His cautious voice had a guilty quaver in it.

"With them bringing me my grub already cut up and only a spoon to eat it with—*huh!*" The murderer grunted. "Why, even the tooth-brush they gave me has got a limber handle on it. And if they let me have a lead-pencil to write with, there's a keeper standing alongside to see I don't try to shove the sharp end of it down my throat. Don't they search my coop every little while? You know they do. Anyhow, I ain't craving to make a messy job of it and probably be caught before it's done, besides. I'm going clean and I'm going quick. What I want is just a nice little jolt of this here cyanide of potassium. You know about that stuff? You swallow it and it's all over in a minute. That's what I want—one little shot of that cyanide stuff. I ain't going to take it till the last hope's gone—a miracle might happen with that governor yet. But when they come to take me out to be juiced in that chair, why, down goes the little pill and out goes Tony, laughing in their foolish faces. I ain't scared to go my way, you understand, but"—he sucked in his breath—"but I'm scared to go their way and I might as well admit it."

Still on the defensive and the negative, Finburg had been shaking his head through this, but his next speech belied his attitude. Being rent between two crossed emotions—a sinking fear for his own safety and a climbing, growing avarice, he said in a soft, wheedling tone: "You mentioned just now about my making something out of—this? Not that I'd even consider such a dangerous proposition," he added hastily. "I—I just wanted to know what you had on your mind, that's all?"

"I thought that'd interest you! Listen, Finburg. All along, I've been holding out on you. I been keeping an ace in the hole in case we should lose out on the appeal. You thought you'd taken the last cent of fall-money I could dig up for fighting my case for me, didn't you? Well, kid, you guessed wrong there. You remember the big Bergen Trust Company hold-up down in New Jersey early last spring, don't you?"

"Yes." Finburg's jaws relaxed the least bit to let a greedy tongue lick out.

"Then you remember, probably, that quite a chunk of negotiable securities—bonds and things—wasn't never recovered?"

"Yes, I recall." Finburg suggested a furtive jackal, tense with a mounting hunger and smelling afar off a bait of rich but forbidden food.

"And that the trust company people offered a reward of ten thousand for the return of that stuff and no questions asked?"

"Yes, go on."

"Well, Finburg, you're smart but here's something you never knew before. I was in on that hold-up—I engineered it. And inside of three weeks afterwards, while I was waiting for the squawk over that job to die down, I came up here and got in this jam and had to plug this cop and they nailed me. But, Finburg, I've got a safe-deposit box in a bank on Third Avenue and I've got a key to it stuck away in another place where a pal's keeping it for me—a pal I can trust. I'll leave you guess what's in that safe-deposit box. Or, if you want me to, I'll tell—"

"No, don't tell me—that would be illegal," said the lawyer very uneasily and yet very eagerly. "It would be more regular, you understand, if I didn't actually have knowledge of what the contents were—that is, beforehand. I've been double-crossed before by some of you hard-boiled people. There was the time when I almost worked my head off defending Roxie McGill and her mob for shoving phony money, and every time I think of how that McGill skirt slipped it over on me, when it came time to settle up"—he winced on what plainly was a most painful recollection—"well, it's made me careful, Tony, awfully careful. Not that I'm doubting you, understand. If a man can't trust a—" He broke off, looking, for him, a trifle embarrassed.

"Say it!" prompted Scarra grimly. "If you can't trust a dying man you can't trust nobody—that's what you had in your mind, wasn't it? Well, I'm as good as dead right now and you won't never regret it, playing my game. It could be fixed up, according to law, couldn't it, like a will, that me not having any kinfolks, I was leaving you what was in that safe-deposit box on account of you having been my lawyer and having worked so hard for me?"

"Oh, yes, I'd know how to phrase the instrument properly. There'd be no trouble about that, none whatever, Tony."

"All right, then, you fix up the paper and I'll sign it right here any day it's ready. And I'll give you a written order on that pal of mine for the key, telling him to hand it over to you the day after I'm gone. You ain't got a thing to worry about. And in payment all you got to do for me is just the one little favor of getting that little pill made up and—"

"I'm telling you there's entirely too much risk," interrupted Finburg, in a timorous sweat of almost over-powering temptation, but still clinging to safety. "I wouldn't dare risk trying to slip you poison, Tony—I couldn't."

"Nobody's asking you to."

"What? What's that you're saying, Tony?" The lawyer shoved his peaked nose between two wattles of the steel.

"I say, nobody's asking you to. Knowing you, I've doped out that part of it so you won't have to take a chance. Listen, Finburg—there's a guard here named Isgrid—a Swede or something. And he comes from down on the East Side, the same as you and me. I've been working on him. We've got friendly. Maybe him and me both having been born on the same block over there beyond the Bowery was what made him sort of mushy towards me—he's one of those big thick slobs. But it ain't for friendship only that he's willing to help. He wants his bit out of it. He's aiming to quit this job he's got here and he wants to take a piece of money with him when he quits. Now, here's what he tells me: He'll be on the death-watch on me. That last night he'll slip me the pill, see? Nobody ain't going to suspect him, he says, and even if anybody does, they ain't going to be able to hang it on him, let alone get you mixed in with the plant."

"I suppose I'll have to see this man," conceded Finburg; "not that that means I'm committing myself to this undertaking."

"I thought of that too. Day after tomorrow is Sunday, and Sunday is his day off. He'll run down to New York and meet you in your office or at your flat, and you can size him up and talk it over with him."

"It can't do any harm to see the man, I suppose." It was plain that the lawyer was convincing himself. "Tell him—only, mind you, this is just an accommodation to you—tell him the address of my rooms and tell him to be there at ten o'clock."

"One thing more," stated the killer. "Isgrid wants one grand for his cut."

"One grand—a thousand dollars!"

"That's his lowest price. I had to work on him to cut it down to that. And, Finburg, you'll have to dig up the thou'. He wants it in advance, see? You can pay yourself back—afterwards. That's up to you."

"That makes it still more complicated," lamented the wavering Finburg. "I don't know—I don't know." Figuratively he wrung his hands in an anguish born of desire and doubt.

"Well, I'll give you till over Sunday to make up your mind, then," said Scarra, he secretly being well content with the progress that had been made. "If by Monday you've decided to go through with your share of the deal, you can come back here and bring that will with you and I'll sign it. If you don't show up on Monday I'll know you're too chicken-hearted for your own good. Remember this, though, Finburg—one way or another I'm going to get that pill. If you don't want to help, that's your lookout—you'll only be kissing good-by to what's down in them safe-deposit vaults on Third Avenue. And if you do—well, I guess you're wise enough to protect yourself at every angle. It's easy pickings for you, Finburg—easy pickings. So think it over before you decide to say no. Well, so long, see you Monday."

He fell back from the grating and to the keeper at the farther end of the corridor motioned to indicate that his interview with his counsel was ended and that he was ready to be returned to his cell.

Monday morning, good and early, Mr. Finburg was back again. His mind had been made up for many hours. In fact it was made up before he left on Friday afternoon. Only, at the time, he had not cared to say so or to look so. To wear a mask was one part of Mr. Finburg's professional attitude. To do things deviously was another. For him always, the longest way round was the shortest way across. His mind was a maze of detours, excepting when he was collecting his retainers or pressing for his principal fees. Then he could be straightforward enough to satisfy anybody. The practice of the criminal law does this to some of its practitioners.

It was because of this trait of Mr. Finburg's that certain preliminary steps in the working-out of his share in the plot were elaborated and made intricate. Since Friday evening when his train landed him at the Grand Central, he had been a reasonably busy young man. From the station he went directly to the Public Library and there, at a table well apart from any other reader, he consulted a work on toxicology, with particular reference to the effects of the more deadly poisons. Before midnight he was in touch with a chemist of his acquaintance who served as laboratory sharp and chief mixer for a bootlegging combine specializing in synthetic goods with bogus labels on them. His real purpose in this inquiry was, of course, carefully cloaked; the explanation he gave—it referred to experiments which a purely supposititious client was making with precious metals—apparently satisfied the expert, who gave information fully.

By virtue of a finely involved ramification of underworld connections, Mr. Finburg was enabled next to operate through agents. Three separate individuals figured in the transaction. But no one of the three beheld more than his particular link in a winding chain and only one of the three had direct dealings with the principal, and this one remained in complete ignorance of what really was afoot. All he knew, all he cared to know, was that, having been dispatched on a mission which seemed to start nowhere and lead nowhere, he had performed what was expected of him and had been paid for it and was through. By such deft windings in and out, Mr. Finburg satisfied himself the trail was so broken that no investigator ever could piece it together. There were too many footprints in the trace; and too many of them pointing in seemingly opposite and contrary directions.

He was quite ready for the man Isgrid when that person came to his apartment on Sunday morning. Whether Isgrid studied Finburg is of no consequence to this narrative, but we may be quite assured that Finburg studied Isgrid, seeing the latter as a stolid, dull person, probably of Scandinavian ancestry and undoubtedly of a cheap order of mentality. About Isgrid as interpreted by Finburg, there was nothing to suggest any personal initiative. He appeared close-mouthed and secretive, though— in short, a man who being committed to a venture would go through it with a sort of intent and whole-hearted determination. This greatly pleased the little lawyer. For the rôle of an unthinking middleman Isgrid seemed an admirable choice. He had such a dependable dumb look about him. Nevertheless it suited Mr. Finburg's book that his conspirings with this man should be marked by crafty play-acting. There sat the two of them, entirely alone, yet Mr. Finburg behaved as though a cloud of witnesses hovered to menace him.

He asked Isgrid various questions—leading questions, they would be called in court—but so phrased that they might pass for the most unsuspicious of inquiries. Then, being well satisfied by the results of such cross-examination, the lawyer came to business.

"Look here," he said, pointing, "on this table is a little box with the lid off. See it? Well, in it are twelve five-grain capsules same as you'd get from any drug-store if you had a touch of grippe and the doctor gave you a prescription to be filled. Between ourselves we'll just say it is a grippe cure that we've got here. Well, one of these capsules is stronger than the others are. If I'm not mistaken, it's this one here"—his finger pointed again—"the last one in the bottom row, the one with a little spot of red ink on it. It's marked that way so a fellow will be wised up to handling it pretty carefully.

"Now then, I'm going into the next room. I've got a wall safe there where I keep some of my private papers and other valuables, including money. I'm going to get a bill—a nice new United States Treasury certificate for one thousand dollars—out of my safe. It may take me two or three minutes to work the combination and find the bill. When I come back, if one or two of those capsules should happen to be missing, why I'll just say to myself that somebody with a touch of grippe, or somebody who's got a friend laid up somewhere with the grippe, saw this medicine here and helped himself to a dose or so without saying anything about it. It won't stick in my mind; what difference does a measly little drug-store pill or two mean to me or to anybody else, for that matter? Inside of ten minutes I'll have forgotten all about it.

"Make yourself at home, please—I'll be back in a jiffy."

He entered the inner room of the two-room flat, closing and snapping shut the connecting door behind him. When he came back, which was quite soon, he glanced at the open box. The twelfth capsule, that one which was red-dotted, and one neighboring capsule had disappeared. Isgrid was sitting where he had been seated before Finburg's temporary withdrawal.

"See this?" resumed Finburg, and he held up what he was holding in his hands. "It's a nice slick new one that's never been in circulation. Well, I've about made up my mind to slip this bill to you. You've been kind to a party that's in trouble—a party that I've had considerable dealings with. He's grateful and naturally I'm grateful, too. As I understand it, you're going to keep on being good to this party. He's in a bad way—may not live very long, in fact—and we'll both appreciate any little attentions you might continue to show him. But this is a hard world—people get careless sometimes; you can't always depend on them. Not knocking you or anything, but still I'd like to make certain that you won't go back on any little promise you might have made to him lately. You get me, I think—just a precaution on my part. See what I'm going to do next?"

From his desk he took up a pair of scissors and with one swift clip of their blades sheared the yellow-back squarely in two across the middle. Isgrid said nothing to this but kept eying him intently.

"Now, then, I put one-half of this bill into my pocket," proceeded Finburg; "and the other half I'm handing over to you"—doing so. "Separated this way, these halves are no use to anybody—none to me, none to you. But paste them together again and you've got a thousand-dollar bill that's just as good as it ever was. For the time being, you keep your half and I'll keep my half. I'll have it right here handy on my person and ready to slip it over to you when the contract that I've been speaking of is completed.

"Now, I expect to be seeing our sick friend tomorrow. Tonight I'll be fixing up a document or two for him to sign and I'm going to take them up to where he is in the morning. I'll tell him of this little arrangement between us and I'm certain he'll endorse it. I may not see him again until the twenty-seventh of this month." He dwelt meaningly upon the date. "It looks as though he couldn't last much longer than that—not more than a few hours. And on the twenty-seventh, if the prospects are that he'll pass out within the next twenty-four hours—which, as I say, is the present outlook—I'll pay him a farewell visit. If everything has worked out right—if you've done him any little last favor that he's counting on—why, he'll tip me the word while we're alone together. You won't have to wait much longer than that for what's coming to you. Just as soon as he gives me the word I'll meet you in some private corner that we'll decide on, and hand you over the other half of your bill. Is everything understood—everything agreeable to you?"

Still mute, Isgrid nodded. They shook hands on it after Isgrid had named a suitable place for their rendezvous on the twenty-seventh; then the silent caller took himself away. All told, he had not contributed a hundred words, counting in grunts as words, to the dialogue.

Being left alone, Mr. Finburg mentally hugged himself before he set to the task of drawing up the papers for his client's signature. This same Sunday he decided not to go to the governor of that near-by state with any futile plea for executive clemency. He'd tell Scarra, of course, that he was going; would pretend he had gone. But what was the use of a man wasting his breath on a quest so absolutely hopeless? He salved his conscience—or the place where his conscience had been before he wore it out—with this reflection, and by an effort of the will put from him any prolonged consideration of the real underlying reason. It resolved itself into this: Why should a man trifle with his luck? With Scarra wiped out—and certainly Scarra deserved wiping out, if ever a red-handed brute did—the ends of justice would be satisfied and the case might serve as a warning to other criminals. But if that governor should turn mush-headed and withhold from Scarra his just punishment, where would Scarra's lawyer be? He'd be missing a delectable chunk of jack by a hair—that's where he would be.

Let the law take its course!

The law did. It took its racking course at quarter past one o'clock on the morning of the twenty-eighth.

Those who kept ward on Tony Scarra, considering him as scientists might consider an inoculated guinea-pig waiting patiently for this or that expected symptom of organic disorder to show itself, marveled more and more as the night wore on at the bearing of the condemned man. His, they dispassionately decided among themselves, was not the rehearsed but transparent bravado of the ordinary thug. That sort of thing they had observed before; they could bear testimony that very often toward the finish this make-believe fortitude melted beneath the lifting floods of a mortal terror and a mortal anguish, so that the subject lost the use of his members and the smoothness of his tongue, and babbled wild meaningless prayers and flapped with his legs and must be half-dragged, half-borne along on that first, last, short journey of his through the painted iron door to what awaited him beyond.

Or, fifty-fifty, it might be that imminent dread acted upon him as a merciful drug which soothed him into a sort of obedient coma wherein he yielded with a pitiful docility to the wishes of his executioners and mechanically did as they bid him, and went forth from his cell meek as a lamb, thereby simplifying and easing for them their not altogether agreeable duties. These experienced observers had come to count on one or the other of these manifestations. In Scarra neither of them was developed.

He seemed defiantly insulated against collapse by some indefinable power derived from within; it was as though a hidden secret reservoir of strength sustained him. He gibed the death-watch and he made a joke of the prison chaplain coming in the face of repeated rebuffs to offer the sustaining comfort of his Gospels. He betrayed no signs whatsoever of weakening—and this, to those who officiated at those offices, seemed most remarkable of all—when they clipped the hair off the top of his skull for the pad of the electrodes and again, later in the evening, when they brought him the black trousers with the left leg split up the inside seam.

All at once though, at the beginning of the second hour after midnight, when the witnesses were assembled and waiting in the lethal chamber, his jaunty confidence—if so, for lack of a better description, it might be termed—drained from him in a single gush. He had called, a minute or two before, for a drink of water, complaining of a parched throat. A filled cup was brought to him. Sitting on a stool in his cell he turned his back upon the bringer and took the draught down at a gulp, then rose and stood looking through the bars at the keepers, with a mocking, puzzling grin on his lips and over all his face and in his eyes a look of expectancy. The grin vanished, the look changed to one of enormous bewilderment, then to one of the intensest chagrin, and next he was mouthing with shocking vile words toward the eternity waiting for him. He resisted them when they went in then to fetch him out, and fought with them and screamed out and altogether upset the decorum of the death-house, so that the surviving inmates became excessively nervous and unhappy.

He did not curse those whose task it was now to subdue and, if possible, to calm him. He cursed somebody or other—person or persons unknown—for having deceived him in a vital matter, crying out that he had been imposed on, that he had been double-crossed. He raved of a pill—whatever that might mean—but so frightful a state was he in, so nearly incoherent in his frenzy of rage and distress and disappointment, that the meaning of what he spoke was swallowed up and lost.

Anyhow, his sweating handlers had no time to listen. Their task was to muffle his blasphemy and get him to the chair, which they did. Practically, they had to gag him with their hands, and one of the men had a finger bitten to the bone.

Since he continued to struggle in the presence of the audience, the proceedings from this point on were hurried along more than is common. His last understandable words, coming from beneath the mask clamped over the upper part of his distorted face, had reference to this mysterious double-crossing of which plainly, even in that extremity, he regarded himself the victim, and on which, as was equally plain, his final bitter thoughts dwelt. The jolt of the current cut him off in a panted, choking mid-speech, and the jaw dropped and the body strained up against the stout breast-harness, and the breath wheezed and rasped out across the teeth and past the lips, which instantly had turned purple, and there was a lesser sound, a curious hissing, whispering, slightly unpleasant sound as though the life were so eager to escape from this flesh that it came bursting through the pores of the darkening skin. Also, there was a wisp of rising blue smoke and a faint, a very faint smell of something burning. There nearly always is; a feature which apparently cannot be avoided. Still, after all, that's but a detail.

For absolute certainty of result, they gave Scarra's body a second shock, and the physicians present observed with interest how certain of the muscles, notably certain of the neck muscles, twitched in response to the throb and flow of the fluid through the tissues. But of course the man was dead. It merely was a simple galvanic reaction—like eel-meat twisting on a hot griddle, or severed frogs' legs jumping when you sprinkle salt on them—interesting, perhaps, but without significance. Except for Scarra's unseemly behavior immediately after drinking the water, this execution, as executions go, and they nearly always go so, was an entire success.

Conceded that as to its chief purpose, the plan unaccountably had gone amiss, Mr. Finburg nevertheless felt no concern over the outcome. Privately he preferred that it should have been thus—there being no reason for any official inquiry, naturally there would be no official inquiry. Happy anticipations uplifted him as, sundry legal formulas having been complied with, he went as Scarra's heir to Scarra's bank on Third Avenue and opened Scarra's safe-deposit box.

It would seem that he, also, had been double-crossed. All the box contained was a neat small kit of burglars' tools. It was indeed a severe disappointment to Mr. Finburg, a blow to his faith in human nature. We may well feel for Mr. Finburg.

Of that triumvirate of East Side connivers, there remains the third and least important member, Isgrid, he who, scheming on his own account and in his own protection, had played for safety by smuggling to the late Scarra not number twelve, the poisonous capsule, but number eleven, the harmless one. Let us not spend all our sympathy upon Mr. Finburg but rather let us reserve some portion of it for Isgrid. For this one, he too suffered a grievous disappointment. It befell when, having patched the parted halves of his thousand-dollar bill, he undertook to pass it. It was refused, not because it was pasted together but because it was counterfeit.

The Cowboy and the Lady—And Her PA

FROM up on the first level of the first shelf of the wagon road above Avalanche Creek came the voice of Dad Wheelis, the wagon-train boss, addressing his front span. The mules had halted at the head of the steep grade to twist about in the traces and, with six 'cello-shaped heads stretched over the rim and twice that many somber eyes fixed on the abyss swimming in a green haze beneath them, to contemplate its outspread glories while they got their wind back. It was evident Dad thought the breathing space sufficiently had been prolonged. On a beautiful clearness his words dropped down through the spicy dry air.

"Git up!" he bade the sextet with an affectionate violence, and you could hear his whip-lash where it crackled like a string of firecrackers above the drooping ears of the lead team. "Git up, you scenery-lovin' *so-and-soes!*"

There was an agonized whine of tires and hubs growing faint and fainter and Mrs. Hector Gatling sighed with a profound appreciation.

"How prodigal nature is out here in these Western wilds!" she said.

"Certainly does throw a wicked prod," agreed her daughter, Miss Shirley Gatling. But her eyes were not fixed where her mother's were.

"Such a climate!" affirmed the senior lady, flinching slightly that the argot of a newer and an irreverent generation should be invoked in this cathedral place. "Such views! Such picturesque types everywhere!"

"Not bad-looking mountains across over yonder, at that," said Mr. Gatling, husband and father of the above, giving his gestured indorsement to an endless vista of serrated peaks of an average height of not less than seven thousand feet. "Not bad at all, so long as you don't have to hoof up any of 'em."

"*Mong père*, he also grows poetic, is it not?" murmured Miss Gatling. "Now, who'd have ever thunk it, knowing him in his native haunts back in that dear Pittsburgh!"

Her glance still was leveled in a different direction from the one in which her elders gazed. Mr. Gatling twisted about so that a foldable camp-chair creaked under his weight, and looked through his glasses in the same quarter where his daughter looked. His forehead drew into wrinkles.

Miss Gatling stood up, a slim, trim figure in her riding-boots and well-tailored breeches and with a gay little sweater drawn snugly down inside her waistband and held there by a broad brilliant girdle of squaw's beadwork. She settled a white sombrero on her bobbed hair and stepped away from them over the pine-needles and thence down toward the roaring creek. The morning sunlight came slanting through the lower tree boughs and picked out and made shiny glitters of the heavy Mexican silver spurs at her heels and the wide Navaho silver bracelet that was set on her right wrist. She passed between two squared boulders that might have been lichened tombs for Babylon's kings.

"Continue, I pray you, dear parents, to sit and invite your souls, if any," she called back. "I go to make sure they're putting plenty of cold victuals in the lunch kit. Yesterday noon, you'll remember, we darn' near starved. For you, the beckon and the lure of the wonderland. But for me and my girlish gastric juices—chow and lots of it!"

Mr. Gatling said nothing for a minute or two, but he took off his cap as though to make more room for additional furrows forming on his brow. A deer-fly alighted where he was baldest and promenaded to and fro there, across the great open spaces. The thinker too deeply was abstracted to shoo away the little stranger; he let her promenade.

"Mmph!" he remarked presently. Mrs. Gatling emerged promptly from her own reverie. It was his commonest way of engaging her attention—that *mmphing* sound was. Lacking vowels though it did, its emphasis of uneasiness was quite apparent to her schooled ears.

"What's wrong, dear?" she asked. "Still sore from all that dreadful horseback riding?"

"It's that girl," he told her; "that Shirley of ours. She's the one I'm worried about."

"Why, goodness gracious!" she cried; "what's wrong with Shirley?"

"Look at her. That's all I ask—just look at her."

Mrs. Gatling, who was slightly near-sighted in more ways than one, squinted at the withdrawing figure.

"Why, the child never seemed happier or healthier in her life," she protested, still peering. "Why, only last Monday—or was it Tuesday; no, Monday—I remember distinctly now it was Monday because that was the day we got caught in the snow-storm coming through Swift Current Pass—only last Monday you were saying yourself how well and rosy she was looking."

"I don't mean that—she's a bunch of limber young whalebones. Look where she's going! That's what I mean. Look what she's doing!"

"Why, what is she doing that's out of the way, I'd like to know?" demanded his puzzled wife, now jealously on the defensive for her young.

"She's doing what she's been doing every chance she got these last four-five days, that's what." Mr. Gatling was manifesting an attitude somewhat common in husbands and fathers when dealing with their domestic problems. He preferably would flank the subject rather than bore straight at it, hoping by these round-about tactics to obtain confirmation for his suspicions before he ever voiced them. "Got eyes in your head, haven't you? All right then, use 'em."

"Hector Gatling, for a sane man, you do get the queerest notions in your brain sometimes! What on earth possesses you? Hasn't the child a perfect right to stroll down there and watch those three guides packing up? You know she's been trying to learn to make that pearl knot or turquoise knot or whatever it is they call it. What possible harm can there be in her learning how to tie a pearl knot?"

"Diamond hitch, diamond hitch," he corrected her testily. "Not pearls, but diamonds; not knots, but hitches! You'd better try to remember it, too—diamonds and hitches usually figure in the thing that I've got on my mind. And, if you'll be so kind as to observe her closely, you'll see that it isn't those three guides she's so interested in. It's one guide out of the three. And it's getting serious, or I'm all wrong. Now then, do you get my drift, or must I make plans and specifications?"

"Oh!" The exclamation was freighted with shock and with sorrow but with incredulity too.

"Oh!" said Mrs. Gatling again and now she was fluttering her feathers in alarm, if a middle-aged lady dressed in tweed knickerbockers and a Boy Scout's shirt may be said to have any feathers to flutter. "Oh, Hector, you don't mean it! You can't mean it! A child who's traveled and seen the world! A child who's had every advantage that wealth and social position and all could give her! A child who's a member of the Junior League! A child who's—who— Hector, you're crazy. Hector, you know it's utterly impossible—utterly! It's preposterous!" Womanlike, she debated against a growing private dread. Then, still being womanlike, she pressed the opposing side for proof to destroy her counter-argument: "Hector, you've seen something—you've overheard something. Tell me this minute what it was you overheard!"

"I've overheard nothing. Think I'm going snooping around eavesdropping and spying on Shirley? I've never done any of that on her yet and I'm too old to begin now—and too fat. But I've seen a-plenty."

"Oh, pshaw! I guess if there'd been anything afoot I'd have seen it myself first, what with my mother's intuition and all! Oh, pshaw!" But Mrs. Gatling's derisive rejoinder lacked conviction.

"I've had the feeling for longer than just these last few days," continued Mr. Gatling despondently. "But I couldn't put my hand on it, not at first. I tried to fool myself by saying it was this Wild Western flubdub and stuff getting into her blood and she'd get over it, soon as the attack had run its course. First loading up with all that Indian junk, then saying she felt as though she never wanted to do anything but be natural and stay out here and rough it for the rest of her life, and now here all of a sudden getting so much more flip and slangy than usual. That's the worst symptom yet—that slang is.

"In your day, ma'am, when a girl fell in love or thought she had, she went and got all mushed-up and sentimental; went mooning around sentimentalizing and rhapsodizing and romanticking and everything. All of you but the strong-minded ones did and I guess they must have mushed-up some too, on the sly. Yes'm, that's what you did—you mushed-up." His tone was accusing, condemning, as though he dealt with ancient offenses which not even the passage of the years might condone. "But now it's different with them. They get slangier and flippier and they let on to make fun of their own affections. And that's what Miss Shirley is doing right now, this very minute, or else I'm the worst misled man in the entire state of Montana."

"Maybe—maybe—" The matron sputtered as her distress mounted. "Of course I'm not admitting that you're right, Hector—the mere suggestion of such a thing is simply incredible—but on the bare chance that the child might be getting silly notions into her head, maybe I'd better speak to her. I'm so much older than she is that—"

"You said it then!" With a grim firmness Mr. Gatling interrupted. "You're so much older than she is; that's your trouble. And I'm suffering from the same incurable complaint. People our age who've got children growing up go around bleating that young people are different from the way young people were when we were young. They're not. They're just the same as we were—same impulses, same emotions, same damphoolishness, same everything—but they've got a new way of expressing 'em. And then we say we can't understand them. Knock thirty years off of our lives and we'd understand all right because then we'd be just the same as they are. So you'll not say a word to that youngster of ours—not yet awhile, you won't. Nor me, neither." Grammar, considered as such, never had meant very much to Mr. Gatling, that masterful, self-educated man.

"But if I pointed out a few things to her—if I warned her—"

"Ma'am, you'll perhaps remember your own daddy wasn't so terribly happy over the prospect when I started sparking you. After I'd come courting and had gone on home again I guess it was as much as the old man could do to keep from taking a shovel and shoveling my tracks out of the front yard. But he had sense enough to keep his mouth shut where you were concerned. Suppose he'd tried to influence you against me, tried to break off the match—what would have happened? You'd have thought you were oppressed and persecuted and you'd have grabbed for me even quicker than you did."

"Why, Hector Gatling, I never grabbed—"

"I'm merely using a figure of speech. But no, he had too much gumption to undertake the stern-father racket. He locked his jaw and took it out in nasty looks and let nature take its course, and the consequence was we got married in the First Methodist Church with bridesmaids and old shoes and kins folks and all the other painful details instead of me sneaking you out of a back window some dark night and us running off together in a side-bar buggy. No, ma'am, if you'll take a tip from an old retired yardmaster of the Lackawanna, forty-seven years, man and boy, with one road, you'll—"

"You never worked a day as a railroad man and you know it."

"Just another figure of speech, my dear. Understand now, you're to keep mum for a while and I keep mum and we just sit back in our reserved seats up in the grandstand and see how the game comes out. A nice polite quiet game of watchful waiting—that's our line and we're both going to follow it. We'll stand by for future developments and then maybe I'll frame up a little campaign. With your valuable advice and assistance, of course!"

With a manner which she strove to make casual and unconcerned, the disturbed Mrs. Gatling that day watched. It was the manner rather of a solicitous hen with one lone chick, and she continually oppressed by dreads of some lurking chicken-hawk. It would have deceived no one who closely studied the lady's bearing and demeanor. But then, none in the party closely studied these.

The camp dunnage being miraculously bestowed upon the patient backs of various pack-animals, their expedition moved. They overtook and passed Dad Wheelis and his crew, caravaning with provender for the highway contractors on up under the cloud-combing parapet of the Garden Wail Wall, and behind them heard for a while his frank and aboveboard reflections upon the immediate ancestries, the present deplorable traits, the darkened future prospects of his work stock. They swung away from the rutted wagon track and took the steeper horseback trail and for hours threaded it like so many plodding ants against the slant of a tilted bowl. They stopped at midday on a little plateau fixed so high toward heaven that it was a picture-molding on Creation's wall above a vast mural of painted buttes and playful cataracts and a straggling timber-line and two jeweled glaciers.

They stretched their legs and uncramped their backs; they ate and remounted and on through the afternoon single-filed along the farther slope where a family herd of mountain-goats browsed among the stones and paid practically no heed to them. They saw a solitary bighorn ram with a twisted double cornucopia springing out of his skull and likewise they saw a pair of indifferent mule-deer and enough landscapes to fill all the souvenir postcard racks of the world; for complete particulars consult the official guide-book of Our National Playgrounds.

Evening brought them across a bony hip of the Divide to within sight of the distant rear boundary of the governmental domain. So they pitched the tents and coupled up the collapsible stove there in a sheltered small cove in the Park's back yard and watched the sun go down in his glory. When the moon rose it was too good to believe. You almost could reach up and jingle the tambourines of little circling stars; anyhow, you almost thought you could. It was a magic hour, an ideal place for love-making among the young of the species. Realizing the which, Mrs. Gatling had a severe sinking and apprehensive sensation directly behind the harness buckle on the ample belt which girthed her weary form amidships. She'd been apprehensive all day but now the sinking was more pronounced.

She strained at the tethers of her patience though until supper was over and it was near hushaby-time for the tired forms of the middle-aged. Within the shelter of their small tent she spoke then to her husband, touching on the topic so stedfastly uppermost in her brain.

"Oh, Hector," she quavered, "I'm actually beginning to be afraid you're right. They've been together this livelong day. Neither one of them had eyes for anything or anybody else. The way he helped her on and off her horse! The way he fetched and carried for her! And the way she let him do it! And they're—they're together outside now. Oh, Hector!"

"They certainly are," he stated. "Sitting on a slab of rock in that infernal moonlight like a couple of feeble-minded turtle-doves. Why in thunder couldn't it 'a' rained tonight—good and hard? Romola, I don't want to harry you up any more than's necessary but you take, say, about two or three more nights like this and they're liable to do considerable damage to tender hearts."

"Don't I know it? O-oh, Hector!"

"Well, anyhow, I had the right angle on the situation before you tumbled," he said with a sort of melancholy satisfaction. "I can give myself credit for that much intelligence anyhow." It was quite plain that he did.

He stepped, a broad shape in his thick pajamas and quilted sleeping-boots, to the door flap and he drew the canvas back and peeped through the opening.

The pair under discussion had found the night air turning chill and their perch hard. They got up and stood side by side in the shimmering white glow. Against a background of luminous blue-black space, it revealed their supple figures in strong, sharp relief. The youth made a handsome shadowgraph. His wide-brimmed sugar-loaf hat; his blue flannel blouse with its flaunting big buttons; his Angora chaps with wings on them that almost were voluminous enough for an eagle's wings; his red silk neckerchief reefed in by a carved bone ring to fit a throat which Mr. Gatling knew to be sun-tanned and wind-tanned to a healthy mahogany-brown; his beaded, deep-cuffed gauntlets; his sharp-toed, high-heeled, silver-roweled boots of a dude cowboy—they all matched and modeled in with the slender waist and the flat thighs and the sinewy broad shoulders and the alert head of the wearer.

His name was Hayes Tripler, but the other two guides generally called him "Slick" and they looked up to him, for he had ridden No Name, the man-killer, at last year's Pendleton Round-up and hoped this year to be in the bulldogging money over the line at Calgary. Within his limitations he was an exceedingly competent person and given to deporting himself accordingly.

At this present moment he appeared especially well pleased with his own self-cast horoscope. There was a kind of proud proprietary aura all about him.

The watcher inside the tent saw a caressing arm slip from about his daughter's body and he caught the sounds but did not make out the sense of words that passed between them. Then the two silhouettes swung apart and the boy laughed contentedly and flung an arm aloft in a parting salute and began singing a catch as he went teetering off toward the spot where his mates of the outfit already were making the low tilt of a tarpaulin roof above them pulse to some very sincere snoring. But before she betook herself to quarters, the girl bided for a long minute on the verge of the cliff and looked off and away into the studded void beyond her. She seemed to be checking up on the minor stars to see whether any of them were missing. But her father knew better than that. The sidewise cant of her head showed that one of the things she did was to listen while her late companion served due notice on the night to such effect as this:

"You monkey with my Lulu,
Tell you what I'll do:
Take out a gun and shoot you,
And carve you plenty too!"

Mr. Gatling drew the flaps together in an abstracted way and *mmphed* several times.

"Pretty dog-gone spry-looking young geezer at that," he remarked absently. "Yes, sir, pretty spry-looking."

"Who?"

"Him."

"You actually mean that cowboy?"

"None other than which."

"Oh, Hector! That—that vulgarian, that country bumpkin, that clodhopper!"

"Now hold on there, Romola. Let's try to be just even if we are prejudiced. All the clods that kid ever hopped you could put 'em in your eye without interfering with your eyesight. He's no farm-hand; he's a cow-hand or was before he got this job of steering tourists around through these mountains—and that's a very different thing, I take it. And what he knows he knows blame' well. I wish I could mingle in with a horse the way he does. When he gets in a saddle he's riveted there but I only come loose and work out of the socket. And I'd give about five years off my life to be able to handle a trout-rod like he can. I claim that in his departments he's a fairly high-grade proposition. He's aware of it, too, but I don't so much blame him for that, either. If you don't think well of yourself who else is going to?"

"Why, Hector Gatling, I believe you're really—but no, you couldn't be! Look at the difference in their stations! Look at their different environments! Look at their different view-points!"

"I'm looking—just as hard as you are. You don't get what I'm driving at. I wouldn't fancy having this boy for a son-in-law any more than you would—although at that I'm not saying I couldn't maybe make some use of him in another capacity. Still, you needn't mind worrying so much about their respective stations in life. I didn't have any station in life to start from myself—it was a whistling-post. And yet I've managed to stagger along fairly well. I'd a heap rather see Shirley tied up to pretty near any decent, ambitious, self-respecting young cuss that came along than to have her fall for one of those plush-headed lounge-lizards that keep hanging round her back home. I know the breed. In my day they used to be guitar-pickers—and some of 'em played a snappy game of Kelly pool. Now they're Charleston dancers and the only place most of 'em carry any weight is on the hip.

"But that's not the point. The point is that if Shirley fell for this party she'd probably be a mighty regretful young female when the bloom began to rub off the peach. They haven't been raised to talk the same language—that's the trouble. I don't want her to make a mistake that'll gum up her life before it's fairly started; don't want that happening any more than you do. I don't want her to have a husband that she's liable later on to be ashamed to show him off before the majority of her friends, or anyhow one that she'd maybe have to go around making excuses for the way he handled his knife and fork in company; or something. Right now, the fix she's in, she's probably saying to herself that she could be perfectly satisfied to settle down in a cabin somewhere out here and wet-nurse a lot of calves for the next forty or fifty years. But that's only her heart talking, not her head. After a while she'd get to brooding on Palm Beach.

"But if she's set her mind—and you know how stubborn she is when she gets her mind set—thank Heavens she didn't get that from my side of the family!—I say, if she's set her mind on him, Heavens above only knows what's going to happen. She's bewitched, she's hypnotized; it's this free-and-easy Western life that's fascinated her. I can't believe she's in love with him!"

"Well, I don't know. Maybe she's in love with a two-gallon hat and a pair of cowboy pants with silver dewdabs down the sides, or then again on the other hand maybe it's the real thing with her, or a close imitation of it. That's for us to find out if we can."

"I won't believe it. She's distracted, she's glamoured, she's—"

"All right, then, let's get her unglammed."

"But how?"

"Well, for one thing, by not rushing in and interfering with her little dream. By not letting either one of 'em see how anxious we are over this thing. By remaining as calm, cool and collected as we can."

"And in the meanwhile?"

"Well, in the meanwhile I, for one, am going to tear off a few winks. I hurt all over and there's quite a lot of me measured that way—all over."

"You can go to sleep with that—that dreadful thought hanging over us?"

"I can and I will. Watch me for about another minute and you'll see me doing it." He settled himself on his air mattress and drew the blankets over him.

"Well, I know I won't close my eyes this whole night through."

"I've heard you say that before and then had to shake you like a dish towel in the morning to make you snap out of it."

"This time I won't. I don't want to sleep. I want to plan something since you won't help me. Hector"—she reached across from her side and plucked at his top coverlid—"Hector, listen, I've got an idea—let's break off this trip tomorrow. Let's bundle right up and start back East. You can say you've got a message calling you back to the office—say you forgot something important, say—"

"And tip our hands just at the most critical time! We will not!... Mmph!" With a drowsy scornfulness he added this. Ten seconds later he *mmphed* again, then again. But the third one merged into a snore.

Undeniably Mr. Hector Gatling could be one of the most aggravating persons on earth when he set out to be. Any husband can.

Speaking with regard to the ripening effect of summer nights upon the spirits of receptive and impressionable youth, Mr. Gatling had listed the cumulative possibilities of three moonlit ones hand-running. Specifically he had not included in his perilous category those languishing soft gloamings and those explosive sunrises and those long lazy mornings when the sun baked resiny perfumes out of the cedars, and the unseen heart-broken little bird that the mountaineers call the lonesome bird sang his shy lament in the thickets; nor had he mentioned slow journeys through deep defiles where the ferns grew with a tropical luxuriance out of the cinders of old forest-fires and, in a paradoxical defiance, shook their fronds toward the never-melting snow-caps on the *sierras* across the cañon; nor yet the fordings of tumbling streams when it might seem expedient on the part of a thoughtful young man to push up alongside and steady a young equestrian of the opposite sex while her horse's hoofs fumbled over the slick, drowned boulders. But vaguely he had lumped all these contingencies.

Three more nights of moon it was with three noble days of pleasant adventuring in between; and on the late afternoon of the third day when camp was being made beside a river which mostly was rapids, Miss Shirley Gatling sought out her father in a secluded spot somewhat apart from the rest. It was in the nature of a rendezvous, she having told him a little earlier that presently she desired to have speech with him. Only, her way of putting it had been different.

"Harken, O most revered Drawing Account," she said, dropping back on a broad place in the trail to be near him. "If you can spare the time for being saddle-sore I want to give you an earful as soon as this procession, as of even date, breaks up. You find a quiet retreat away from the flock and wait there until I find you, savvy?"

So now he was waiting, and from yonder she came toward him, stepping lightly, swinging forward from her hips with a sort of impudent freedom of movement; and to his father's eyes she never had seemed more graceful or more delectable or more independent-looking.

"Dad," she began, without preamble, and meeting him eye to eye, "in me you behold a Sabine woman. I'm bespoken."

"Mmph," he answered, and the answer might be interpreted, by a person who knew him, in any one of half a dozen ways.

"Such is the case," she went on, quite unafraid. "That caveman over there in the blue shirt"—she pointed—"he's the nominee. We're engaged."

"I can't plead surprise, kid," he stated, taking on for the moment her bantering tone. "The report that you two had come to a sort of understanding has been in active circulation on this reservation for the past forty-eight hours or so—maybe longer."

Her eyebrows went up.

"I don't get you," she said. "Who circulated it?"

"You did, for one," he told her. "And he did, for another. I may be failing, what with increasing age and all, but I'm not more than half blind yet. Have you been to your mother with this piece of news?"

"I came to you first. I—I"—for the first time she faltered an instant—"I figured you might be able to get the correct slant a little quicker than she would. This is only the curtain-raiser. I'm saving the big scene with the melodramatic touches for her. I have a feeling that she may be just a trifle difficult. So I picked on something easy to begin with."

"I see," he said. "Kind of an undress rehearsal, eh?" He held her off at arm's length from him, studying her face hungrily. "But what's the reason your young man didn't come along with you or ahead of you, in fact? In my time it generally was the young man that brought the message to Garcia."

"He wanted to come—he wasn't scared. I wouldn't let him. I told him I'd been knowing you longer than he had and I could handle the job better by myself. Well, that's your cue. What's it going to be, daddy—the glad hand of approval and the parental bless you, my children, bless you, or a little line of that go-forth-ungrateful-hussy-and-never-darken-my-doors-again stuff? Only, we're a trifle shy on doors around here."

He drew her to him and spoke downward at the top of her cropped head, she snuggling her face with a quick nervous little jerk against his wool-clad breast.

"Baby," he said, "when all's said and done, the whole thing's up to you, way I look at it. I don't suppose there ever was a man who really loved his daughter but what he figured that, taking one thing with another, she was too good for any man on earth. No matter who the lucky candidate is he says to himself: 'Well, if I have to have a son-in-law I suppose maybe you'll do, but alongside of her you're a total loss.' That's what any father who's worth his salt is bound to think. And that's what I'd still think no matter who you picked out. I'm not saying now what sort of a husband I'd try to pick out for you if the choice had been left to me. I'd probably want to keep you an old maid so's I could have you around and then I'd secretly despise myself for doing it, too. What I'm saying is this: If you're certain you know your own mind and if you've decided that this boy is the boy you want, why what more is there for me to do except maybe to ask you just one or two small questions?"

"Shoot!" she bade, without looking up, but her arms hugged him a little tighter. "Probably one of the nicest old meal-tickets in the world," she added, confidentially addressing the top buttonhole of his sweater.

"Has it by any chance entered into your calculations at this early stage of the game, how you are going to live—you two? Or where? Or, if I may be so bold, what on?"

"That's easy," she said, and now she was peering up at him through a tousled short forelock. "You're going to set us up on a place out here somewhere—a ranch. We're going to raise beef. He knows about beef. And I'm going to learn. I aim to be the leading lady beefer of the Imperial Northwest before I'm done."

"Whose notion was that?" His voice had sharpened the least bit.

"Mine, of course. He doesn't know anything about it. His idea is that we start in on what he can earn. But my idea is that we start in on a few of the simoleons that have already been earned—by you. And that's the idea that's going to prevail."

"Lucky I brought a fountain pen and a check-book along," he said. "Nothing like being prepared for these sudden emergencies. Still, I take it there's no great rush. Now, I tell you what: You run along and locate your mother and get *that* over with. She knows how I stand—we've been discussing this little affair our own selves."

"Oh," she said. "Oh, you have?" She seemed disappointed somehow—disappointed and slightly puzzled.

"Oh yes, several times. And on your way kindly whisper to the young man that I'm lurking right here behind these rocks ready to have a few words with him—if he can spare the time."

"Righto!" She reached up and kissed him and went swinging away, suspecting nothing, and for just a moment Mr. Gatling's conscience smote him, that she did not suspect.

"I've got to do it," he said to himself, excusing himself. "I've just got to find out—for her sake and ours—yes, and for his, too. It looks like an impossible bet and I've got to make sure."

With young Tripler he had more than the few words he had specified. They had quite an interview and as they had it the youth's embarrassment, which at the outset of the dialogue had made him wriggle and mumble and kick with his toes at inoffensive pebbles, gradually wore off until it vanished altogether and his native assurance reasserted itself. A proposition was advanced. It needed little pressing; promptly he fell in with it. It appealed to him.

"So we're agreed there," concluded his prospective father-in-law, clinching the final rivets. "We'll all go right ahead and finish out this tour—it's only a couple of days more anyhow and there's still a few cutthroats I want to catch. Then I'll take Shirley and her mother and run on out to Spokane. We'll hustle one of the other boys back tomorrow to the entrance to tell my chauffeur to load some bags in the car and run around to this side and meet us where we come out. We'll leave you there and you can dust back to the starting point through that short cut over the Garden Wall you were just speaking of. The business that I've got in Spokane will keep me maybe two or three days. That'll give you time to get those new clothes of yours and then we'll all meet over at Many Glacier—I'll wire you in advance—and in a day or two we'll all go on East together so's you can get acquainted with Shirley's friends and so forth. But of course, as I said before, that's our secret—all that part of it is. You've never been East, I believe?"

"Well, I've been as far as Minot, North Dakota."

"You'll probably notice a good deal of territory the other side of there. You'll enjoy it. Sure you can pick up all the wardrobe you need out in this country?" His manner was solicitous.

"Oh yes, sir, there's those two swell fellows named Steinfelt and Immergluck I was telling you about that they've got the leading gents' furnishing goods store down in Cree City."

"Good enough! I'd suggest that when picking out a suit you get something good and brisk as to pattern. Shirley likes live colors." Mr. Gatling next stressed a point which already had been dwelt upon: "You understand of course that she's not to know a single thing about all this—it's strictly between us two?"

"Yes, sir."

"You see, that'll make the surprise all the greater when she sees you all fixed up in a snappy up-to-date rigging like young college fellows your age wear back where she comes from. Seems like to me I was reading in an advertisement only here the other day where they're going in for coats with belts on 'em this season. Oh yes, and full-bottomed pants; I read that, too.

"One thing more occurs to me: Your hair is a little bit long and shaggy, don't you think? That's fine for out here but back East a young fellow that wants to be in style keeps himself trimmed up sort of close. Now I saw a barber working on somebody about as old as you are just the other day. Let me see—where was it? Oh yes, it was the barber at that town of Cree City—I dropped in there for a shave when we motored down last week. He seemed to have pretty good ideas about trimming up a fellow's bean, that barber."

"I know the one you mean—Silk Sullivan, next door to the bank. I've patronized him before."

"That's the one. Well, patronize him again before you rejoin us. He knows his business all right, your friend Sullivan does.... Now, mind you, mum's the word. All this part of it is absolutely between us."

"Oh yes, sir."

"O. K. Shake on it.... Well, suppose we see how they're coming along with supper."

Mr. Gatling's strategy ticked like a clock. After they got to Spokane he delayed the return by pretending a vexatious prolongation of a purely fictitious deal in ore properties, his privy intent being to give opportunity for Cree City's ready-made clothing princes to work their will. Since a hellish deed must be done he craved that they do it properly. Then on the homeward journey when they had reached the Western Gate and were preparing to ship the car through the non-negotiable sixty-mile stretch across the summit, he suddenly remembered he had failed to complete his purchases of an assortment of game heads at Lewis's on Lake McDonald. He professed that he couldn't round out the order by telephone; unless he personally selected his collection some grievous error might be made.

"You go on across on this train, Shirley," he said. "I telegraphed your young man that we'd be there this morning and he'll be on the lookout. Your mother and I'll dust up to the head of the lake on the bus and I'll finish up what I've got to do there and we'll be along on the Limited this evening. After being separated for a whole week you two'll probably enjoy a day together without any old folks snooping around. Meet us at the hotel tonight for a reunion."

So Shirley went on ahead. It perhaps was true that Shirley's nerves had suffered after six days spent in the companionship of a devoted mother who trailed along with yearning, grief-stricken eyes fixed on her only child—a mother who at frequent intervals sniffed mournfully and once in a while broke into low moaning and sighing sounds. Mrs. Gatling was bearing up under the blow as well as could be expected, but, even so, there had been hours when depression enveloped her as with sable trappings and at no period had she been what the kindliest of critics would call good company. Quite willingly Shirley went.

"I—I feel as though I were giving her up forever," faltered Mrs. Gatling, following with brimming eyes her daughter's departing form.

"Romola," commanded Mr. Gatling, "don't be foolish in the head. You're going to be separated from her exactly nine hours—unless the evening train's late, in which event it may be as long as nine hours and a half."

"You know what I mean, Hector."

"Don't I? Mmph!"

"But she tripped away so gaily—so gladly. It was exactly as though she wanted to leave us. And yet, Heaven knows I've tried and tried ever since that—that terrible night to show her what she means to me.... Have you got a handkerchief to spare? Mine's sopping."

"You've done more than try, Romola—you've succeeded, if that's any consolation to you. You've succeeded darned well." He stared almost regretfully down the line at the rear of an observation-car swiftly diminishing into a small square dot where the rails came together. "Since you mention it, she did look powerfully chipper and cheerful a minute ago, hustling to climb aboard that Pullman—cheerfuller than she's looked since we quit the trail last Wednesday. Lord, how I wish I could guarantee that kid was never going to have a minute's unhappiness the rest of her life!" Something remotely akin to remorse was beginning to gnaw at Mr. Gatling's heart-cockles.

Indeed, something strongly resembling remorse beset him toward the close of this day. At the station when they detrained, no Shirley was on hand to greet them; nor was there sign of Shirley's affianced. Up the slope from the tracks at the hotel a clerk wrenched himself from an importuning cluster of newly arrived tourists for long enough to tell them the numbers of their rooms and to say Miss Gatling had left word she would be awaiting them there.

So they went up under escort of two college students serving as bell-hops. Collegians as a class make indifferent bell-hops. These two deposited the hand-baggage in the living-room of the suite, accepted the customary rewards and departed. As they vanished, a bedroom door opened and out came Shirley—a crumpled, wobegone Shirley with a streaky swollen face and on her cheek the wrinkle marks where she had ground it into a wadded pillow.

"It's all right, mater," she said with a flickering trace of her usual jauntiness. "The alliance between the house of Gatling and the house of Tripler is off. So you can liven up. I'll be your substitute for such crying as is done in this family during the next day or two. I've—I've been practicing all afternoon."

She eluded the lady's outstretched arms and clung temporarily at her father's breast.

"Dad," she confessed brokenly, "I think I must have been a little bit loony these last two weeks. But, dad, I've taken the cure. It's not nice medicine and it makes you feel miserable at first but I guess it's good for what ails me.... Dad, have you seen—him?"

"Not yet." Compassion for her was mixed in with his own secret exultation, as though he tasted a sweet cake that was iced with a most bitter icing.

"Well, when you do, you'll understand. Even if he doesn't!"

"Have you told him?"

"Of course I have. Did you think I'd try to wish that little job off on you? I didn't tell him the real reason—I couldn't wound him that much. I told him I'd changed. But he—he's really the one that's changed. That's what makes it harder for me now. That's what makes it hurt so."

"Here, Romola," he said, kissing the girl and relinquishing her into her mother's grasp. "You swap tears awhile—you'll enjoy that anyhow, Romola. I've got business down-stairs—got to make some sleeper reservations for getting out of here in the morning. And as soon as we hit Pittsburgh I figure you two had better be booking up for a little swing around Europe."

The lobby below was seething—seething is the word commonly used in this connection so we might as well do so, too—was seething with Easterners who mainly had dressed as they imagined Westerners would dress, and with Westerners who mainly had dressed as they imagined Easterners would dress, the resultant effect being that nobody was fooled but everybody was pleased. Working his way through the jam on the search for a certain one, Mr. Gatling's eye almost immediately was caught by a startling color combination or rather a series of startling color combinations appertaining to an individual who stood half hidden in the protection of a column, leaning against it head down with his back to Mr. Gatling.

To begin at the top, there was, surmounting all, a smug undersized object of head-gear—at least, it would pass for head-gear—of a poisonous mustard shade. It perched high and, as it were, aloof upon the crest of its wearer's skull. Below it, where the neck had been shaved, and a good portion of the close-clipped scalp as well, a sort of crescent of pink skin blazed forth in strong contrast to an abnormally long expanse of sun-burnt surface rising above the cross-line of an exceedingly low, exceedingly shiny blue linen collar.

Straying on downward, Mr. Gatling's wondering eye was aware of a high-waisted Norfolk jacket belted well up beneath the armpits, a jacket of a tone which might not be called mauve nor yet lavender nor yet magenta but which partook subtly of all three shades—with a plaid overlay in chocolate superimposed thereon. Yet nearer the floor was revealed a pair of trousers extensively bell-bottomed and apparently designed with the intent to bring out and impress upon the casual observer the fact that their present owner had two of the most widely bowed legs on the North American continent; and finally, a brace of cloth-top shoes. Tan shoes, these were, with buttoned uppers of a pale fawn cloth, and bulldog toes. They were very new shoes, that was plain, and of an exceedingly bright and pristine glossiness.

This striking person now moved out of his shelter, his shoulders being set at a despondent hunch, and as he turned about, bringing his profile into view, Mr. Gatling recognized that the stranger was no stranger and he gave a gasp which became a choked gurgle.

"Perfect!" he muttered to himself; "absolutely perfect! Couldn't be better if I'd done it myself. And, oh Lordy, that necktie—that's the finishing stroke! Still, at that, it's a rotten shame—the poor kid!"

He hurried across, overtaking the slumping figure, and as his hand fell in a friendly slap upon one drooped shoulder the transformed cowboy flinched and turned and looked on him with two sad eyes.

"Howdy-do, sir," he said wanly. Then he braced himself and squared his back, and Mr. Gatling perceived—and was glad to note—that the youngster strove to take his heartache in a manly fashion.

"Son," said Mr. Gatling, "from what I'm able to gather I'm not going to have you for a son-in-law after all. But that's no reason why we shouldn't hook up along another line. I've been watching you off and on ever since we got acquainted and more closely since—well, since about a week ago, and it strikes me you've got some pretty good stuff in you. I've been thinking of trying a little flier in the cattle game out here—had the notion in the back of my mind for quite a while but didn't spring it until I found the party that I figure could maybe run it right. Well, I think I've found him. You're him. If you think you'd like a chance to start in as foreman or boss or superintendent or whatever you call it and maybe work up into a partnership if you showed me you had the goods, why, we'll talk it over together at dinner. The womenfolks won't be down and we can sit and powwow and I'll give you my ideas and you can give me yours."

"I'd like that fine, sir," said young Tripler.

"Good boy! I'll keep you so busy you won't have time to brood on any little disappointment that you may be suffering from now.... Say, son, don't mind my suggesting something, do you? If I was you I'd skin out of these duds you've got on and climb back into your regular working clothes—somehow, you don't seem to match the picture the way you are now."

"Why, you advised me to get 'em your own self, sir!" exclaimed the youth.

"That's right, I did, didn't I? Well, maybe you had better keep on wearing 'em." A shrewd and crafty gleam flickered under his eyelids. "You see—yes—on second thoughts, I think I want a chance to get used to you in your stylish new outfit. Promise me you'll wear 'em until noon tomorrow anyhow?"

"Yes, sir," said his victim obediently.

Mr. Gatling winked a concealed deadly wink.

A Close Shave

ON a certain day the young governor—Gov. G. W. Blankenship—left the Executive Mansion and motored up to the State Penitentiary.

As the car spun him north over good roads through the crisp morning air, he took stock of himself and of his past life and of his future prospects, nor had cause for disappointment or doubt regarding any one of these three. This was a fine large world—large yet cozy—and he gave it his unqualified indorsement while he rode along.

He took the penitentiary unawares. The warden was not expecting him. Nobody was—not even the warden's pretty, amorous little wife. Of this, his first visit to the institution since his inauguration six months before, the governor meant to make a surprise visit. An announcement sent on ahead would have meant preparations for his arrival—an official reception and a speeding-up of the machinery. His design was to see how the place looked in, as you might say, its week-day clothes.

It looked pretty good. After a painstaking inspection he was bound to conclude that, for a prison, this prison came very near to being a model prison. The management was efficient, that was plain to be seen. The discipline, so far as he might judge, was strict without being cruel.

The climax to a very satisfactory forenoon came, when the warden at the end of the tour invited him to stay for luncheon.

"It'll just be a simple meal, Governor," said Warden Riddle, "with nobody else there except Mrs. Riddle. But I'd mightily like to have you take pot-luck with us."

"Well, I believe I will do just that very thing," said Governor Blankenship, heartily. Privately he was much pleased. "That is, if I'm not putting your household out on my account?"

"Of course not," stated Riddle. "I'll just chase a trusty across the road to tell the missis to put a third plate on the table—that's all that's necessary." He spoke with the pride of a contented husband in a well-ordered home.

"Then I'll get in my car and go find a barber shop," said the governor, sliding the palm of his hand across his chin. "I started up country so soon after breakfast this morning that I forgot to shave."

"No need for you to do that," Riddle told him. "Don't you remember seeing the little shop over back of the main building—not the big shop where the inmates are trimmed up, the little one where the staff have their barbering done? We've got a lifer over there who's a wiz' at his trade. I'll guarantee you'll get as good a shave from him as you ever had in your life, Governor."

So, escorted by the warden, Governor Blankenship recrossed the enclosure to a wing behind the infirmary. From the doorway of a small, neat shop, properly equipped and spotlessly clean, the warden addressed the lone occupant, a young man in convict gray.

"Shave this gentleman right away," he ordered. "A good quick job."

"Yes, sir," replied the prisoner.

"You needn't wait, Warden," said the governor. "I'll rejoin you in your office in a few minutes."

The warden accordingly departed, the barber closing the door behind him. The governor climbed into the chair and was tilted back. A crisp cloth was tucked about his collar, warm, soft suds were applied to his face and deft fingers kneaded the soap and rubbed it in among the hair roots, then the razor began mowing with smooth, even strokes over the governor's jowls—first one jowl, then the other. This much was done in a silence broken only by the gentle scraping sound of the steel against the bristles.

It was the convict who spoke first, thereby violating a prison rule. He had finished with his subject's jaws; the razor hovered above the Adam's apple.

"I know you," he said coldly; "you're the governor."

"Yes," said his Excellency, "I am."

"Then you ought to recognize me, too," continued the barber. "Take a look!"

Slightly startled, Governor Blankenship blinked and peered upward into a face that was bent just above his own face.

"No," he said, "I don't believe I remember you. Where did we ever meet before?"

"In a courtroom," said the prisoner, "in a courtroom at — —," he named the principal city of the state, which also was the city where the governor held his citizenship. "You prosecuted me—you sent me here."

All at once his voice grew shaky with passion; his features, which until now he had held in a composed blank, became distorted—a twisted mask of hatred.

Sudden apprehension stirred inside the young governor. He made as though to straighten up. A strong hand pressing on his breast kept him down, though.

"Stay still!" commanded the convict. "You haven't got a chance. I locked the door there when the head-screw left. And don't try to yell for help, either—I can take that head of yours off your shoulders at one swipe. Stay still and listen to me."

As white under the patchings of lather as the lather was—yes, whiter—Governor Blankenship lay there, rigid with a great fear, and hearkened as his tormentor went on:

"Probably you wouldn't remember me. Why should you? I was just one of the poor stiffs you persecuted when you were district attorney, building up the record that landed you in the governor's chair. 'Blood Hound' Blankenship—that's what they called you. And how you worked to put me away! Well, you had your wish. Here I am, in for keeps. And here you are, helpless as a baby, and a sharp razor right against your neck. Feel it, don't you? I'll make you feel it!"

The stricken man felt it, pressing at his throat, fraying the skin, ready to slice downward into his crawling flesh. The mere touch of it seemed to paralyze his vocal cords. He strove to speak, but for the life of him—and his life was the stake, he realized that—he couldn't get the words out.

In a terrible relentless monotone the torturer went on:

"I don't so much blame the judge—he seemed almost sorry for me when he was hanging the sentence on me. And I don't blame the jury, either. But you—what you said about me, the way you went at me on cross-examination, the names you called me when you were summing up! I swore then that if ever I got a chance at you I'd fix you. And now I've got my chance—and I've got you right where I want you!"

"Wait—for God's sake, wait!" In a strangled frenzied gurgle the helpless man pumped forth the entreaty.

"Why should I wait? They don't have capital punishment any more in this state. All they can do is pile another life term on the one I'm already doing."

"But wait—oh, please wait! I do seem to remember you now. Maybe—maybe I was too severe. If I took your case under advisement—if I pardoned you—if-if—" He was begging so hard that he babbled.

The pressure of that deadly thing at his throat was relaxed the least bit.

"Now you're getting reasonable," said the lifer. "I thought the thing I wanted most in the world was to kill you. But after four years here, liberty would be pretty sweet too. There's one thing they've always said about you—that you keep your word. Swear you'll keep your trap shut about what's happened in this shop today, and on top of that swear to me you'll turn me out of here, and you can go!"

On these terms then the bargain was struck. The governor, having given his promise, had a good shave, twice over, with witch-hazel for a lotion, and having somewhat mastered his jumping nerves and regained his customary dignity, went home with the warden for luncheon.

From the foot of the table, little Mrs. Riddle shot covert smiles at him—and soft languishing glances. There was meaningness in her manner, in her caressing voice. Her husband talked along, suspecting nothing. He thought—if he gave it a thought—that she was flattered at having the governor at her board. As for the governor, even in his shaken state he had a secret glowing within.

As he was leaving, he remarked in a casual tone to his host:

"That pet barber of yours—Wyeth, I believe his name is. He interested me—aroused my sympathy, in fact."

"My wife feels the same way about him," said the warden. "But then, you know how women are. He's young and well-mannered and she's full of kindness for every human being."

"Then probably she'd be pleased in case—*h'm*—in case I should grant him a pardon?"

Warden Riddle gave a start.

"She might," he said, "but nobody else would. Governor, take it from me, that fellow's bad all the way through. And the crime that landed him here—a cold-blooded, brutal murder—it was an atrocious thing, utterly unprovoked. No mitigating circumstances whatsoever, just plain butchery.

Governor, as your friend I beg you, don't be swept off your feet by any rush of misguided sentimentality for such a wretch. To turn him loose would kill you politically. You're in line to be our next United States Senator. Already they're saying over the country that you're Presidential timber. There's no telling how high or how far you'll go if only you don't make some fatal mistake. And this—this would be fatal. It would rouse the whole state against you. It would destroy you, not only with the party but with the people. You know what ruined your predecessor—he made too free a use of the pardoning power. Governor, if you let that man loose on society, you're wrecked."

That night, back at the Executive Mansion, the bachelor governor slept not a wink.

Was ever a man strung between the horns of a worse dilemma? Warden Riddle had been right. To open the prison doors for so infamous a creature as Wyeth was, would be damnation for all his ambitions. And Governor Blankenship was as ambitious as he was godly. And probably no more godly man ever lived. On the other hand, he had given his pledge to Wyeth.

There was this about Governor Blankenship: he had been named for the father of his country—that man who could not tell a lie. And, wittingly, Governor Blankenship had never in all his blameless life told a lie either. To keep the faith with himself and the world, to wear truth like a badge shining upon his breast, had from boyhood been his dearest ideal. Off that course he never intentionally had departed. With him it was more than a code of ethics and more than a creed of personal conduct—it was the holiest of religions. He unreservedly believed that one guilty falsehood—just one—would consign his soul to the bottommost pit of perdition forever. Here was a real Sir Galahad, a perfect knight of perfect honor.

Through days and weeks he walked between two invisible but ever-present mentors. One of them, whose name was Expediency, constantly tempted him.

"You passed your word under duress and in mortal fear," Expediency whispered in his ear. "Let that man rot in his cell. 'Tis his just desert."

But the other counselor, called Conscience, as repeatedly said to him: "You never told a lie. Can you tell one now?"

In such grievous plight, he received a secret message, sent by underground from Wyeth.

"I'm getting impatient," was Wyeth's word. "Are you, or are you not, going to come clean?"

This enhanced his desperation. From sleeplessness, from gnawing worry he lost flesh. People about him said the noble young governor was not like himself any more. They predicted a breakdown unless he was cured of what hidden cause it was which distressed him.

One morning he rose, haggard and red-eyed, from the bed upon which since midnight he had tossed and rolled. He had made his decision. Selfishness had won. He would break his promise to Wyeth. But since he must go to eternal Hell for a lie, he would go there for another and a sweeter reason.

Until now, his romantic dealings with little Mrs. Riddle had been mild and harmless, if clandestinely conducted. He had not philandered with her; he merely had flirted. On his side it had been an innocent flirtation—an agreeable diversion. But he knew the lady's mind—knew she was weak and willing, where he had been strong and straightforward.

So be it then. For a crown to his other and lesser iniquity he would corrupt the wife of his devoted friend.

For the first time in a month he had zest for his breakfast. Conscience was so thoroughly drugged she seemed as though dead.

From the table he went to the long-distance telephone. He would call her up and arrange for an assignation. There was considerable delay in establishing the connection—a buzzing over the wire, a confusion of vague sounds. Finally his ringing was answered by a strange voice.

"I wish to speak with Mrs. Riddle," he said.

There was a little pause. Then, in a fumbling, evasive fashion the voice made reply.

"She's not here. She's—she's out."

It occurred to the governor that he might as well tell the warden he had abandoned the idea of pardoning the barber.

"Then I'd like to talk with Mr. Riddle," he said.

"He's—he's not here either. Who is this, please?"

In his double disappointment the governor forgot the possible need for caution. "This," he said, "is Governor Blankenship."

"Oh!" The voice became warmer. "Is that you, Governor? I've been trying for an hour to get you on your private line. This is Warden Riddle's brother at the 'phone—you know, Henry Riddle? They got me up at daylight when this—this terrible thing was discovered, and I've been here ever since, doing what I could."

"What terrible thing do you mean?"

"Haven't you heard the news? Why, sir, the worst man in the penitentiary got away last night—Wyeth, the desperado. He—he had help. That's why the warden's away, why I'm in charge. My poor brother's out with the posse trying to get trace of the scoundrel. I guess he'll shoot him if he finds him."

"But why is Mrs. Riddle absent at such a time?"

"Governor, that's the worst part of it. She was the one that helped that devil to escape. And she—she went with him!"

To the end of his days Governor G. W. Blankenship was known as the man who never told a lie. When he died they carved something to that general effect upon his tombstone.

Good Sam

FROM the foot of the lake where most of the camps were, everybody had been driven out by the forest-fire. Among those who fled up to our end and took temporary quarters on the hotel reservation was my friend, the Native Genius.

My friend, the Native Genius, was a cowboy before he became a painter. He became a great man and was regarded in our Eastern art circles, but in his feelings and his language he remained a cowboy. He also was an historian of the folk-lore of the Old West that has ridden over the ultimate hill of the last free grazing and vanished forever and ever, alas! With none of the conscious effort which so often marks such an undertaking, he could twine a fragrant fictional boscage upon the solid trellis of remembered fact and make you like it. To my way of thinking, this was not the least of his gifts. Indeed not.

He joined us the evening before, bringing the tools of his trade and various finished or unfinished canvases. During the night my slumber was at intervals distracted by the far-off wails of a wind-instrument in travail. It was as though someone, enraged by its stubborn defiance, had put the thing to the torture. Distance muffled those moaning outcries but in them, piercing through the curtains of my sleepiness, were torment and anguish.

In the morning early, when I walked past the row of log houses at the farther side of the grounds, I came upon the author of this outrage. A male of the refugees sat at an open window and contended with a haunted saxophone for the lost soul of a ghostly tune.

He was young enough to have optimism. On the other hand, he was old enough to know better. He had the look about him—a wearied and red-eyed and a wannish look it was—of one who never knows when he is licked. Except among amateur musicians I would regard this as an admirable trait.

My friend was squatted on the top step of his cabin, two numbers on beyond. He greeted me and the new-born day with a wide yawn.

"Would you maybe like to buy a horn?" he asked, and flirted with his thumb toward the place next-door-but-one.

"I don't think so," I answered.

"I'm making a special inducement," he said. "There's a man's hide goes with it."

His mien changed then from the murderous to the resigned. "Lead me away from here," he pleaded. "I don't know which distresses me the most—the sight of so much suffering or the sound of it."

We went by the scene of the unfinished crime and sat in the lee of the hotel veranda with the lake below us, blinking like a live turquoise in its rough matrix of gray mountains. The wind was in our favor there; to our ears reached only faint broken strains of that groaning and that bleating. But from other sources other interruptions ensued, all calculated to disturb the pious reflections of the elderly.

A domestic group, exercising rights of squatter sovereignty on the slope of the lawn in a tent, emerged therefrom and swarmed about us. Of parents there was but the customary pair, but of offspring there were seven or eight and although plainly of the same brood, a family resemblance marking each as brother or sister to the rest, these latter seemed miraculously all to be of substantially the same age or thereabouts. The father told a neighbor fifty yards away of their narrow escape; the mother joined in and was shrill in her lamentations for a threatened homestead over the hills across the water; the overalled little ones got underfoot and scuffled around and by their loud childish clamor still further interfered with our ruminations.

Then one of the big red busses hooted and drove up and disgorged upon us a locust plague of arriving tourists. The responsible strangers went within to claim reservations but the juveniles inundated the porches and the lawn, giving hearty indorsement to the scenery and taking snap-shots of it, and inquiring where souvenir postcards might be had and whether the fishing was any good here; and so on and so forth, according to their tribal habits. Hillocks of hand-baggage accumulated about us and trunks descended from a panting auto-truck in a thunderous cascade. A bobbed-haired camera bandit in search of picturesque local types came within easy shooting distance and aimed her weapon at us, asking no leave of her victims but shooting repeatedly at will; and she wore riding breeches and boots. Presumably she had been wearing them aboard the train. An oversized youth stumbled with his large undisciplined feet against an outlying suitcase and struck the wall and caromed off and almost upset us from our tilted chairs. Here plainly was an undergraduate—a perfect characteristic specimen. He was in the immature summer plumage.

"I always feel sorry for one of those college boys this season of the year in this climate," said my friend as the gigantic fledgling lunged away toward the boat dock. "It's too late for his coon-skin ulster and too early yet for him to tie a handkerchief around his scalp and go bareheaded."

He arose, tagging me on the arm.

"Let's ramble down the line a piece," he suggested, "and maybe find us a hollow snag to hide in. After what I went through last night my nerves ain't what they used to be, if they ever were."

Below the creek we quit the paved highway and took the lower trail. Through the brush we could see where the vast blue eye of the lake had quit winking and was beginning to scowl. The wind must have changed quarters; it no longer brought us smells of ashes and char, but a fresher, sweeter smell as of rain gathering; and puffed clouds were forming over the range to the westward. The sunshine shut itself off with the quickness of a stage effect. Along the shore toward us limped a blackened smudge of a man, like a ranger turned chimney-sweep. For a fact, that precisely was what he was—Melber, assistant chief of the park forestry service. From tiredness he was crippled. He could shamble and that was about all.

"Well, we've got her whipped," he told us, and leaned against a tree. He left smears like burnt cork on the bark where his shoulders rubbed. "This breeze hauling around ought to finish the job. She'll burn herself out before dark, with or without showers. I'm on my way now to long-distance to notify the chief that we won't need any reinforcements."

"Much damage?"

"The colony is saved. By backfiring we held the flames on the upper edge of the road leading in from the station. But Ordman's ranch is gone up in smoke, and the Colfax & Webster sawmill and eighteen thousand acres of the handsomest virgin pine on this side of the Divide. Man, you'd weep to see those raped woodlands—and all because some dam'-fool hiker didn't have sense enough to put out his cigarette! Or hers, as the case may be!" He grinned through his mask and we were reminded of nigger minstrels.

"How close up did the burning get to my shebang?" inquired the Native Genius.

"Dog-gone close, Charley. But that wasn't the big blaze—that was the other blaze which broke out soon after midnight. We got her—the second one, I mean—licked just over the rise behind your studio. My force fought till they dropped and even that bunch of I.W.W.'s that they rushed in on the special from Spokane did fairly well. I've revised some of my opinions about Wobblies. But there's a million dead cinders in the grass around your cottage right now, Charley. And your back corral fence is all scorched.

"I leave it to you—wouldn't you think with that first example before our eyes that everybody in both gangs would have sense enough not to be careless? But you never can tell, can you? When most of the crew knocked off late last night, seeing she was under control, one idiot builds a fire to heat himself up a pot of coffee. Would you believe it?—with the timber all just so much punk and tinder after this long dry spell, he kindles up a rousing big blaze right among the down-stuff and then drops off to sleep? I don't much blame him for wanting to sleep—I'm dead on my own feet this minute—but to make a fire that size in such a place! He's the kind that would call out the standing army to kill a cockroach! Well, when this poor half-wit wakes up, the fire is running through the tree-tops for a quarter of a mile south of him and we've got another battle on our hands that lasts until broad daybreak. It's a God's blessing we had the outfit and the emergency apparatus handy."

"Who's the guilty party?"

"Not one of my staff, you can gamble on that. And not one of the Spokane gang either. It was a green hand—fellow named Seymour working as a brakeman on the railroad and one of the few volunteers who refused to take any pay. And he was square enough to own up to what he'd done, too. Oh, I guess he had good intentions. But, thunderation, good intentions have ruined empires!

"Well, I've got to be getting along. I'm certainly going to put somebody's nice clean bathroom on the bum as soon as I get through telephoning."

Melber straightened himself and lurched off into the second-growth. He moved like a very old man, his blistered hands dangling.

"What he just now said about good intentions puts me in mind of Samson Goodhue," said Charley. "There was one of the best paving contractors Hell ever had." I knew what the expression on his face meant. It meant he was letting down a mental tentacle like a baited hook into the thronged private fish-pool of his early reminiscence. Scenting copy, I encouraged him.

"What about this Samson person?"

"I'm fixing to tell you," he promised. "This looks to me like a good loafing place."

We reposed side by side on a lichened log with our toes gouging the green moss, and he rolled a cigarette and proceeded:

Like I was just now telling you, his name was Samson Goodhue. So you can see how easy it was to twist that around into Good Samaritan and then to render that down for kitchen use into Good Sam. It was a regular trick name and highly suitable, seeing that he counted that day lost which, as the poet says, its low descending sun didn't find him trying to help somebody out of a jam.

In fact, he really made a profession out of it. You might say he was an expert promoter. He wasn't one of your meek and lowly ones, though.

They say the meek shall inherit the earth but I reckon not until everybody else is through with it.

Not Good Sam. He was just as pushing and determined and persisting in his work as though he was taking orders for enlarging crayon portraits. And probably it wasn't his fault that about every time he tackled a job of philanthropping the scheme seemed to go wrong. You had to give him credit for that. But after a while it got so that when the word spread that Good Sam was going around doing good, smart people ran for cover. They didn't know but what it might be their turn next, and they figured they'd had enough hard luck already without calling in a specialist.

I remember like it was yesterday the first time I ever saw him operating—down in Triple Falls, this state. I hadn't been there very long. Winter-time had driven a bunch of us beef-herders in off the range and we were encouraging the saloon industry—in fact, you might say we were practically supporting it. That was before I quit. I haven't taken a drink for fifteen years now but, at that, I figure I'm even with the game. The day I quit I had enough to last me fifteen years.

Good Sam hadn't been there much longer than we had. He blew in from somewhere back East and to look at him you'd have said offhand that here was just an average pilgrim, size sixteen-and-a-half collar, three-dollar pants, addicted to five-cent cigars and a drooping mustache; otherwise no distinguishing marks. He didn't look a thing in the world like a genius. His gifts were hidden. But it didn't take him long to begin showing them.

One bright cold morning Whiz Bollinger came in from his place proudly riding in a brand-new buckboard that had cost him thirty-two dollars, and right in front of Billy Grimm's filling-station the cayuse he was driving balked on him. You understand I'm speaking of a filling-station in the old-fashioned sense. We'd read about automobiles and seen pictures of them but they hadn't penetrated to our parts as yet. If a fellow was going somewhere by himself he generally rode a hoss and if he was moving his womenfolks he packed 'em in a prairie-schooner. Sometimes he'd let 'em live in one for a few years so they could have constant change of scene and air. I recall one day a bunch of old-timers were discussing the merits of different wagons—Old Hickory and South Bend and even Conestoga—and old Mar'm Whitaker spoke up and says: "Well, boys, I always have claimed and always will that the Murphey wagon is the best one they is for raisin' a family in."

So Billy Grimm's sign was a pile of empty beer kegs racked up alongside the front door. Sometimes in mild weather he'd have another sign—some wayfarer that had been overtaken just as he got outside and was sleeping it off on the sidewalk. After the first of November all the flies in the state that didn't have anywhere else to go went to Billy's place and wintered there. He was Montana's leading house-fly fancier. He was getting his share of my patronage and I happened to be on the spot when this Bollinger colt decided to stop right where he was and stay there until he froze solid.

You know how it is when a hoss goes balky. In less than no time at all the entire leisure class of Triple Falls were assembled, giving advice about how to get that hoss started again. They twisted his ear and they tried stoving in his ribs by kicking him in the side and they pushed against his hind quarters and dragged at the bit, and through it all that wall-eyed, Roman-nosed plug remained just as stationary as an Old Line Republican. Alongside of him, the Rock of Gibraltar would seem downright restless.

And then this Samson Goodhue comes bulging into the circle and takes charge. "Stand back, everybody, please," he says, "while I show you how to unbalk a horse. Get me a few pieces of kindling wood, somebody," he says, "and some paper or some straw or something." Various persons hurry off in all directions, eager to obey. In every crowd there are plenty of suckers who'll carry out any kind of orders if somebody who acts executive will give them. So when they've assembled his supplies for him he makes a little pile of 'em on the packed snow right under the cayuse's belly and is preparing to scratch a match and telling Whiz Bollinger to climb back on his seat and take a strong grip on the reins, when Mrs. Oliver J. Doheny, who's among the few ladies present, interferes with the proceedings.

Now this here Mrs. Oliver J. Doheny is at that remote period our principal reform element. She's 'specially strong on cruelty to dumb beasts, being heartily against it. It's only been a few weeks before this that a trapper trails down from across the international boundary with one of those big Canada bobcats that he's caught in a trap and he's got it on exhibition in a cage in Hyman Frieder's Climax Clothing Store, when Mrs. Doheny happens along and sees how the thing sort of drags one foot where the trap pinched it and she begins tongue-lashing the Canuck for not having bound up its wounds.

When she's slowed down for breath he says to her very politely: "Ma'am, in reply to same I would just state this: Ma'am, when my dear old mother was layin' on her death-bed she called me to her side and she whispered to me, 'My son, whatever else you do do, don't you never try to nurse no sick lynxes.' And, ma'am, I aim to keep that farewell promise to my dear dyin' mother! But I ain't no objections to your tryin'. Only, ma'am, I feels it my Christian duty to warn you right now that if you would get too close to this here unfortunate patient of mine he's liable to turn you every way you can think of except loose."

So on that occasion Mrs. Doheny thought better of her first impulse but now she is very harsh toward this stranger. "Do you mean to tell me," she says, "that it is your deliberate intention to ignite a fire beneath this poor misguided animal's—er—person?" Although a born reformer she was always very ladylike in her language.

"That, madam," he says, "is the broad general idea."

"How dare you!" she says. Then she says it again: "How dare you! Think of the poor brute's agony!" she says.

"Madam," he says right back at her, "you do me a grave injustice. Not for worlds would I inflict suffering upon any living creature. The point is, madam, that the instant this here chunk of obstinacy feels the heat singeing of him he will move. Observe, madam!" And before she can say anything more he has lighted the match and stuck it in the paper and the flames shoot up and, just as he's predicted, Whiz Bollinger's balked cayuse responds to the appeal to a dormant better nature.

You never saw a horse move forward more briskly or more willingly than that one did. There was just one drawback to the complete success of the plan and, as everybody agreed afterwards when the excitement had died down and there was time for sober reason, this Goodhue party as we called him then, or Good Sam as we took to calling him afterwards, couldn't really be held responsible for that. The hoss moved forward but he stopped again when he'd gone just exactly far enough for the fire to get a good chance at Whiz's shiny beautiful new buckboard, which it blazed up like a summer hotel, the paint being fresh and him having only that morning touched up the springs with coal-oil. A crate of celluloid hair combs burning up couldn't have thrown off any prettier sparks or more of them. Before the volunteer fire department could put their uniforms on and get there that ill-fated buckboard was a total loss with no insurance.

This was Good Sam's first appearance amongst us in, as you might say, a business capacity. It wasn't long, though, before he was offering us more and more and still more evidences of his injurious good toward afflicted humanity. It was no trouble to show samples. With that misguided zealot it amounted to a positive passion.

For instance, one night in December little Al Wingate came into Billy Grimm's where a gang of us were doing our Christmas shopping early and, as usual when he had a load aboard, he was leaking tears and lamentations with every faltering step he took. Talk about your crying jags, when this here Little Al got going he had riparian rights. It made you wonder where he kept his reservoirs hid at, him not weighing more than about ninety pounds and being short-waisted besides. Maybe he had hydraulic legs; I don't know. Likewise always on such occasions, which they were frequent, he acted low and suicidal in his mind. He was our official melancholi*hic*.

So he drifted in out of the starry night and leaned up against the bar, and between sobs he says to Billy Grimm, "Billy," he says, "have you got any real deadly poison round here?"

"Only the regular staple brands," says Billy. "What'll it be—rye or Bourbon?"

"Billy," he says, "don't trifle with a man that's already the same as dead. Licker has been my curse and downfall. It's made me what I am tonight. Look at me—no good to myself or anybody else on this earth. Just a poor derelick without a true friend on this earth. But this is the finish with me. I've said that before but now I mean it. Before tomorrow morning I'm going to end everything. If one of you boys won't kindly trust me with a pistol I'd be mighty much obliged to somebody for the loan of a piece of rope about six or seven or eight feet long. Just any little scrap of rope that you happen to have handy will do me," he says.

I put in my oar. "Why, you poor little worthless sawed-off-and-hammered-down," I says to him, "don't try to hang yourself without you slip an anvil into the seat of your pants first."

One of the other boys—Rawhide Rawlings, I think it was—speaks up also and says, "And don't try jumping off a high roof, neither; you'd only go up!"

You see we were acquainted with Little Al's peculiarities and we knew he didn't mean a word he said, and so we were just aiming to cheer him up. But Good Sam, who'd joined our little group of intense drinkers only a few minutes before, he didn't enter into the spirit of it at all. He motioned to us to come on down to the other end of the rail and he asks us haven't we got any sympathy for a fellow being that's sunk so deep in despondency he's liable to drown himself in his own water-works plant any minute?

"You don't want to be prodding him that-away," he says; "what you want to do is humor him along. You want to lead him so close up to the Pearly Gates that he can hear the hinges creaking; that'll make him see things different," he says. "That'll scare him out of this delusion of his that he wants to be a runt angel."

"I suppose then you think you could cure him yourself?" asks one of the gang.

"In one easy lesson," says Good Sam, speaking very confident. "All I ask from you gents is for one of you to let me borrow his six-gun off of him for a little while and then everybody agree to stand back and not interfere. If possible I'd like for it to be a big unhealthy-looking six-gun," he says.

Well, that sounded plausible enough. So Rawhide passes over his belt, which it's got an old-fashioned single-action Colt's swinging in its holster, and Good Sam buckles this impressive chunk of hardware around him and meanders back to where Little Al is humped up with his shoulders heaving and his face in his hands and a little puddle forming on the bar from the salty tears oozing out of his system and running down his chin and falling off.

"My poor brother," says Good Sam, in a very gentle way like a missionary speaking, "are you really in earnest about feeling a deep desire to quit this here vale of tears?"

"I sure am," says Little Al; "it's the one ambition I've got left."

"And I don't blame you none for it neither," says Good Sam. "What's life but a swindle anyhow—a brace game—that nobody ever has beaten yet? And look at the fix you're in—too big for a midget in a side-show and too little for other laudable purposes. No sir, I don't blame you a bit. And just to show you my heart's in the right place I'm willing to accommodate you."

"That's all I'm craving," says Little Al. "Just show me how—ars'nic or a gun or the noose or a good sharp butcher-knife, I ain't particular. If it wasn't for the river being frozen over solid I wouldn't be worrying you for that much help," he says.

"Now hold on, listen here," says Good Sam, "you mustn't do it that way—not with your own hands."

"How else am I going to do it, then?" says Little Al, acting surprised.

"Why, I'm going to do it for you myself," says Good Sam, "and don't think I'm putting myself out on your account neither. Why, it won't be any trouble—you might almost say it'll be a pleasure to me. Because if you should go and commit suicide you'll be committing a mortal sin that you won't never get forgiveness for. But if I plug you, you ain't responsible, are you? I've already had to kill seven or eight fellows in my time," says this amiable liar of a Good Sam, "or maybe the correct count is nine; I forget sometimes. Anyhow, one more killin' on my soul won't make a particle of difference with me. And to bump off a party that's actually aching to be done so, one that'll thank me with his last expiring breath for the favor— why, brother," he says, "it *will* be a pleasure! Just come on with me," he says, "and we can get this little matter over and done with in no time at all."

With that he leads the way to a little shack of a room that Billy Grimm's got behind his saloon. Al follows along but I observe he's quit weeping all of a sudden and likewise it looks to me like he's lost or is losing considerable of his original enthusiasm. He's beginning to sort of hang back and lag behind by the time they've got to the doorway, and he casts a sort of pitiful imploring look backwards over his shoulder; but Good Sam takes him by the arm and leads him on in and closes the door behind them. The rest of us wait a minute and then tiptoe up to the door and put our ears close to the crack and listen.

First we hear a match being struck. "Now then, that's the ticket," we hear Good Sam say very cheerfully; "we don't want to take any chances on messing this job up by trying to do it in the dark." So from that we know he's lighted the coal-oil lamp that's in there. Then he says: "Wait till I open this here back window, so's to let the smoke out—these old black powder cartridges are a blamed nuisance, going off inside a house." There's a sound of a sash being raised. "Suppose you sit down here on this beer box and make yourself comfortable," is what Good Sam says next. There's a scuffling sound from Little Al's feet dragging across the floor. "No, that won't hardly do," goes on Good Sam, "sitting down all caved in the way you are now, I'd only gut-shoot you and probably you'd linger and suffer and I'd have to plug you a second time. I'd hate to botch you all up, I would so.

"Tell you what, just stand up with your arms down at your sides.... There, that's better, brother. No, it ain't neither! I couldn't bear afterwards to think of that forlorn look out of your eyes. The way they looked out of their eyes is the only thing that ever bothers me in connection with several of the fellows I've had to shoot heretofore. Maybe you'll think I'm morbid but things like that certainly do prey on a fellow's mind afterward—if he's kind-hearted which, without any flattery, I may say I'm built that way. So while I hate to keep pestering you with orders when you're hovering on the very brink of eternity, won't you please just turn around so you'll have your back to me? Thank you kindly, that'll do splendid. Now you stay perfectly still and I'll count three, kind of slow, and when I get to 'three' I'll let you have it slick as a whistle right between the shoulders.... *One!*" And we can hear that old mule's ear of a hammer on that six-gun go *click, click.* Then: "*Two-o-o!*... Steady, don't wiggle or you're liable to make me nervous.... *Thr—*"

Somebody lets out the most gosh-awful yell you ever heard and we shove the door open just in time to see Little Al sailing out of that window, head first, like a bird on the wing; and then we heard a hard thump on the frozen ground 'way down below, followed by low moaning sounds. In his hurry Little Al must have plumb forgot that while Billy Grimm's saloon was flush with the street in front, at the far end it was scaffolded up over a hollow fifteen or twenty feet deep.

So we swarmed down the back steps and picked him up and you never saw a soberer party in your life than what that ex-suicider was, or one that was gladder to see a rescue party arrive. Soon as he got his wind back he clung to us, pleading with us to protect him from that murdering scoundrel of a man-killer and demanding to know what kind of a fellow he was not to be able to take a joke, and stating that he'd had a close call which it certainly was going to be a lesson to him, and so on. Pretty soon after that he began to take note that he was hurting all over. You wouldn't have believed that a man who wasn't over five-feet-two could be bunged up and bruised up in so many different localities as Little Al was. Even his hair was sore to the touch.

When he got so he could hobble around he joined an organization which up until then it'd only had one other charter member in good standing, the same being Whiz Bollinger, former owner and chief mourner of that there late-lamented buckboard. It was a club with just one by-law—which was entertaining a profound distrust for Samson Goodhue, Esquire—but there were quite a good many strong rich cuss-words in the ritual.

Still, any man who devotes himself to the public welfare is bound to accumulate a few detractors as he goes along. Good Sam went booming ahead like as if there wasn't a private enemy on his list or a cloud in his sky. He'd do this or that or the other thing always, mind you, with the highest and the purest motives and every pop it would turn out wrong. Was he discouraged? Did he throw up his hands and quit in the face of accumulating ingratitude? Not so as to be visible to the naked eye. The milk of human kindness that was sloshing about inside of him appeared to be absolutely curdle-proof. I wish I knew his private formula—I could invent a dandy patent churn.

Let's see, now, what was his next big outstanding failure? I'm passing over the little things such as him advising Timber-Line Hance about what was the best way to encourage a boil on his neck that wouldn't come to a head and getting the medicines mixed in his mind and recommending turpentine instead of hog-lard. I'm trying to pick out the high points in his career. Let's see? Now I've got it. Along toward spring, when the thaws set in, somebody told him how Boots Darnell and Babe Louder had been hived up all winter in a shanty up on the Blue Shell with nobody to keep them company except each other, and how Babe was laid up with a busted leg and Boots couldn't leave him except to run their traps. So nothing would do Good Sam but what he must put out to stay a couple of days with that lonesome pair and give 'em the sunshine of his presence.

They welcomed him with open arms and made him right to home in their den, such as it was. I ought to tell you before we go any further that this here Babe and this here Boots were a couple of simple-minded, kind-hearted old coots that had been baching it together for going on fifteen or twenty years. It was share and share alike with those two. Living together so long, they got so they divided their thoughts. One would know what was on the other's mind before he said it and would finish the sentence for him. They'd actually split a word when it was a word running into extra syllables. "Well, I'll be dad—" Boots would say; "—gummed," Babe would add, signifying that they were going partners even on the dad-gumming. Their conversation would put you in mind of one of these here anthems.

They certainly were glad to see Good Sam. In honor of the occasion Boots cooked up a muskrat stew and made a batch of sour-dough biscuits for supper and Babe sat up in his bunk and told his favorite story which Boots had already heard it probably two or three million times already but carried on like he enjoyed it. They showed him their catch of pelts and, taking turn and turn about, they told him how they'd been infested all winter by a worthless stray hound-dog. It seems this hound-dog happened along one day and adopted them and he'd been with 'em ever since and he'd just naturally made their life a burden to them—getting in the way and breeding twice as many fleas as he needed for his own use and letting them have the overflow; and so on.

But they said his worst habit was his appetite. He was organized inside like a bottomless pit, so they said. If they took him along with them he'd scare all the game out of the country by chasing it but never caught any; and if they left him behind locked up in the cabin he'd eat a side of meat or a pack-saddle or something before they got back. A set of rawhide harness was just a light snack to him, they said—sort of an appetizer. And his idea of a pleasant evening was to sit on his haunches and howl two or three hours on a stretch with a mournful enthusiasm and after he did go to sleep he'd have bad dreams and howl some more without waking up, but they did. Altogether, it seemed he had more things about him that you wouldn't care for than a relative by marriage.

They said, speaking in that overlapping way of theirs, that they'd prayed to get shut of him but didn't have any luck. So Good Sam asked them why somebody hadn't just up and killed him. And they hastened to state that they were both too tender-hearted for that. But if he felt called upon to take the job of being executioner off their hands, the hound being a stranger to him and he not a member of the family as was the case with them, why, they'd be most everlastingly grateful. And he said he would do that very little trick first thing in the morning.

Now, of course, the simplest and the quickest and the easiest way would have been for Good Sam to toll the pup outdoors and bore him with Boots' old rifle. But no, that wouldn't do. As he explained to them, he was sort of tender himself when it came to taking life, but I judge the real underlying reason was that he liked to go to all sorts of pains and complicate the machinery when he was working at being a philanthropist. Soon as supper was over he reared back to figure on a plan and all at once his eye lit on a box of dynamite setting over in a corner. During the closed season on fur those two played at being miners.

"I've got it now," he told them. "I'll take a stick of that stuff there with me and I'll lead this cussed dog along with me and take him half a mile up the bottoms and fasten him to a tree with a piece of line. Then I'll hitch a time-fuse onto the dynamite and tie the dynamite around his neck with another piece of rope and leave him there. Pretty soon the fuse will burn down and the dynamite will go off—*kerblooie!*—and thus without pain or previous misgivings that unsuspecting canine will be totally abolished. But the most beautiful part of it is that nobody—you nor me neither—will be a witness to his last moments."

So they complimented him on being so smart and so humane at the same time and said they ought to have thought up the idea themselves only they didn't have the intellect for it—they admitted that, too—and after he'd sopped up their praise for a while and felt all warm and satisfied, they turned in, and peace and quiet reigned in that cabin until daylight, except for some far-and-wide snoring and the dog having a severe nightmare under the stove about two-thirty A. M.

Up to a certain point the scheme worked lovely. Having established the proper connections between the dog and the tree, the fuse and the dynamite, Good Sam is gamboling along through the slush on his way back and whistling a merry tune, when all of a sudden his guiding spirit makes him look back behind him—and here comes that pup! He's either pulled loose from the rope or else he's eaten it up—it would be more like him to eat it. But the stick of dynamite is dangling from his neck and the fuse is spitting little sparks.

Good Sam swings around and yells at the animal to go away and he grabs up a chunk of wood and heaves it at him. But the dog thinks that's only play and he keeps right on coming, with his tail wagging in innocent amusement and his tongue hanging out like a pink plush necktie and his eyes shining with gratefulness for the kind gentleman who's gone to all the trouble of thinking up this new kind of game especially on his account. So then Good Sam lights out, running for the cabin, and the dog, still entering heartily into the sport, takes after him and begins gaining at every jump. It's a close race and getting closer all the time and no matter which one of 'em finishes first it looks like a mortal cinch that neither winner nor loser is going to be here to enjoy his little triumph afterwards.

Inside the cabin Boots and Babe hear the contestants drawing nearer. Mixed in with much happy frolicsome barking is a large volume of praying and yelling and calls for help, and along with all this a noise like a steam snow-plow being driven at a high rate of speed. Boots jumps for the door but before he can jerk it open, Good Sam busts in with his little playmate streaking along not ten feet behind him, and at that instant the blast goes off and the pup loses second money, as you might say, by about two lengths.

It's a few minutes after that when Boots and Babe reach the unanimous conclusion that they've been pretty near ruined by too much benevolence. Boots is propping up the front side of the cabin, the explosion having jarred it loose, and Babe is still laying where he landed against the back wall and nursing his game leg. The visiting humanitarian has gone down the ridge to get his nerves ca'mmed.

"Babe," says Boots, "you know what it looks like to me?"

"What it looks like to us two, you mean," says Babe.

"Sure," says Boots; "well, it looks like to both of us that we've been dern near killed with kindness."

"As regards that there pup," says Babe, continuing the clapboarded conversation, "we complained that he was all over the place and—"

"Now he's all over us," states Boots, combing a few more fine fragments of dog-hash out of his hair.

"I'd say we've had about enough of being helped by this here obliging well-wisher, wouldn't you?" says Babe.

"Abso—" says Boots.

"—lutely!" says Babe.

"I've run plum out of hospi—" says Boots.

"—tality!" says Babe. "What we ought to do is take a gun and kill him good—"

"—and dead!" says Boots.

But they didn't go that far. They make it plain to him though, when he gets back, that the welcome is all petered out and he takes the hint and pikes out for town, leaving those two still sorting what's left of their housekeeping junk out of the wreckage.

So it went and so it kept on going. Every time Good Sam set his willing hands to lifting some unfortunate fellow citizen out of a difficulty he won himself at least one more sincere critic before he was through. Even so, as long as he stuck to retailing it wasn't so bad. Certain parts of town he was invited to stay out of but there were other neighborhoods that he could still piroot around in without much danger of being assassinated. It was only when he branched out as a jobber that his waning popularity soured in a single hour. That was when the entire community clabbered on him, as you might say, by acclamation.

It happened this way: Other towns east and west of us were having booms, but our town, seemed like, was being left out in the cold. She wasn't growing a particle. So some of the leading people got up a mass-meeting to decide on ways and means of putting Triple Falls on the map. One fellow would rise up and suggest doing this and another fellow would rise up and suggest doing that; but every proposition called for money and about that time money was kind of a scarce article amongst us. So far as I was concerned, it was practically extinct.

Along toward the shank of the evening Good Sam took the floor.

"Gents," he said, "I craves your attention. There's just one sure way of boosting a town and that's by advertising it. Get its name in print on all the front pages over the country. Get it talked about; stir up curiosity; arouse public interest. That brings new people in and they bring their loose coinage with 'em and next thing you know you've got prosperity by the tail with a down-hill pull. Now, I've got a simple little scheme of my own. I love this fair young city of ours and I'm aiming to help her out of the kinks and I ain't asking assistance from anybody else neither. Don't ask me how I'm going about it because in advance it's a secret. I ain't telling.

You just leave it to me and I'll guarantee that inside of one week or less this'll be the most talked-about town of its size in the whole United States; with folks swarming in here by every train—why, they'll be running special excursions on the railroad. And it's not going to cost a single one of you a single red cent, neither."

Of course his past record should have been a plentiful warning. Somebody ought to have headed him off and bent a six-gun over his skull. But no, like the misguided suckers that we were, we let him go off and cook up his surprise.

I will say this: He kept his promise—he got us talked about and he brought strangers in. Inside of forty-eight hours special writers from newspapers all over the Rocky Mountains were pouring in and strangers were dropping off of through trains with pleased, expectant looks on their faces; and Father Staples was getting rush telegrams from his bishop asking how about it, and the Reverend Claypool—he was the Methodist minister—was hurrying back from conference all of a tremble, and various others who'd been away were lathering back home as fast as they could get here.

What'd happened? I'm coming to that now. All that happened was that Good Sam got the local correspondent for the press association stewed, and seduced him into sending out a dispatch that he'd written out himself, which it stated that an East Indian sun worshiper had lighted in Triple Falls and started up a revival meeting, and such was his hypnotic charm and such was the spell of his compelling fiery eloquence that almost overnight he'd converted practically the entire population—men, women, children, half-breeds, full-bloods, Chinks and Mexies—to the practice of his strange Oriental doctrines, with the result that pretty near everybody was engaged in dancing in the public street—without any clothes on!

So it was shortly after that, when cooler heads had discouraged talk of a lynching, that Good Sam left us—by request. And I haven't seen him since.

The Native Genius pointed up the trail. Toward us came Eagle Ribs, titular head of the resident group of members of the Blackfeet Confederacy, now under special retainers by the hotel management to furnish touches of true Western color to the adjacent landscape. The chief was in civilian garb; he was eating peanut brittle from a small paper bag.

"You'll observe that old Ribs has shucked his dance clothes," said my friend, "which means the official morning reception is over and the latest batch of sight-seers from all points East have scattered off or something. I guess it'll be safe for us to go back."

We fell into step; the path was wide enough for two going abreast.

"So you never heard anything more of the Good Samaritan?" I prompted, being greedy for the last tidbitty bite of this narrative.

"Nope. I judge somebody who couldn't appreciate his talents must have beefed him. But I'm reasonably certain he left descendants to carry on the family inheritance. One of 'em is in this vicinity now, I think."

"You're referring to what's-his-name who started the second fire last night—aren't you?" I asked.

"Not him. If he'd had a single drop of the real Good Sam blood in him his fire would be raging yet and my camp would be only a recent site.

"No, the one I've got in mind is the party with the saxophone. Did you get some faint feeble notion of the nature of the tune he was trying to force out of that reluctant horn of his? Well, it would be just like Good Sam's grandson to practice up on some such an air as that—and then play it as a serenade at midnight under the window of a sick friend."

How to Choke a Cat Without Using Butter

THIS writer has always contended that the ability to make a great individual fortune is not necessarily an ability based on superior intelligence—that in the case of the average multi-millionaire it merely is a sort of sublimated instinct, in a way like the instinct of a rat-terrier for smelling out hidden rats. The ordinary dull-nosed dog goes past a wainscoting and never suspects a thing; then your terrier comes along and he takes one whiff at the bottom of that baseboard and immediately starts pawing for his prey. He knows. It's his nature to know. Yet in other regards he may be rather an uninteresting creature, one without special gifts.

And so it is with many of our outstanding dollar-wizards, or at least so it would appear to those on the outside looking in. They differ from the commonplace run of mortals only in their ken for detecting opportunities to derive dividends from quarters which we cannot discern. Peel off their financial ratings from them and they'd be as the rest of us are—or even more so.

Now Mr. E. Randall Golightly, the pressed-brick magnate, would impress you as being like that. When it came to amassing wealth—ah, but there was where he could show you something! Otherwise he offered for the inspection of an envying planet the simple-minded easy-going unimportant personality of a middle-aged gentleman who was credulous, who was diffident in smart company, who was vastly ignorant of most matters excepting such matters as pertained to his particular specialty which, as just stated, was getting rich and richer. Out in the world away from his office and his plants, he had but little to say, thus partly concealing the fact that on the grammar side at least his original education wofully had been neglected. He was quiet and self-effacing, also he was decent and he was kindly.

But when a smart young man representing Achievements came by appointment, asking for an interview on the general subject of his early struggles, Mr. Golightly became properly flattered and suddenly vocal. Achievements was a monthly magazine devoted to purveying to the masses recipes for attaining success in business, the arts, the crafts, the sciences and the professions, the theory of its editors being that the youth of the land, reading therein how such-and-such leaders attained their present prominence, would be inspired to step forth and do likewise. Deservedly it had a large national circulation. Rotarians all over the country bought it regularly and efficiency experts prescribed it for their clients as doctors prescribe medicine for ailing patients.

Mr. Golightly was no bookworm, but he knew about Achievements, as what seasoned go-getter did not? The project outlined by the caller appealed to him. It resuscitated a drowned vanity in his inner being. So willingly enough he talked, giving dates and figures, and the young scribe took notes and still more notes and then went back to his desk and wrote and wrote and wrote. He wrote to the extent of several thousand words and his pen was tipped with flaming inspiration. He had such a congenial theme, such a typical Achievementalesque topic. Lord, how he ripped off the copy!

In due time a messenger brought to Mr. Golightly sundry long printed slips of an unfamiliar aspect called "galley proofs." Mr. Golightly read these through, making a few minor corrections. He told nothing at home regarding what was afoot; he was saving it up as a pleasant surprise for Mrs. Golightly and the two Misses Golightly. Anyhow, he had got out of the habit of telling at home what happened at the office.

One day in advance of publication date he received a copy of the issue of the magazine containing the interview with him. It was more than a mere content. Practically it dominated the number; it led everything else. And it was more than an interview. It was a character study, a eulogy for honest endeavor, a tribute to outstanding performance, an example to oncoming generations—and fully illustrated with photographs and drawings by a staff artist. It was what they called in the Achievements shop a whiz and a wow.

A happy pride, almost a boyish pride, puffed up Mr. Golightly as he walked into his thirty-thousand-a-year apartment on upper Park Avenue that afternoon after business hours. A terrible and a devastating humility deflated him an hour later when, without waiting for dinner, he escaped thence to his club, there to sit through a grief-laden evening in a secluded corner of the reading-room. Regret filled him; elsewise he had a sort of punctured look as though all joy and all hope of future joy had seeped out of his body through many invisible leaks.

As for domestic peace, future fireside comfort, agreeable life in the collective bosom, if any, of his family—ha, ha! To himself within he laughed a hollow despairing laugh. He began to understand why strong men in their prime might look favorably upon suicide as an escape from it all.

In his ears, like demoniac echoes, rang the semi-hysterical laments of his womenfolk. There was, to begin with, the poignant memory of what that outraged woman, Mrs. Golightly, had cried out:

"Wouldn't it be just like him to disgrace us this way? I ask you, wouldn't it?" Ignoring his abased presence she was addressing her two daughters, her deep voice rising above their berating tones. "What else could we have expected from such a father and such a husband? Does he think of us? Does he give a thought to my efforts to be somebody ever since we moved here to New York? Does he care for all my scheming to get you girls into really exclusive society? Or to get you married off into the right set? Do our ambitions mean anything to him? No, *no*, NO! What does he do? To gratify his own cheap cravings for notoriety he lets this shameful detestable vulgar rag expose us before the whole world. We'll be the laughing stock of everybody. Can you hear what the Hewitt Strykers will say when they read these awful admissions?"

In her agony, the poor mother waved aloft the clutched copy of Achievements and seared him with a devastating sidewise glare. "Can't you hear the Pewter-Walsbergs gloating and snickering when they find out that your father's first name is Ephraim and that he used to be called 'Eph' for short and that he started life as a day-laborer and that then he worked at the trade of a bricklayer and that secretly all these years he's been paying his dues in a dirty old union and carrying a dirty old union card—a thing which even I, knowing his common tastes as I did, never suspected before! But here's a picture of it printed in facsimile to prove it!" And now she beat with a frenzied forefinger on a certain page of the offending periodical. "And then he goes on to tell how with his own hands he made some of the very bricks that went into the office-building where his office is now! And then—then—then—oh, how can I ever hold up my head again?—then he says that when we were first married we had to live on twelve dollars a week and do all our own housework and that I even used to wash out his undershirts!"

"Oh, mommer!" This was the senior Miss Golightly, bemoaning their ruin.

"And well may you say 'Oh, mommer'—with the invitations out for your formal début next week!"

"Oh, popper!" exclaimed the stricken Miss Golightly. In the shock of the moment she had temporarily forgotten about her scheduled début. "Oh, popper, how could you do such a thing to me!"

"And Evelyn here expecting to join the Junior League—what chance has the poor child now? How can she ever forgive you?"

"Oh, oh, oh!" screamed the younger Miss Golightly, not addressing anyone in particular.

It was at this point that Mr. Golightly had grabbed his hat and clamped it on his degraded head and fled from this house of vain and utter repinings.

Late at night he crept in, almost as a burglar might creep in, and sought the seclusion of his room, not daring again to face his three women. Early next morning before any of them had risen to intercept him with her further lamentations, he crept out again and at his office spent a haunted forenoon. Every time his telephone buzzed he flinched. And when, following lunch for which he had absolutely no appetite, the girl on the private switchboard rang to tell him Mrs. Golightly herself was on the line he flinched more than ever as he told the exchange to plug in the connection, then braced himself for the worst. If his daughters were resolved never again to speak to him, so be it. At least he would take the blow standing. If it was to be a separation, a divorce even, so be that, too. He had only himself to blame.

"Hello," he said, wanly; and awaited the explosion.

"Oh, Ephie!" Mrs. Golightly was calling him by an old pet name—a beloved, homely name he had not heard her speak for years—and over the singing wire her voice came to him flutingly, yes, actually with affectionate flutings and thrills in it. "Oh, Ephie, you'll never guess what has happened! Oh, Ephie, Mrs. Pewter-Walsberg just called up! You know what she stands for in society? You know how I've worked and schemed to get in with her crowd and how I've subscribed for her pet charities and offered to serve on her tiresome committees and all? Well, she just called up. She's going to let her daughter, Millicent, be on the receiving line for Harriet's début. She's going to see that Evelyn gets into the Junior League right away. Her word is just law there. And she's invited you and me to dine with them next Thursday—one of those small intimate dinners that she's so famous for. Isn't it wonderful? And it's all due to you, dear, and I'm so grateful and the girls are both so grateful that I just had to ring you up to tell you."

"Humphphe-e-e!" Mr. Golightly got his breath back, as a diver emerging from an ice-water bath might. "Did you say grateful?"

"Of course, you dear old stupid! It seems—listen to this, Ephie—it seems that Mr. Pewter-Walsberg saw a copy of that adorable magazine on the news-stand this morning and saw your name on the cover and bought it out of curiosity and he read what it said about you and he was so delighted with it that he didn't wait until tonight to show it to her— Mrs. Pewter-Walsberg, I mean. He came right on uptown with it and read it to her. And she says—they both say, in fact—it took a great strong silent resolute man like you to see that the trend of the day is for democracy; and that it's high time the lower orders who aren't in society should know that there are no barriers to keep out those who rise by their own efforts from humble beginnings, but just the other way around; and that when ordinary people find out how far you've climbed—your position in business and our position in society and all—it's calculated to make them more satisfied with their lot and keep down anarchy and socialism and all such dreadful things. And she says Mr. Pewter-Walsberg will take it as a very great favor if you can arrange for these clever magazine people to interview him next—it seems they started forty years ago without a cent out in Illinois or some such outlandish place. Think of it, dear—a man like Herbert Pewter-Walsberg, with a hundred and fifty millions behind him—asking for a favor from you! Isn't it just too wonderful?... Hold the wire, Ephie, the girls are here waiting to congratulate you on being so smart in their behalf and to beg your pardon, as I do, for being so sort of excited as we all three were last night. But they didn't understand then, and neither did I. But now we do, and we do so appreciate it all—you splendid brilliant shrewd old darling, you! Ephie dearest, tell me this—how did you ever come to figure out such a marvelous stroke of genius all by yourself?"

"Maria," answered Mr. Golightly, and, as he answered, his chest expanded perceptibly and brushed against the edge of his desk, "if you'd been in the pressed-brick game as long as I have, you'd know there are several ways of killing a cat besides choking it to death with butter."